The
POLAR
BEAR

EXPLORERS' CLUB

Also by Alex Bell

The Polar Bear Explorers' Club

The Forbidden Expedition

The POLAR BEAR

EXPLORERS' CLUB

Book 1

Alex Bell

Illustrated by Tomislav Tomić

Simon & Schuster Books for Young Readers
NEW YORK LONDON TORONTO SYDNEY NEW DELHI

SIMON & SCHUSTER BOOKS FOR YOUNG READERS
An imprint of Simon & Schuster Children's Publishing Division
1230 Avenue of the Americas, New York, New York 10020

This book is a work of fiction. Any references to historical events, real people, or real
places are used fictitiously. Other names, characters, places, and events are products of
the author's imagination, and any resemblance to actual events or places or persons,
living or dead, is entirely coincidental.

Text copyright © 2017 by Alex Bell
Cover and interior illustrations copyright © 2018 by Tomislav Tomić
Originally published in Great Britain in 2017 by Faber & Faber Limited
First US edition December 2018
All rights reserved, including the right of reproduction in whole or in part in any form.
SIMON & SCHUSTER BOOKS FOR YOUNG READERS
is a trademark of Simon & Schuster, Inc.
For information about special discounts for bulk purchases, please contact
Simon & Schuster Special Sales at 1-866-506-1949
or business@simonandschuster.com.
The Simon & Schuster Speakers Bureau can bring authors to your live event.
For more information or to book an event, contact
the Simon & Schuster Speakers Bureau at 1-866-248-3049 or visit our website at
www.simonspeakers.com.
Also available in a Simon & Schuster Books for Young Readers hardcover edition
Cover design by Chloë Foglia and Tiara Iandiorio
Interior design by Hilary Zarycky
The text for this book was set in Granjon.
The illustrations for this book were rendered in
pen and ink and digitally.
Manufactured in the United States of America I 1019 OFF
First Simon & Schuster Books for Young Readers paperback edition November 2019
2 4 6 8 10 9 7 5 3 1
The Library of Congress has cataloged the hardcover edition as follows:
Names: Bell, Alex, 1986– author.
Title: The Polar Bear Explorers' Club / Alex Bell.
Description: First edition. I New York : Simon & Schuster Books for Young Readers,
[2018] I Series: The Polar Bear Explorers' Club ; 1 I Summary: "Stella Starflake Pearl
just wants to be part of the Polar Bear Explorers' Club. But Stella's a girl, and everyone
knows that girls aren't allowed to be explorers. Stella's ready to prove everyone
wrong"— Provided by publisher.
Identifiers: LCCN 2017031123 I
ISBN 9781534406469 (hardcover) I ISBN 9781534406476 (pbk)
ISBN 9781534406483 (eBook)
Subjects: I CYAC: Fantasy. I Adventure and adventurers—Fiction. I
Identity—Fiction. I Explorers—Fiction. I Clubs—Fiction. I Sex
role—Fiction. I Foundlings—Fiction. I Adoption—Fiction.
Classification: LCC PZ7.B388875 Pol 2018 I DDC [Fic]—dc23
LC record available at https://lccn.loc.gov/2017031123

For my soul mate, Neil Dayus

They slipped
briskly
into an intimacy from which they never recovered
—F. SCOTT FITZGERALD

Polar Bear Explorers' Club Rules

ALL Polar Bear explorers will keep their mustaches trimmed, waxed, and well groomed at all times. Any explorer found with a slovenly mustache will be asked to withdraw from the club's public rooms immediately.

EXPLORERS with disorderly mustaches or unkempt beards will also be refused entry to the members-only bar, the private dining room, and the gentlemen's billiards room without exception.

ALL igloos on club property must contain a flask of hot chocolate and an adequate supply of marshmallows at all times.

ONLY polar bear–shaped marshmallows are to be served on club property. Additionally, the following breakfast items will be prepared in polar bear–shape only: pancakes, waffles, crumpets, sticky pastries, fruit jellies, and donuts. Please do not request alternative animal shapes from the kitchen—including penguins, walruses, woolly mammoths, and yetis—as this offends the chef.

MEMBERS are kindly reminded that when the chef is offended, insulted, or peeved, there will be nothing on offer in the dining room whatsoever except for buttered toast. This toast will be bread-shaped.

EXPLORERS must not hunt or harm unicorns under any circumstances.

ALL Polar Bear Explorers' Club sleighs must be properly decorated with seven brass bells and must contain the following items: five fleecy blankets, three hot water bottles in knitted sweaters, two flasks of emergency hot chocolate, and a warmed basket of buttered crumpets (polar bear–shaped).

PLEASE do not take penguins into the club's saltwater baths; they *will* hog the Jacuzzi.

ALL penguins are the property of the club and are not to be removed by explorers. The club reserves the right to search any suspiciously shaped bags. Any bag that moves by itself will automatically be deemed suspicious.

ALL snowmen built on club property must have appropriately groomed mustaches. Please note that a carrot is not a suitable object to use as a mustache. Nor is an eggplant. If in doubt, remember that the club president is always available for consultation regarding snowmen's mustaches.

IT is considered bad form to threaten other club members with icicles, snowballs, or oddly dressed snowmen.

WHISTLING ducks are not permitted on club property. Any member found with a whistling duck in his possession will be asked to leave.

Upon initiation, all Polar Bear explorers shall receive an explorer's bag containing the following items:

- One tin of Captain Filibuster's Expedition-Strength Mustache Wax
- One bottle of Captain Filibuster's Scented Beard Oil
- One folding pocket mustache comb
- One ivory-handled shaving brush, two pairs of grooming scissors, and four individually wrapped cakes of luxurious foaming shaving soap
- Two compact pocket mirrors

Desert Jackal Explorers' Club Rules

MAGICAL flying carpets are to be kept tightly rolled when on club premises. Any damage caused by out-of-control flying carpets will be considered the sole responsibility of the explorer in question.

ENCHANTED genie lamps must stay in their owners' possession at all times.

PLEASE note: Genies are strictly prohibited at the bar and at the bridge tables.

TENTS are for serious expedition use only and are not to be used to host parties, gatherings, chin-wags, or chitchats.

CAMELS must not be permitted—or encouraged—to spit at other club members.

JUMPING cacti are not allowed inside the club unless under exceptional circumstances.

PLEASE do not remove flags, maps, or wallabies from the club.

CLUB members are not permitted to settle disagreements via camel racing between the hours of midnight and sunrise.

THE club kangaroos, coyotes, sand cats, and rattlesnakes are to be respected at all times.

MEMBERS who wish to keep all their fingers are advised not to torment the giant desert hairy scorpions, irritate the bearded vultures, or vex the spotted desert recluse spiders.

EXPLORERS are kindly asked to refrain from washing

their feet in the drinking water tureens at the club's entrance, which are provided strictly for our members' refreshment.

SAND forts may be constructed on club grounds, on condition that explorers empty all sand from their sandals, pockets, bags, binocular cases, and helmets before entering the club.

EXPLORERS are asked not to take camel decoration to extremes. Desert Jackal Explorers' Club camels may wear a maximum of one jeweled necklace, one tasseled headdress and/or bandana, seven plain gold anklets, up to four knee bells, and one floral snout ornament.

Upon initiation, all Desert Jackal explorers shall receive an explorer's bag containing the following items:

- One foldable leather safari hat or one pith helmet
- One canister of tropical-strength giant desert hairy scorpion repellent
- One shovel (please note this object's usefulness in the event of being buried alive in a sandstorm)
- One camel-grooming kit, consisting of organic camel shampoo, camel eyelash curlers, head brush, toenail trimmers, and hoof polishers (kindly provided by the National Camel-Grooming Association)
- Two spare genie lamps and one spare genie bottle

Jungle Cat Explorers' Club Rules

MEMBERS of the Jungle Cat Explorers' Club shall refrain from picnicking in a slovenly manner. All expedition picnics are to be conducted with grace, poise, and elegance.

ALL expedition picnicware must be made from solid silver and kept perfectly polished at all.times.

CHAMPAGNE carriers must be constructed from high-grade wicker, premium leather, or teakwood. Please note that champagne carriers considered "tacky" will not be accepted onto the luggage elephant under ANY circumstances.

EXPEDITION picnics will not take place unless there are scones present. Ideally, there should also be magic lanterns, pixie cakes, and an assortment of fairy jellies.

EXOTIC whip snakes, alligator snapping turtles, horned baboon tarantulas, and flying panthers must be kept securely under lock and key while on club premises.

DO NOT torment or tease the jungle fairies. They *will* bite and may also catapult tiny, but extremely potent, stink-berries. Please be warned that stink-berries smell worse than anything you can imagine, including unwashed feet, moldy cheese, elephant poo, and hippopotamus burps.

JUNGLE fairies must be allowed to join expedition picnics if they bring an offering of any of the following: elephant cakes, striped giraffe scones, or fizzy tiger punch from the Forbidden Jungle Tiger Temple.

JUNGLE fairy boats have right of way on the Tikki Zikki River under *all* circumstances, including when there are piranhas present.

SPEARS are to be pointed away from other club members at all times.

WHEN traveling by elephant, explorers are kindly asked to supply their own bananas.

IF and when confronted by an enraged hippopotamus, a Jungle Cat explorer must remain calm and act with haste to avoid any damage befalling the expedition boat (please note that the Jungle Navigation Company expects all boats to be returned to them in pristine condition).

MEMBERS are courteously reminded that owing to the size and smell of the beasts in question, the club's elephant house is not an appropriate venue in which to host soirees, banquets, galas, or shindigs. Carousing of any kind in the elephant house is strictly prohibited.

Upon initiation, all Jungle Cat explorers shall receive an explorer's bag containing the following items:

- An elegant mother-of-pearl knife and fork, inscribed with the explorer's initials
- One silverware polishing kit

- One engraved Jungle Cat Explorers' Club napkin ring and five luxury linen napkins—ironed, starched, and embossed with the club's insignia
- One magic lantern with fire pixie
- One tin of Captain Greystoke's Expedition-Flavor Smoked Caviar
- One corkscrew, two cheese knives, and three wicker grape baskets

Ocean Squid Explorers' Club Rules

SEA monster, kraken, and giant squid trophies are the private property of the club, and cannot be removed to adorn private homes. Explorers will be charged for any decorative tentacles that are found to be missing from their rooms.

EXPLORERS are not to fraternize—or join forces—with pirates or smugglers during the course of any official expedition.

POISONOUS puffer fish, barbed-wire jellyfish, saltwater stingrays, and electric eels are not appropriate fillings for pies or sandwiches. Any such requests sent to the kitchen will be politely rejected.

EXPLORERS are kindly asked to refrain from offering to show the club's chef how to prepare sea snakes, sharks, crustaceans, or deep-sea monsters for human consumption. This includes the creatures listed in the rule immediately above. Please respect the expert knowledge of the chef.

THE Ocean Squid Explorers' Club does not consider the sea cucumber to be a trophy worthy of reward or recognition. This includes the lesser-found biting cucumber, as well as the singing cucumber and the argumentative cucumber.

ANY Ocean Squid explorer who gifts the club with a tentacle from the screeching red devil squid will be rewarded with a year's supply of Captain Ishmael's Premium Dark Rum.

PLEASE do not leave docked submarines in a submerged state; it wreaks havoc with the club's valet service.

EXPLORERS are kindly asked not to leave deceased sea monsters in the hallways or any of the club's communal rooms. Unattended sea monsters are liable to be removed to the kitchens without notice.

THE South Seas Navigation Company will not accept liability for any damage caused to their submarines. This includes damage caused by giant squid attacks, whale ambushes, and jellyfish plots.

EXPLORERS are not to use the map room to compare the length of squid tentacles or other trophies. Please use the marked areas within the trophy rooms to settle any private wagers or bets.

PLEASE note: Any explorer who threatens another explorer with a harpoon cannon will be suspended from the club immediately.

Upon initiation, all Ocean Squid explorers shall receive an explorer's bag containing the following items:

- One tin of Captain Ishmael's Kraken Bait
- One kraken net
- One engraved hip flask filled with Captain Ishmael's Expedition-Strength Salted Rum
- Two sharpened fishing spears and three bags of hunting barbs
- Five tins of Captain Ishmael's Harpoon Cannon Polish

CHAPTER ONE

STELLA STARFLAKE PEARL RUBBED frost from the turret window and scowled out at the snow. She ought to be in the most splendid mood—it was her birthday tomorrow, and the only thing Stella loved more than birthdays was unicorns. But it was hard to be cheerful when Felix was still refusing to take her on his expedition. Even though she'd begged, pleaded, cajoled, threatened, and stormed—none of it had done any good at all. The thought of being packed off to stay with Aunt Agatha again made Stella feel positively sick. Aunt Agatha didn't know much about children, and sometimes she got things completely wrong, like the time she gave Stella a cabbage for her packed school lunch. No chocolate dinosaurs, or marshmallow cake, or treats of any kind—just a single, solitary, useless cabbage. Plus, Aunt Agatha had nostril hair. It was almost impossible not to sometimes stare at it.

Stella had wanted to be an explorer ever since she was old enough to know what the word meant. More specifically, she wanted to be a navigator. She never got tired of looking at maps and globes, and as far as she was concerned, a compass was just about the most beautiful thing in the whole entire world. After unicorns, obviously.

And if she wasn't meant to be an explorer, then why had the fairies given her a middle name? Everyone knew that only explorers had three names. Felix had given her his last name, Pearl, but then hadn't known what to do about a first name, so he'd asked the fairies to name her instead. This was probably a good thing, because Felix was fond of peculiar names like Mildred and Wilhelmina and Barbaretta. But the fairies had given her not one name, but two: Stella and Starflake. And surely that meant that she was absolutely destined to be an explorer.

Stella scrambled onto the turret window seat and pulled her legs up to rest her chin on her knees. It was getting dark outside, and she knew Felix would be looking for her to give her her twilight present. It was a tradition they had—Stella was always allowed to open one present the night before her birthday. But right now she was too angry and disappointed for presents, so she'd come up to the turret to hide. And if she tucked herself into the window seat she couldn't be seen from the end of the corridor.

Unfortunately, though, Gruff liked the turret too, and

he had come lumbering over almost as soon as Stella had sat down, and was now poking his nose into her pockets in search of cookies. Mrs. Sap, their housekeeper, hadn't been very happy when Felix brought an orphaned polar bear cub home one day, but the bear would have died otherwise. Not only was he an orphan, he had a deformed paw as well, and would never have been able to survive in the wild. Stella thought it was the best thing ever to have a polar bear in the house, even if he did almost flatten her sometimes when he wanted to cuddle. Polar bears were quite startlingly huge.

She reached into her pocket for a fish cookie and held it out to Gruff, who took it from her with extreme gentleness and then crunched it up happily, covering her in crumbs and bear slobber. Stella was used to the bear slobber, so she didn't mind, but the downside of Gruff coming to see her was that he gave her presence away when Felix entered the corridor a few minutes later.

"Ah, there you are," he said, stopping by the window seat. "I've been searching high and low for you."

Stella looked up into his face—her favorite face in the whole world, the first one she could ever remember seeing. Stella had been a snow orphan, just like Gruff. If Felix hadn't found her when she was a baby, she would probably have died out there, alone on the ice. Stella had never met anyone with hair as white as hers, or skin as pale, or eyes her particular shade of ice-chip blue. Most people had pink, or black, or brown skin, but Stella was white as a pearl from head to toe. It was something that had always bothered her. She wished she looked more like her adoptive father.

Felix wasn't particularly handsome or distinguished, and he didn't sport a mustache, whiskers, or sideburns, as was the current fashion. This was in large part because those things required quite a significant time commitment in terms of grooming and maintenance, and Felix said he had (so far) counted up a total of 134 more interesting ways that he would rather spend his time, including making numbered lists of interesting ways he would rather spend his time. His nose was bent at the top, and Stella loved the way his eyes crinkled at the corners. His golden-brown hair was usually just a little bit too long, curling around his collar—and his mouth always wanted to smile. Felix didn't like frowning. He said it was a waste of good muscle use.

Stella had always thought of him as a special person, and the fact that he was a fairyologist proved it beyond doubt. There weren't many humans that fairies would speak to, but they had always liked Felix. He could hardly leave the house in the summer months without one of them perching on the brim of his hat or landing on his shoulder to whisper into his ear. So if he forgot to brush his hair sometimes, or put on odd socks, or did the buttons of his shirt up wrong, none of that mattered one bit to Stella. Besides which, Felix knew how to ride a unicycle, perform card tricks, and make little flying birds out of paper—and if that wasn't enough to make someone a favorite person, Stella didn't know what was.

"It's twilight-present time," he announced, holding up a white box wrapped with a wonky pink bow.

It took all of Stella's discipline to say, "I don't want it." She turned her head to stare out the window.

"I cannot believe you are serious," said Felix. He tried to nudge Gruff—who had lain down next to the window seat—out of the way, but nudging a polar bear is a bit like nudging a mountain and really isn't any use at all, so Felix climbed over the bear instead and sat on the seat opposite Stella.

"I'd take you in a heartbeat," Felix said quietly. "If girls were allowed on expeditions, then you know I would take you."

"It's not fair that girls can't be explorers!" Stella said. "It's stupid and it doesn't make sense!"

The injustice of it made her whole body tremble. Stella had grown up listening to Felix's stories whenever he returned home from an expedition, and had always loved them, but there comes a time when a girl gets tired of hearing about other people's adventures and wants to start having a few of her own.

Plenty of explorers took their sons with them on expeditions. Even Stella's friend Beanie was going on this next one with his uncle, the renowned entomologist Benedict

Boscombe Smith. Beanie was the same age as Stella, but he was part elf and not quite like the other children at their school. He had a long list of dislikes that, so far, included small talk, sarcasm, handshakes, hugs, and hair-cuts. Basically anything that involved physical contact was a definite no.

"You're absolutely right," Felix replied. "It is stupid, and it does not make sense. I'm sure it will be different one day. But the world doesn't always change as quickly as we'd like it to."

Stella continued to look out the window, preferring to stare at the snow than meet Felix's eye. "I thought rules didn't matter to you," she said, biting her lip.

Felix had always said that some rules were okay to break and, in fact, some should be broken regularly for one's health. When Aunt Agatha said that Stella needed a woman in the house to bring her up properly, Felix was always on Stella's side about stuff like being allowed to gal-lop around the grounds on her unicorn, or build a fort out of books in the library, or learn how to make balloon ani-mals rather than sew ugly embroidery.

"There are some rules that absolutely cannot be bro-ken," he'd say. "Like being kind and treating others as you'd like to be treated yourself. But whether or not people laugh at you, or think you peculiar or different from them, doesn't much matter in the grand scheme of things."

"It's not like it would hurt anyone if I went on the expedition, is it?" Stella asked, trying to use Felix's own logic against him. "And if people think it's strange for a girl to be an explorer, then that's their problem. Not mine."

Felix sighed and put the present down on the seat between them. "My dear thing, I wish it were that simple. But I don't make the rules at the Polar Bear Explorers' Club." He nudged the present along the seat toward her. "Let's not let it ruin your birthday. Why don't you open your present?"

"Take it away. I don't want it," Stella said in her coldest voice. But she felt awful as soon as she spoke, and she hated herself for being cruel, and she hated being angry with Felix too. It felt so unnatural not to be friends—it made her stomach feel all twisted up and wrong.

"I'm sorry," she blurted quickly. "That was mean."

Felix picked up the present and pressed it into her hands. "Open it," he said again. "The poor things will be getting terribly stuffy in there by now."

That piqued Stella's curiosity, so she tugged off the bow, removed the lid from the box, and stared down at a tiny igloo, nestled in a bed of pink tissue paper. Exclaiming in delight, she lifted it free of the box and realized it was made from actual ice. Each minute brick felt freezing against her fingers, and frost sparkled along the curved surface like dozens of tiny diamonds.

7

"It's enchanted," Felix said. "That's why it doesn't melt. I got it from a magician I met on my travels through Snuffleville. Look inside."

Stella lifted it to peer through the open doorway and gasped at the sight of a family of tiny penguins happily sliding about on the ice inside.

"They're Polar Pets," Felix told her. "They're part of the magic trick, so they don't require feeding or anything, although the magician said they like to be sung to every once in a while. One of the other igloos had polar bears in it and another had seals, but I thought you'd like the penguins best."

"I love them!" Stella replied.

"There was even one igloo that had tiny snow goblins inside, but that one struck me as just plain worrying. What on earth are you supposed to think if someone presents you with an igloo full of snow goblins? When I looked in, they seemed to be trying to poke each other's eyes out with twigs. It was all getting quite violent."

"Sounds like the kind of present Aunt Agatha would give," Stella said, immediately feeling glum again as soon as she said her name.

Stella loved the tiny penguins in their tiny igloo, just as she had loved all the other oddities, treasures, and knick-knacks that Felix had brought back from his travels. But what she *really* wanted—more than anything—was to find her own marvels and rarities to bring back home with her.

She wanted to have her very own study, the walls lined with maps and charts, where she could spend as much time as she liked drawing up packing lists, inspecting her curiosities, and planning her next adventure to strange lands on the other side of the world.

"Your aunt does her best," Felix said. "She just . . . well, she finds our ways a little odd, that's all. But she does care . . ." A faint frown line appeared between his eyes as he looked out the window. "In her own way."

Stella wasn't at all sure about that. Felix had always introduced Stella to people as his daughter, and she knew he loved her as much as any father ever could, even if she was just another orphaned foundling he'd discovered in the snow. But Aunt Agatha had always looked at her with the same kind of mild distaste with which she looked at Gruff after he'd just done one of his long, loud, fish-biscuit burps.

Stella didn't want to argue with Felix anymore, though, so she gave him a kiss good night, scrambled over Gruff, and returned to her room. She set the igloo by the side of her bed, got changed, and then climbed under the sheets, where she stared up at the slowly revolving mobile that hung from the ceiling. She knew she was too old for mobiles now, but Felix had made this one for her when she was very small to make her feel more at home, and Stella loved it.

He'd designed it to remind her of where she'd come from, stringing it with shaggy-haired yetis, snow-white unicorns, massive woolly mammoths, and glimmering silver stars. There were even abominable snowmen and cloven-hoofed yaks on there, all painstakingly created from clay and beads and wool and sparkling glass stones. Stella had only been a couple of years old when Felix had found her—too young to remember anything about her life before. And yet, sometimes she'd dream she was a baby again, sitting on a bed, playing with a tiara covered in crystals and pearls and ice-white gems. Then the image would shift, and she'd be outside and there would be blood splattered across the snow. . . .

Stella knew she would never find out what had happened to her or her biological family, but the frozen wilderness out there had been her home once and she wanted to see it again for herself.

And when Felix and his expedition attempted to be the first explorers to reach the coldest part of the Icelands, Stella wanted to be there with them. She just needed to think of a way to get Felix to let her come.

Finally, she sighed, turned over in bed, and snuggled down deeper into the covers, where she fell asleep to the sound of the quiet, happy honking of the penguins in their igloo.

CHAPTER TWO

STELLA WOKE UP THE next morning to the sun streaming through her bedroom windows and warming her toes where they stuck out the end of her bed. She sat up and wondered whether she might feel different now that she was twelve. Not that they could know her real age for sure, but Felix thought she'd been about two when he first found her. He said everyone should celebrate their birthday once a year (ideally twice), so he'd decided that the day he found Stella in the snow would be her official birthday.

The muffled sound of a party whistle drew her attention to the tiny igloo at her bedside, and she picked it up and peered in at the family of penguins. It looked like one of them must be having a birthday too, because the penguins all wore paper party hats and were blowing party whistles, and there was a cake in the shape of a fish with a whole load of candles stuck in it. One of the penguins—presumably the birthday boy or girl (it was hard to tell with penguins)—was clapping its flippers together and making little honking noises of excitement. Remembering what Felix had said about singing to them, Stella sang "Happy Birthday" through the door of the igloo, which immediately caused a great furor, with all the penguins running around in circles, their big feet slapping noisily on the ice. Stella smiled and put the igloo back by the side of her bed.

With an effort, she pushed all thoughts of Felix's imminent departure, and her own dreary imprisonment with Aunt Agatha, out of her mind. It would be a terrible waste to let it ruin her birthday. You only turned twelve once, after all.

She put on her most favorite special-occasion dress. It was powder blue, with tiny white buttons in the shape of polar bears, and a glorious petticoat skirt, which puffed up beautifully when Stella spun around in a circle, making her feel rather like one of the sugar plum fairies she sometimes saw dancing in the backyard at midnight.

She tied her white hair back with a blue ribbon, then went down the vast staircase that led to the lower floor. Like most explorers, Felix was extremely wealthy, and their mansion of a home had several kitchens and dining rooms, with a whole host of cooks and chefs and servants. If they had explorers staying with them—which they often did

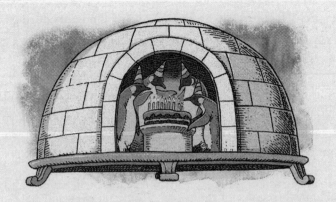

whenever there was an expedition being planned—then they ate breakfast in the parlor. But when it was just the two of them, they always ate in the orangery. Felix still called it the orangery, although there hadn't been any orange trees in there for years. There was an entirely different type of thing in the glass conservatory now.

Stella opened the door, and warmth washed over her, along with the faint smell of long-gone oranges. With its glass roof and walls, the orangery was the warmest part of their home, which made it the ideal environment for pygmy dinosaurs. Some people called them fairy dinosaurs because of their minute size—even the T-rex, Stella's absolute favorite, was no bigger than a kitten. His name was Buster, and he came rushing up to meet her the moment she stepped inside. Stella scooped him up and lightly ran a finger over his scaly head. He immediately squirmed in delight, his front claws curling tightly around her thumb.

Felix had first discovered the pygmy dinosaurs during a trip to the Spice Islands of the Exotic South, and had been studying them for some time. Word of his studies had gotten around, and whenever a sick or injured pygmy dinosaur turned up anywhere, Felix would be contacted and asked if he would take it in. He never turned any away, and the orangery was now home to dozens of little dinosaurs.

"Ah, there's the birthday girl!" Felix called from the table in the center of the room. "Come on over and have some breakfast."

Stella was delighted to see that they were having ice cream, complete with sprinkles, wafers, and gooey chocolate toffee sauce. She was also thrilled that Felix had made dozens and dozens of balloon animals—all unicorns—and strung them up from the pterodactyl houses hanging from the ceiling. Every now and then, a pygmy pterodactyl would fly up to inspect one of the bright pink balloon unicorns, only to flutter away hastily, looking terribly confused.

Stella sat down with Buster on her lap, gave him a wafer—which he snatched from her fingers greedily—and then picked up her spoon and dug in before the ice cream could melt. Everything was going superbly until a rapid tapping on the glass wall made them turn, to see Aunt Agatha standing outside, peering in at them with a grim expression on her broad face.

Stella's heart sank. "I thought she wasn't coming to pick me up until this afternoon," she said, giving Felix an accusing look.

"So did I. She must have caught an earlier train," he replied. Then he sighed. "Well, there's no use trying to hide from her now that she's seen us, I suppose." He waved at her through the glass and raised his voice: "Come in, Agatha. The door is open."

Stella returned her attention to her ice cream as her aunt navigated herself to the door. She came stomping in a moment later, dressed in a matching purple skirt and jacket, as well as a big floppy purple hat with a feather in it. Aunt Agatha was a stout woman, and Stella thought the outfit made her look rather like a giant violet frog—definitely the kind that you shouldn't touch, just in case it turned out to be poisonous.

"How nice to see you, Agatha," Felix said politely, standing up to pull out a chair for her. "Would you care for some ice cream?"

"Ice cream?" Aunt Agatha repeated in a tone of horror. Anyone would have thought that Felix had just said: "Would you care for some minced squid lips?"

"Ice cream for breakfast?" she went on. "Oh, really, Felix, really."

"It's Stella's birthday," he replied as he sat back down in his seat.

"Oh, yes. Happy birthday, dear," Aunt Agatha said, acknowledging Stella for the first time.

"Thank you, Aunt Agatha," Stella replied.

Her aunt plonked herself down in a chair, clutching her handbag on her lap as if she feared someone was about to snatch it from her. She scowled at the table. "Felix, why on earth is there a dinosaur sitting in that cereal bowl?"

"That's Mildred," Felix said mildly. "She's a diplodocus."

The tiny dinosaur was indeed nestled in the bowl at Felix's elbow, her body partially submerged in milk and cereal.

"I didn't ask what type it was; I asked why it's in the bowl," Aunt Agatha said with a sigh.

"Skin complaint," Felix said. "I'm treating her with milk and cereal. It's working well so far. Are you sure I can't interest you in some ice cream? Do have a wafer, at least."

"It can't be hygienic for you to be eating in here," Aunt Agatha replied. "Not with these dinosaurs running amok all over the place. It's far too warm in this room, besides." She took an enormous fan from her bag and began fluttering it in front of her face in an agitated manner.

Stella scraped the last of her ice cream from her bowl and held her spoon out for Buster to lick before setting him down on the floor. Unfortunately, he charged straight over to Aunt Agatha and started worrying at her shoelaces with his teeth. Aunt Agatha let out a squeal and went to slap him with her fan, but Felix's hand instantly shot out to prevent her.

"Steady on," he said. He scooped Buster up and set him down on his lap. The T-rex glared across the table at Aunt Agatha. He had quite a good glare. It was one of Stella's favorite things about him.

She was just going to ask if she could be excused, as she'd rather be down in the stables with her unicorn (or pretty much anywhere else, come to that) than sitting here with her disapproving aunt, but then Aunt Agatha turned to her and said, "Stella, dear, why don't you run along and play outside for a little bit? I have some things to discuss with my brother in private."

Aunt Agatha always called Felix "my brother." Never "your father." Stella shrugged and hopped down from her chair as if she didn't mind and had far more important things to be doing anyway. But if Aunt Agatha wanted to talk to Felix "in private," that could only mean that she wanted to talk about Stella. And like any self-respecting child, Stella fully intended to eavesdrop on all conversations that concerned her.

So she went back into the house the way she'd come, grabbed her cloak, and then went outside to the marshmallow shrub at the side of the orangery. It wasn't a very large shrub but it was just big enough to hide her from view if she gathered up her petticoats, crouched down low in the snow, and didn't move an inch. From there she could peer through the leaves and fluffy pink marshmallows at Aunt Agatha and Felix, and quite clearly hear every word that was being said.

"Really, Felix, it's too much!" Aunt Agatha was complaining. "Bats in the belfry, dinosaurs in the orangery, fairies in the woodpile . . . I mean, where will it all end?"

"Agatha, please," Felix replied. "There are no bats in the belfry. I'm not even sure what a belfry is, to be quite honest with you, but I'm reasonably certain we don't have one here. The bats are in the smoking room. They used to favor the library, but ever since that falling out with the bookworms, they—"

"Oh, I don't care about the bats!" Agatha interrupted impatiently—which Stella thought was pretty rude, considering that she was the one who'd brought up the bats in the first place. "I care about what's going to become of this girl."

"'This girl,'" Felix repeated in a quiet voice. "Are you, perhaps, referring to my daughter, Stella?"

"Felix, please be serious. She isn't your daughter. Not really."

Felix stood up abruptly and there was a pause, which Stella knew meant that he was counting to ten inside his head. Felix said you should always count to ten if you feared you were in danger of getting angry with someone, although Stella very rarely saw Felix angry. In fact, Aunt

Agatha seemed to be the only person who could succeed in spoiling his typically cheerful mood.

"She is my daughter," Felix finally said, "in every way that can possibly matter."

"Listen, I came early because I wanted to speak to you seriously about just what you intend to do with her. I mean, she's not going to be a child forever. What's going to become of her when she grows up? She can't just live here indefinitely, can she?"

Felix took a watering can out of an icebox and calmly began to sprinkle fresh cold milk over Mildred, who was still happily soaking in her cereal bowl. "And what would you suggest, Agatha?" he asked.

"Well, I have some wonderful news, Felix. In fact, I've solved the problem." The feather in Aunt Agatha's hat wobbled as she drew herself up in her chair. "I've secured a place for Stella at a finishing school for young ladies."

Felix set the watering can down. "But Stella already goes to school with the local children here. And I'm seeing to her education as well—"

Aunt Agatha pointed a finger at him. "You've been filling her head up with a lot of silly nonsense from books. Stella needs to learn how to do useful things, like sew and embroider and wear a dress without ruining it in five seconds."

Stella couldn't help glancing guiltily down at her party dress. She saw that Buster had pulled some of the threads loose with his claws when he'd been on her lap earlier, and that the petticoat hem was looking rather bedraggled from trailing in the snow. It seemed Buster had drooled a little on the fabric too. Stella sighed. Pygmy T-rex were prone to drooling something terrible when there were wafers around.

"At a finishing school for young ladies she will be taught how to sing and draw," Aunt Agatha went on. "She will be made to see that it's incorrect for a girl to gallop about on unicorns and pore over dusty old maps. Her posture will be corrected. The girls there spend an hour every day walking up and down with books on their heads."

Felix gaped at her. "Do they really?"

Aunt Agatha gave an emphatic nod. "Yes, indeed. Two hours, sometimes."

"That time would be better spent *reading* the books, surely?"

"It is a quite splendid establishment," Aunt Agatha said, pretending not to have heard him. "If Stella were to spend even one term there, you would be amazed at the change in her, Felix, really you would."

"I don't doubt that for a moment," Felix replied.

"They'll show her how to do her hair in the latest fashion," Aunt Agatha said, warming to her theme. "And she'll be taught how to dance, and apply powder and rouge, and make herself attractive to a gentleman. Then, when she's older, a suitable marriage can be made for her and she will be someone else's responsibility. I've thought it all through, Felix, and this is the only way. I know you're fond of taking in these snow orphans, but a girl is quite different from a polar bear—I mean, even you must realize that."

Stella held her breath, her heart hammering in her chest. What if Felix agreed with Aunt Agatha? She was sure it would break her heart if he sent her away. Suddenly she wished she hadn't been so grumpy with him last night. She wished she'd been a better daughter and that she'd told him how much she loved him fifty times every single day.

Felix turned away from the table, and Stella gasped when she realized he was walking over to the glass wall right on the other side from where she was hiding. She slunk down lower in the snow and tried to keep as still as possible while staring at Felix's boots, which had come to a stop right in front of her.

"It's a fine plan, Agatha," she heard him say, and a thrill of dread ran through her entire body. "But I'm not convinced that Stella would care much for embroidery."

Stella risked a glance up through the pink marshmallows of the shrub and was startled to find Felix looking right at her. His mouth quirked upward slightly in a half smile, and he gave her a wink.

"Besides which," he went on, scratching his cheek, "walking up and down with books balanced on one's head seems like the most dreadful waste of one's time. I know I'm no expert on womanly things, but there's got to be more to a young girl's life than singing and dancing, surely? They're not performing monkeys, after all."

"Felix, I really must insist. The arrangements have all been made. Stella will start at the school tomorrow."

"My dear Agatha, I know you mean well, but you have no right to insist. In fact, you have no say in this matter at all. Stella will not start at the school—tomorrow or ever." Felix turned around from the window. "Thank you for coming, but I think, in fact, I won't need you to look after Stella on this occasion."

"You can't mean that you're just going to leave her here with the servants and these awful dinosaur things?" Agatha said. "She needs to be properly supervised!"

"I will supervise her properly. She'll come with me on the expedition."

Stella gasped. Aunt Agatha's mouth gaped open. "You can't take a *girl* on an expedition, Felix! It cannot be done!"

"Why can't it be done?" Felix asked at once. "I'm sure a great number of extraordinary and incredible things have been achieved despite others saying that they cannot be done. Sometimes maybe even because of it."

"Girls can't be explorers! The very idea! Can you honestly imagine a woman tearing about the place with sleighs and compasses, and getting stuck in avalanches, and resorting to cannibalism, and goodness knows what else? No, no—it's all much too dangerous, much too unseemly."

"First of all, I've been a polar explorer for twenty years," Felix said calmly, while ticking the points off on his fingers, "and I have never yet been stuck in an avalanche. Secondly, we use sleds during expeditions, not sleighs, and thirdly, explorers haven't eaten each other for decades. Not for *decades*, Agatha. The field of exploration has come along in leaps and bounds. If twelve-year-old boys can join the expedition, I see no reason why Stella should not."

"You can't be serious, Felix. This is too much, even for you. You simply cannot be serious. I won't believe it."

"I try not to be serious wherever possible, Agatha, but right now, I don't think I've ever been more serious in my whole life. I'm sorry you wasted your trip. Thank you for coming. Please do have some cookies or marmalade or something before you go. You'll forgive me if I don't stay and chat any longer, though. Stella and I have rather a lot of packing to do."

It was the best birthday present Stella could have possibly asked for. Felix left Aunt Agatha fuming in the orangery, and Stella almost tripped over her petticoats as she raced around to meet him back inside the house.

"Did you mean it?" she asked, throwing her arms around his waist.

"Of course I meant it, sweetling," Felix replied. "When do I ever say anything I don't mean?"

"But the rules of the Polar Bear Explorers' Club are—"

"Never mind about that," Felix said. "We'll deal with that when we get there. The important thing right now is to get everything ready so we're in time to catch the train tomorrow. Can you pack your bits and your bobs by yourself, or would you like me to help?"

"I can do it by myself," Stella promised him.

The rest of the day was spent in a whirlwind of preparation. After making one more futile attempt to talk Felix into her way of thinking, Aunt Agatha had left the house in a huff. Felix gave Stella a big old suitcase covered in faded travel stickers. It was dusty and smelled like mothballs, but Stella thought it was the most perfect suitcase she'd ever seen. She ran around throwing clothes in at random, while also trying to work out what else she ought to take with her for a polar expedition.

She peered into her tiny igloo and saw that the penguins all appeared to be busily packing suitcases too—although from the looks of it, the contents consisted entirely of smoked fish. Stella wrinkled her nose at the smell and put the igloo carefully down on her bedside table.

She pulled open the drawer underneath and took out the gold compass Felix had given her for her birthday last year. A proper explorer's compass didn't bother with North, South, East, and West but could have as many as twenty headings—things like Food, Shelter, Yetis, Water, and Angry Gnomes. Stella wasn't too sure what the Angry Gnome heading was about—she'd never met an angry gnome, or any kind of gnome, come to think of it, but she fervently hoped she would see one on this expedition, and that it would be positively furious. Stella wanted to see absolutely everything.

The packing was completed by late afternoon, so Felix took Stella skating on the lake behind the house for an hour before dinner. When they returned home, the cook had prepared all of Stella's favorite foods—miniature hot dogs, giant pizzas, purple macaroons, and jelly dragons—for her birthday dinner, which had been set out on the long table in the parlor. A fire blazed in the huge granite fireplace and Gruff snoozed contentedly on the rug in front of it.

Stella was quite stuffed with food by the time she returned to her bedroom. When she opened the door, she found that the fairies had been in and left her a birthday present as well. Every available surface was covered in magic flowers that glowed in beautiful colors, filling the room with sparkling, shimmering light, and when Stella stroked their petals—which smelled deliciously of buttered popcorn—the flowers unfurled themselves to reveal tiny slices of frosted birthday cake, cotton-candy pink, all in the shape of little unicorns.

Stella found she had a bit more room left after all, because she ate all the unicorn cakes before getting into bed. She was quite sure that she was far too excited to sleep. Her tummy felt like it was full of fluttering butterflies at the thought of going on the expedition with Felix tomorrow. But the excitement of the day had worn her out, and she was asleep before she knew it.

She woke up early the next morning, though, and scrambled straight out of bed, practically trembling with anticipation as she changed out of her pajamas and into a white traveling dress with star-shaped buttons, a fur-lined hood, and extra-long cuffs to keep out the snow.

An hour later, Stella's unicorn, Magic, was harnessed to their sleigh, which was ready to take them to the train station, with all their luggage strapped on the back. Stella and Felix put on their thickest traveling cloaks, lined with the warmest yeti wool, and settled into a pile of furs and blankets in the sleigh. The household staff had been left with detailed instructions regarding the care of Gruff and the pygmy dinosaurs, and so there was nothing more left to do except set off for the station. Mr. Pash, the head groom, climbed up into the driver's seat, gave a flick of the reins— and then Magic was trotting forward and the sleigh was gliding along, the runners singing over the snow, the house getting smaller and smaller behind them.

CHAPTER THREE

T HE POLAR BEAR EXPLORERS' Club was located in Coldgate—the farthest point of civilization before the Icelands took over—and the fastest way to get there was by sea. Soon after disembarking the train that afternoon, Stella found herself on the docks staring up at the most gigantic ship she had ever seen. Granted, that wasn't too difficult given that she'd only ever come across tiny ones printed in the corners of maps, but even so—this was an absolute monster that towered over all the other ships in the harbor. A beautiful mermaid figurehead rose up along the prow, and there was a name painted on the side in great looping letters: *The Bold Adventurer*.

It belonged to the Royal Crown Steam Navigation Company and had been specially commissioned to take the members of the expedition to Coldgate, so they could visit the Polar Bear Explorers' Club, and then continue on to the Icelands.

Stella followed Felix onto the ship by way of a wooden gangplank that creaked and groaned alarmingly beneath their weight, as if it was about to dump them in the freezing sea foaming far below. Up on deck there were supplies for the expedition everywhere, as well as unicorns and wolves. Stella could hear the unicorns snorting and shuffling in their makeshift stalls, and the wolves were already starting to howl.

Stella wasn't sure whether the animals just didn't like the ship, or they could sense that bad weather was coming. The clouds on the horizon looked black and threatening; everything smelled of salt and brine and storms, and there was the constant *slap, slap, slap* of the icy waves against the hull. The deck lurched beneath Stella's feet, causing her to reach out and grab Felix's sleeve for balance. For the first time since she'd left home, some small, traitorous part of her felt a twinge of nervousness, and something that was almost homesickness. She could be sitting in the orangery right now, throwing twigs for Buster, warm and safe and—

"It doesn't do to be too afraid of life and taking chances," Felix announced cheerfully, as if reading her mind. "No one ever had any fun that way." He glanced down at her with a reassuring smile and said, "Let's go and report to the captain."

cocktail party in the gramophone room, with lots of thick cigar smoke and irritatingly loud laughter and flamboyant mustache-twirling, so Stella gave that a wide berth and headed to the lower decks instead. Down in the hold she came across their stored supplies, which included sleds, tents, snowshoes, tin cups—and rifles, in case they came across any woolly mammoths, yetis, or bandits. Or angry gnomes, Stella supposed. There was also a giant crate of iced gems for the unicorns. Stella couldn't resist sneaking a few of the yummy treats on her way past, taking care to pick out only the pink ones.

The ship was now out in open water and bobbing around like a cork, which made walking in a straight line particularly difficult. In no time at all, she was lost again. Stella was delighted. She'd never really had the chance to get lost before and found it a perfectly delicious feeling, not knowing where she might come out next or who she might meet.

You couldn't help where you got lost, so it wasn't entirely Stella's fault that she found herself up on deck where Felix had told her not to go. She'd just happened upon a ladder—which she climbed—only to find herself in the wolf kennels, filled with the smell of wet fur and sweet hay. She tried to tell herself that she wasn't technically *out* on deck, since the kennels had a roof and some canvas walls, but these were flapping about like anything, with icy air whistling in through the gaps, along with occasional flurries of snow and steam from the great ship's funnels. She could hear the wind roaring and the waves beating against the wooden sides.

Stella was just thinking that she really shouldn't be here, and ought to get back down below, when a heavy *thump* made her turn around.

There was a boy at the back of the kennels, shifting great big piles of hay. He looked about a year older than Stella, with very dark hair that reached almost to his shoulders, golden-brown skin, and shirtsleeves rolled up to the elbow.

Stella felt a twinge of jealousy at his light brown skin. Until she'd started at the village school, she'd always assumed that there were other white children like her. But all the other kids at school were pink or black or brown. No one was white like she was, absolutely nobody. She came home from her first day crying, and when she told Felix the reason why, he said, "Oh, my darling, you can't be jealous of other people's skins. Or of their possessions, or good fortune, or little triumphs. Nothing lies down that road but misery. The man—or woman—who walks around constantly comparing their life to others' will never be happy."

"But I'm different from all of them. No one else had white hair or skin. They said I was a ghost girl! Why can't I just be normal?"

Felix scooped her up in his arms and kissed the top of

her head. "I tried to be normal once, and it made me utterly miserable," he said. "So I gave it up and have been perfectly content ever since. It is no great achievement to be the same as everybody else, Stella. Being different is a perfectly fine thing to be, I promise you."

Now, on deck, Stella took a step further into the kennels and called a greeting to the boy at the back, raising her voice to be heard over the gale.

He turned around and raised his eyebrows in surprise at the sight of her. "Hello there," he said. "I didn't expect to see anyone else up here. Haven't you noticed there's a storm coming?"

"You're here, aren't you?"

"Sure, but I'm looking after the wolves." The boy's clothes were covered in hay, and there were even pieces of it sticking out of his hair. He had brown eyes and wore a silver wolf pendant attached to a cord of leather around his neck. He also had an earring dangling from his left ear— Stella was pretty sure it was a wolf's fang. It made him look like a pirate, which meant she liked him instantly.

"What's your name?" she asked.

"Shay Silverton Kipling."

"Captain Kipling's son?" Stella recognized the name of their expedition's captain from all the times Felix had mentioned him.

"That's right," the boy replied.

"I'm Stella Starflake Pearl."

Shay grinned. "I know who you are. You're Felix's daughter. He's visited our house to plan expeditions before. Mum says he's one of the most charming men she's ever met. He talks about you all the time, you know."

Stella was pleased that Felix had talked about her, although she hoped he'd only said nice things and not shared any stories where she had been bad—like the time she had tried to give Gruff a haircut but ended up making him look like a giant white poodle, which had been very embarrassing for them both.

"Can I help?" She gestured toward the canvas wall. "I'm not afraid. I like storms."

"I hate to break it to you, but this isn't the storm. This is just a touch of rain. Trust me, when the storm catches up with us, you'll know about it."

The words were barely out of his mouth before the ship made a great lurching, bucking movement that hurled the children and the wolves against one of the tent's thin canvas walls.

The storm had finally arrived. But the canvas wasn't strong enough to take their weight and instantly tore free of its ropes. Before they knew what was happening, Stella and Shay were out on the open deck, slipping and sliding across the soaking wet boards while the rain lashed at their skin like thousands of salt needles.

"The wolves!" Shay yelled, gesturing at the two that had fallen out with them. "We have to get them back in or they'll be washed overboard!"

As the ship gave another stomach-churning lurch, Stella thought that they were in danger of getting washed overboard themselves. Felix would be absolutely furious if he knew she was up here. But no wolves were going to get swept away tonight if Stella had anything to do with it, so she wrapped her arms around the nearest one—a reddish-colored wolf with soft brown eyes. Shay grabbed the other, picked it up, and hurried back toward the canvas wall of the kennel. Stella tried to follow but she wasn't strong enough to lift the wolf, and the next moment another great wave crashed into the ship.

The wooden deck made a groaning sound, and Stella and the wolf fell back against the railings. For a moment she couldn't tell what was up or down, what was sea and what was stars. Then a great flash of lightning lit up the sky, making it almost as bright as daylight, and a cold, foaming wave reached right over the side of the ship and tried to pluck her from the deck, drenching her in the process.

"It's okay," Stella gasped as the wolf whined and panted in her arms. "It's okay. I've got you. I won't let go."

She struggled back to her feet and took a lurching step in the direction of the kennel. Thunder broke overhead so loudly that it was almost like the sky was being cracked in two. The deck suddenly fell away from Stella's feet as the ship took another plunge over the edge of a giant wave. She fell back, and this time she was higher than the railings and there was nothing to stop her from sailing right over them—out, out, out toward the sea.

As she flew over the side—beyond the point of no return—she couldn't tell whether the roaring in her ears was from the pounding of the waves, or the crack of the thunder, or just the thrumming of her own blood beating against her eardrums. She heard Shay shout her name, but her jaw was too locked up with fear for her to call back. Her arms were still clamped tight around the wolf as she screwed up her eyes and tried to brace herself for the shock of the icy water hitting her skin; the terrible, black, greedy sucking of the ocean that would draw her right underneath the surface with the drowned men and the mermaids and the sunken pirate treasure.

Only it never came. Instead she landed with a crash and a thump on something solid. And then everything went unnaturally, eerily quiet. The wolf squirmed out of her grip and Stella sat up, trying to work out what was happening. Her back gave a twinge of protest but she seemed to be all in one piece. An oar clattered against her foot and she realized that she had landed in one of the lifeboats.

"Are you all right down there?"

Stella looked up and saw Shay peering over the railings at her.

"I think so," she called back.

"Thank the stars! And Kayko?"

"Who?"

"The wolf."

"She's okay too."

"Man, when I saw you go flying over those railings I thought you'd had it for sure! Look, please don't start crying or anything—I'll have you up from there in a jiffy."

"I have no intention of crying," Stella replied, feeling quite indignant at the suggestion. "What happened to the storm, anyway? Is it over?"

Shay hesitated, then shook his head and said, "It's not over."

"Then how come it's so quiet?"

It had completely stopped raining. There wasn't even a puff of wind—just a strange heavy feeling in the air, as if the sky was pressing down on her.

"It's the Eye," Shay said.

"The what?"

"The Eye of the storm," Shay said. "Look there."

He pointed down into the water and Stella craned her neck over the side of the lifeboat. She couldn't work out what she was seeing at first but then, suddenly, she gasped. Where she had expected to see only dark waves, there was a huge great eye staring up at her, shining silver in the moonlight. It was easily the most enormous eye Stella had ever seen. The pupil alone was wider than she was tall—a deep, dark black, the color of strange and terrible secrets. The silvery iris rippled like water, and gigantic eyelashes, as thick as a man, reached right up out of the sea to brush against Stella's lifeboat.

"Great Scott!" she muttered, staring down, torn between fascination and dread. There was something almost hypnotizing about that eye, something that made it hard to look away.

"We don't have much time. Hold tight, I'm going to pull you up," Shay called from the deck, already tugging at the ropes.

Stella looked back over the side. If she were to reach over, she would actually be able to touch one of the eyelashes with her fingertips. The fleeting thought occurred to her that perhaps she should grab hold of one and try to yank it free. An eyelash from the Eye of a storm would, after all, be a fine addition to the curiosities on display at the Polar Bear Explorers' Club. The president was sure to be pleased with her, and such a trophy might help persuade him that she really was cut out to be an explorer. She reached her hand out over the side, all set to do it. But then she recalled something Felix had once said to her.

Sometimes you should let sleeping polar bears lie. . . .

Stella thought that the same general rule probably applied here. Poking the Eye of a storm on her very first voyage seemed like a rather foolhardy thing to do, plus it would have been very rude. Stella had always liked storms and had no wish to offend this one.

"Good-bye, storm," she whispered instead, as Shay hauled on the ropes above and the lifeboat rose steadily up toward the deck.

"Well, you're a sparky thing, aren't you?" Shay said with a grin when she finally drew level. "Exactly what I'd expect from Felix's daughter, really." He gave her his hand and helped her scramble clear before scooping out the wolf. Then he turned back to Stella and, to her surprise, threw his arms around her and squeezed her tight in a great big hug. "You wonderful girl—thank you, thank you, thank you!" he said. "Kayko would have been lost if it weren't for you." He let her go, glanced out toward the horizon, and said, "The calm won't last. Let's batten down the hatches while we still can."

Stella cast one last look down at the Eye before following Shay to the wolf pen. They just had time to get inside and tie the wall firmly down before the Eye of the storm closed and the gale started up around them once again.

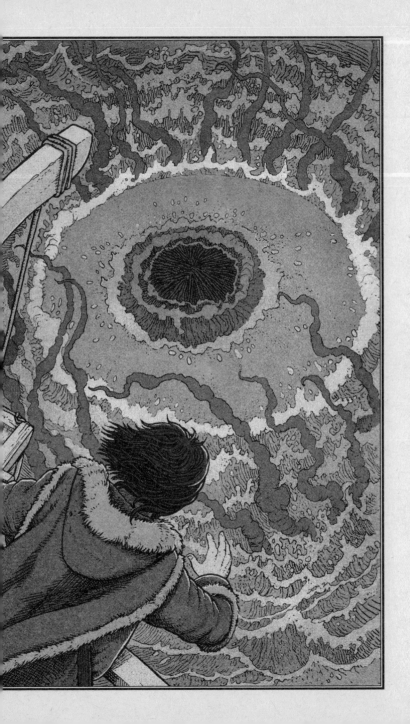

CHAPTER FOUR

How come you're looking after the wolves, anyway?" Stella asked Shay as the two of them set about securing the canvas walls of the kennel.

"Dad says a proper explorer should always see to his animals before seeing to himself," he replied. "Seems only fair. Besides, it's easier for me because I speak their language."

He pulled the silver wolf pendant free of his shirt, and Stella realized that this was no ordinary pendant but a whisperer's wolf—a magical clockwork creature.

"You're a wolf whisperer!" she said.

Felix had told her about whisperers: amazing people who could speak to animals. They were quite rare, and hardly anyone was born with the gift these days. Felix had once met a man who claimed to be a frog whisperer and carried a small frog around with him in a box, telling anyone who would listen that it was a genius who could solve all the problems of the civilized world. But the frog seemed very uninterested in whatever conversation the man was trying to have with it, and Felix wasn't convinced that he was really a frog whisperer at all.

"Can I see the wolf?" Stella asked, a little breathlessly. The ship gave another rolling lurch and she grabbed hold of a rope to steady herself.

"Sure." Shay slipped the pendant from around his neck and dropped it into Stella's palm. The animal had been sitting up with its eyes closed, but as soon as it touched her skin it lay down on her hand in one quick movement, its nose between its paws. The silver was warm and Stella could feel the soft thump of a tiny heartbeat deep within it. Animals like these were only given to whisperers who'd been rigorously tested and vetted and verified by the Royal Guild of Whisperers. Otherwise there was nothing to stop any old person from putting a frog in a box and claiming he could speak to it.

"How does being a whisperer work?" Stella asked.

"I just think whatever I want to say, and the wolves hear me," Shay said with a shrug. "And then they speak back to me inside my head too. Like this, look."

Shay turned his head toward the nearest wolf pen, and although he didn't speak out loud, Stella could tell that he was talking to one of the wolves because the wolf pendant in her hand moved. The silver wolf opened its eyes, which were revealed to be tiny red jewels that gleamed in the lamplight. Stella saw a nearby wolf—the reddish one she had saved earlier—suddenly prick up its ears, raise its head, and look straight at Shay.

"She says thanks a bunch for helping her earlier," Shay said, turning to Stella. "She thought you were very brave. I did too."

Stella shrugged, although she couldn't help being pleased by the compliment. "I wish I was a wolf whisperer," she said, handing the pendant back. "Or any kind of whisperer, really."

A polar bear whisperer would definitely be her first choice. She could have proper conversations with Gruff then, and she was quite sure he would have plenty of fascinating opinions to share and interesting things to say.

The ship was rolling hard enough to send her sprawling, so Stella sat down on the nearest haystack. "Have you ever been to the Royal Guild of Whisperers?" she asked.

Shay nodded as he replaced the whisperer's wolf around his neck and joined her on the haystack. "Yep. Mum took me. When I was tested," he said, settling into a cross-legged position. "They had an entire cabinet there with pendants for different animals. Some of them were pretty unusual, like the duck-billed platypus. And there was a sheep, and a sloth, and a mole," he went on, counting them off on his fingers. "And a ferret, and a duck. I don't think duck whispering would be very useful, though, really."

"About as useful as frog whispering," Stella replied.

"And there was a yeti, of course."

A flash of lightning suddenly lit up the wolf pen and, in those few seconds, Stella clearly saw the dark silhouette of a wolf go by on the other side of the canvas wall.

"Oh!" She leapt to her feet. "Oh no, there's a wolf still out there!"

She was already heading for the exit, horrified at the thought of the poor animal being swept overboard, when Shay caught hold of her arm. Stella noticed that he wore several bracelets, woven from chocolate-colored leather, many of them fastened with beads the shape of wolf heads.

"Hold your horses," he said. "That's just Koa."

"Koa?"

"She's my shadow wolf."

Stella stared at him. "What's a shadow wolf?"

Shay tilted his head, and one side of his mouth quirked upward in a half smile. "Well," he said, "that's a good question. No one quite knows for sure. Most whisperers have them. Some people think they're a kind of guardian angel sent to protect the whisperer. Others believe that the shadow animal is a wild part of the whisperer's own soul, brought to life and given physical form."

He drew back the canvas wall so that Stella could see

45

out onto the shiny wet deck. Through the driving rain, a dark shape moved slowly toward them, and as it got closer, Stella saw that it was an enormous wolf. It wasn't like the wolves in the pen, though. This one was larger, reaching almost to Stella's waist, and its fur was coal black—the exact same shade as Shay's own hair. When it stopped in front of them, Stella saw that the wolf had intelligent, silver eyes that seemed to glow with a faint light all their own.

Shay dropped down into a crouch so that his face was level with the wolf's. The animal gazed back at him with obvious affection.

"Is she friendly?" Stella asked. "Can I pet her?"

"Oh, she's friendly, all right," Shay replied. "But she has no physical substance. She's a shadow wolf, remember?"

He demonstrated by reaching out his hand and bringing it slowly toward Koa's back. Instead of making contact with the fur, his hand just passed straight through the wolf's body, like the animal was made of smoke. And indeed, the next moment, Koa melted away into the shadows, as if she'd never been there at all.

"Where's she gone?" Stella asked, gazing around.

Shay shrugged. "Who knows?" He stood up. "Koa comes and goes as she pleases. I don't always see her, but I feel her close by. She's never too far away."

"What kind of things does she say to you?" Stella asked, desperately curious.

"Secrets, mostly. I couldn't possibly share them. She'd never forgive me." Shay offered her a grin. "Sorry."

"That's okay," Stella replied. The fairies told Felix secrets sometimes, and he had explained to her that it was very important to never betray a friend's trust by sharing a confidence.

"Were you born a wolf whisperer?" Stella asked. "Or was Koa just there one day?"

She very much hoped it was the second option. If Shay's shadow wolf had just suddenly appeared, then perhaps Stella might yet turn out to be a whisperer. Why, she might wake up in her cabin tomorrow to find a shadow unicorn or shadow polar bear peering up at her. Really, even a shadow caterpillar or a shadow duck would be better than nothing.

But Shay said, "You're born a whisperer. Koa's been there for as long as I can remember." He paused, then added, "She saved my sister's life once. I have seven of them, you know." He gave Stella another sudden grin. "Sisters, that is. Not shadow wolves. My youngest sister is a penguin whisperer."

"How absolutely wonderful!" Stella exclaimed.

Shay shrugged. "It's okay, I guess, but her shadow penguin, Honky, is terribly grumpy. He and Koa get on famously, though. Honky likes to stand on Koa's back and ride about on her while flapping his wings up and down."

Stella couldn't help giggling at the image. Just at that

moment, though, a gigantic thunder crack overhead made both children jump. "I'd better go," Stella said reluctantly. She thought of the promise she had made earlier and added, "Felix said I had to go back to the cabin if the storm hit. Will the wolves be okay?"

Shay nodded. "I'll stay with them," he said. "And Koa will keep an eye out. All night long if we have to."

"Well, good night, then."

"Good night, Sparky. And thanks again for your help. You were wonderful."

When Stella woke up the next morning, the ship was already in the harbor at Coldgate. From her top bunk she looked out of the porthole and marveled at the beautiful white sails of the other ships.

"Stella, why on earth are your clothes all wet?" Felix asked from below.

Stella winced and peered over the side of the bunk. She'd been so keen to change into her unicorn pajamas last night that she'd just left her wet clothes in a pile by the bed.

"I was helping Shay Kipling look after the wolves," she said. "And the ship was rocking around so much that I fell into their water trough."

It was only half a lie, after all, and there was no reason to upset Felix unnecessarily. Stella noticed that he had put on his explorer's hooded dress cloak. It was made from

48

pale blue cloth and had a small polar bear stitched on the front, clearly marking him out as a member of the Polar Bear Explorers' Club. Stella had seen the cloak many times before, but normally only hanging on a coat peg or thrown over the back of a chair. Felix hated it for being heavy and itchy and too formal, and was forever taking it off as soon as he got the chance.

They left the ship and stepped onto a dockside bustling with people. Many of them seemed to be selling weird and wonderful things, from mermaid flowers and pirate pancakes to treasure maps and telescopes. Stella would have loved to explore, but there wasn't even time to have breakfast. The other members of the expedition had already left to arrange their final supplies, and Felix and Stella were the last to get going.

A sleigh had been sent for them from the Polar Bear Explorers' Club, ornate and beautiful, adorned with dozens of silver bells, and the explorers' crest painted on the side. And stamping their pearly hooves, and snorting their misted breath into the frosty morning air, were six magnificent zebra unicorns.

Stella and Felix boarded the sleigh and set off into Coldgate, the many tiny bells creating a constant backdrop of silver music. The entire city was made from ice, and dozens of ice towers sparkled as the sleigh rattled along the frozen cobbles. Stella was quite sure it must be one of the most beautiful places in the world. Everything was bright white in the morning sunshine, with ice sculptures and frozen fountains marking every corner.

In no time at all, they'd reached the gates of the Polar Bear Explorers' Club, topped with gold-tipped spikes. There were also glorious polar bear statues crafted from white marble reclining on the pillars at either end. The gates swung open for them, and the sleigh passed down a central path flanked on each side by a vast snow garden. There were ice sculptures designed to look like an entire forest of trees, and Stella glimpsed ice polar bears between the tree trunks.

But even the lovely ice garden couldn't compare with the magnificent building that housed the club itself. It was, officially, the largest igloo-shaped structure in the known world, but rather than being constructed from ice, it was made entirely of white marble, shot through with silver veins that sparkled in the sun. And instead of the usual smooth, round roof, this igloo had dozens of white brick chimneys, all of which were busily puffing out woodsmoke from the many great fires the club kept burning day and night.

The sleigh pulled right up to the front entrance and liveried staff seemed to appear out of nowhere. A man with very white gloves held out a silver tray with steaming cups of hot chocolate on it, and Felix passed one to Stella before taking one for himself. The hot chocolate footman was clearly expecting Felix to go into the club alone, because he suddenly looked quite alarmed when Felix helped her down from the sleigh and said, "Right, then. We'd better go and announce ourselves."

"Um, sir?"

"Yes, Parsons?"

"It's just that, er . . . your companion is, er . . ." He glanced nervously at Stella.

"Yes?"

"It's just that she's a girl, sir."

Felix gazed at Stella for a moment, as if only just seeing her for the first time. Then he gave a shrug and said, "So she is. Well, there you have it. Not much we can do about that now, I daresay."

"But, sir, girls aren't permitted in the Polar Bear Explorers' Club," the hapless footman said.

"Aren't they?" Felix said, as if this was the first he'd heard of it.

"It's forbidden, sir."

"That's all right, Parsons. I'll take responsibility," Felix said in a polite but firm voice. He held his hand out to Stella, who normally considered herself too grown up for hand-holding, but she was starting to feel a little bit intimidated by the club and its disapproving footman, so she took Felix's hand and was glad when he gave her fingers a reassuring squeeze.

Together, they went through the huge double doors and into the club's lobby. It was a thoroughly grand affair, with a gigantic fireplace dominating the far wall. The air smelled of pine needles, and the walls were made of the same white marble bricks as the exterior. All around the room hung huge portraits of the Polar Bear Explorers' Club's most famous and esteemed members, who peered out at them with extremely serious expressions on their faces. They were all men, of course, and they all seemed to have a penchant for monocles and morose mustaches.

The floor was also white marble, and it was scattered about with thick, warm rugs, intricately stitched in silver and blue. But one of them wasn't man-made, and Stella and Felix both winced at the sight of a huge polar bear rug spread out in the center of the room. It still had its entire head, and the mouth had been fixed open to display its teeth, its sightless glass eyes staring blindly ahead. Stella thought of Gruff, and his love of hugs and fish cookies and rolling in the snow, and turned her head away from the sad skinned bear on the floor.

Her eyes instantly fell on a gigantic pair of snow moose antlers displayed over the fireplace—another trophy brought back from some past expedition. The animal skins and rugs and antlers made Stella feel very glum, and she thought she might have preferred the entrance hall of the Jungle Cat Explorers' Club, which was said to be adorned with hundreds and hundreds of piranha teeth.

The footman took their cloaks and said, "If you'd care to follow me, I'll announce you to the president."

Stella and Felix followed him down a corridor, their footsteps muffled by the many thick rugs, although thankfully there were no more polar bear ones. Finally, they stopped in front of a large red door that led to the club president's study. There was a brass nameplate on the door that read: ALGERNON AUGUSTUS FOGG, CLUB PRESIDENT.

Felix indicated some ornate, uncomfortable-looking chairs and said, "Better wait out here, Stella. The old boy is a bit of a stick-in-the-mud and it would be best if I could warm him up to the idea of you slowly."

Stella sighed but sat down on one of the chairs. The footman duly announced Felix, who smiled at her before disappearing into the room on the other side of the door. With a final worried look in Stella's direction, the footman left as well, leaving her alone in the corridor.

She fidgeted around for a while, trying to get comfortable, but the seat was lumpy and smelled funny, as if a wet polar bear had rubbed its fur up against it. For what felt like the longest time, Stella strained her ears, trying to catch a few words of the conversation that was taking place in the other room. She didn't hear anything except for once when a voice that wasn't Felix's exclaimed: "Absolutely out of the question!"

She flinched and knew they must be talking about her.

An hour went by and still Felix hadn't come out. Stella got up, paced around a bit, and looked up and down before finally deciding that she couldn't possibly sit in that lumpy old chair a moment longer. She was in the Polar Bear Explorers' Club, so if Felix wasn't persuasive enough, and the president was about to have her thrown out, then Stella was going to make absolutely sure that she at least got to see the map room before she left.

She figured it couldn't be that difficult to find, and so, with one last guilty look at the club president's door, she turned her back on it and walked away down the corridor.

CHAPTER FIVE

I T TURNED OUT THAT finding the map room wasn't quite as straightforward as Stella had hoped. There were no signs anywhere, for one thing. No handy maps with red *you are here* dots to mark the way. She had no choice but to wander at random. She found the library, which was even larger than the one they had at home, and also stumbled into a couple of cozy-looking drawing rooms, which held a lot of overstuffed armchairs and snoozing explorers and clouds of cigar smoke. The next door she opened led to a steaming saltwater pool in a huge room with a cavernous ceiling and beautiful wall tiles decorated with polar bears and the explorers' club crest. Strangely, the Jacuzzi in the corner was full of happily soaking penguins, who looked quite miffed at being disturbed.

It wasn't long before Stella was completely lost and wouldn't have been able to return to the president's room even if she'd wanted to. She felt a guilty twinge as she realized that Felix was going to have to come looking for her, but there wasn't much she could do to change that now.

Finally, she turned a corner and found herself outside a set of large and impressive-looking double doors. Hoping that these might lead to the map room, Stella pushed them open and slipped inside. However, she didn't find herself in the map room, but in the Hall of Flags.

And it was most definitely a Hall with a capital *H*. The ceiling soared high above her, painted with a white frozen landscape scattered with some of the most important discoveries claimed by members of the Polar Bear Explorers' Club. At one end Stella recognized the polar beans, which were almost like normal beans, except for the fact that they had arms and legs and good singing voices. They were said to be quite delicious, and had saved Coldgate from famine sixty years ago. At the other end were a collection of frost hares and a whole herd of singing ice whales. In the very center of the painting was a great yeti, teeth bared ferociously while the rarest of polar explorers—a yeti whisperer—stood alone and unarmed below it, calming the huge beast with nothing but words.

Lining the walls, in gilt gold frames, was a selection of retired expedition flags. All of them showed signs of wear and tear around the edges, or unidentified stains, or tooth marks—sure indications that they had been out there in the world, proudly displayed throughout their various expeditions.

Stella walked over to the first one and examined the explorers' crest stitched in the center. It combined the four symbols of the world's four explorers' clubs: Polar Bear, Ocean Squid, Jungle Cat, and Desert Jackal. But because these were Polar Bear Explorers' Club flags, the polar bear was stitched in gold thread, while the others were stitched in black. A plaque on the wall beneath it proclaimed that this flag had been taken on the Frozen Waterfall Expedition, the Narrow Gorge Expedition, and the Snow Shark Expedition before being retired to the Hall of Flags. Stella guessed that the snow shark one must have been the last, because the flag had rather an alarming amount of bite marks. It had practically been shredded in some places.

Stella was so absorbed in the flag, and thoughts of the monster that had wrecked it, that she didn't notice there was someone else in the hall with her. She only became aware of his presence when a cold voice spoke behind her: "You shouldn't be here."

Stella yelped in surprise and whirled around on the spot. At first she couldn't see anyone in the vast hall, but then her eyes found a boy sitting in a corner with his back against the wall and his legs drawn up, his arms resting on his knees. Slowly, he unfolded his skinny body, stood up, and took a step toward her.

He was perhaps a year older than Stella, with a thin, pale face and hair so blond it was almost white. Stella narrowed her eyes when she saw he wore the black robes of the Ocean Squid Explorers' Club. These were similar in style to the Polar Bear robes, except that they were made from waxed oilcloth, to protect the wearer from the elements, and had a tiny squid emblem emblazoned on the chest. The boy's white collar was so stiff and straight it looked as if it had been starched, and his hair was brushed back so neatly that Stella thought he must have used a whole tube of hair wax to fix it like that.

"Girls aren't allowed in the explorers' clubs," the boy said. "You're not supposed to be here."

Stella folded her arms over her chest. "Well, neither are you. This is the Polar Bear Explorers' Club, not Ocean Squid."

"How did you get in? Did you sneak over the gates?" the boy asked, ignoring her remark.

"Did you slither up through the drains?" Stella shot back.

The boy glared at her. "I'm here for an expedition. The Ocean Squid Explorers' Club is going to be the first ever to reach the coldest part of the Icelands."

Stella gaped at him. "You can't be. That's what *we're* going to do!"

"Not likely," the boy said.

Stella didn't like the way he was staring so openly at

her hair, which she had tied back into a long ponytail. It wasn't unusual for people to be curious about her appearance on first meeting her, especially when they'd never seen white hair like hers before, but even so, it was terribly rude to stare like that.

Stella lifted her head a little higher, calmly smoothed an imaginary wrinkle from the dove-colored skirts of her traveling dress, and said, "I still don't understand why you're even here, when you're not a Polar Bear club member."

The boy gave her a superior look. "Don't you know anything? We're being hosted as guest explorers. Our two expeditions will take the same ship to the Icelands. It's less expensive that way."

"So what's your role, then?" Stella asked. "Are you a squidologist? You look like a squidologist to me."

"I am *not* a squidologist!" The boy drew himself up to his full height. "My name is Ethan Edward Rook, and I'm a magician."

"Do some magic, then."

Ethan looked momentarily taken aback, but quickly recovered himself and said, "All right, if you want me to. Hold out your hand, girl."

"Don't call me 'girl.' My name is Stella. Stella Starflake Pearl."

Ethan looked down his nose at her. She gave him her fiercest stare right back.

"Only explorers have three names," he said.

"That must make me an explorer, then."

Ethan shrugged, and gestured impatiently for her hand. Stella held it out palm upward. One side of Ethan's mouth twisted in a half smile as he held both his hands over hers and said, "I hope you're not afraid of snakes."

Stella *was* a little bit unsure about snakes, but she gritted her teeth and promised herself that she absolutely *would not* flinch if one magically appeared on her hand. Ethan's eyes narrowed in concentration and the air between their two hands shimmered, causing Stella's skin to tingle. But perhaps part of Ethan's mind was still thinking of the polar beans painted on the ceiling above them, because when the shimmering air formed into a solid shape, there was no fearsome snake—but five polar beans all jumping up and down on Stella's palm, giggling and laughing and clapping their tiny hands together.

Stella gave a snort of amusement and glanced at Ethan, whose pale face was flushed with embarrassment. He clenched his hand into a fist and thumped it against the wall, hard enough to rattle the framed flag that hung there.

"Drat!" he exclaimed.

"No need to be a sore loser about it." Stella laughed. She leaned down to set the polar beans on the floor, where they skipped, cartwheeled, and frolicked their way around the hall. "Squidologists can't make beans out of thin air, so

I believe you're a magician now at least—just not a very good one."

Ethan fixed her with an icy-gray stare. Stella distinctly saw his nostrils flare. "I am an excellent magician," he said. "You're just a stupid girl who doesn't know what she's talking about."

Stella was about to offer the nastiest insult she could think of in return, when the door opened behind them and Felix walked in. "Ah, there you are," he said. "I've been looking high and low for you."

He didn't raise his voice or sound angry, but Stella could hear the edge of disappointment in his tone, which was somehow worse. Suddenly, she felt no bigger than the polar beans merrily sliding up and down the polished floor of the hall.

"I'm sorry, Felix," she said. "I just wanted to see the map room."

Felix raised an eyebrow slightly. "This is the Hall of Flags."

"I got lost," Stella admitted.

Ethan gave a snort beside her.

"Well, I'm glad to see you're making friends, at least," Felix said, walking over to them. He held his hand out to Ethan and said, "Felix Evelyn Pearl. Delighted to meet you."

Ethan looked at Felix's outstretched hand with an

expression of distaste, and Stella decided right then and there that if Ethan didn't shake Felix's hand within the next five seconds, she was going to bop him on the nose. Really, really hard. Fortunately for Ethan, he eventually took Felix's hand and said, "Ethan Edward Rook."

"How do you do?" Felix said. "I just met your father in the corridor."

Ethan instantly looked a little shifty, and Stella wondered whether he had wandered off against instructions too.

Felix turned to her and said, "You'll be pleased to hear that the president has agreed you can come on the expedition with us. You'll need to take the explorers' pledge, and then we'll be off." He turned back to Ethan and said, "We'll see you on the ship, Master Rook."

Stella felt a sense of smug satisfaction at the stunned expression on Ethan's face, and she couldn't resist poking her tongue out at him as she followed Felix from the room. She really was going on the expedition! The president hadn't forbidden it after all. And there was nothing Ethan Edward Rook, or anyone else, could do to stop her.

CHAPTER SIX

I REALLY AM SORRY," STELLA said to Felix as they walked down the corridor.

"What are you sorry for, Stella?" he asked.

"Well, for not staying outside like you asked me to. And for . . . for disappointing you."

Felix stopped and turned toward her. "Listen," he said, "this is your first expedition, so everything is going to seem new and strange and exciting to you. But, Stella, you absolutely *must* do as I say from now on. It wasn't easy getting the president to agree to you coming along. And if anything goes wrong with the expedition as a result, then I will certainly lose my membership in the Polar Bear Explorers' Club. Do you understand?"

Stella nodded. The last thing she wanted was for Felix to regret bringing her, and she would hate herself forever if she somehow got him thrown out of the club that he loved so much. "Yes, Felix. I promise I'll be good and do as you say and not let you down."

"Excellent. And in fact, while we're on the subject, there's one particular thing you can agree to do for me right now."

"Anything," Stella said. "I'll do anything you want."

"I want you to be nice to Ethan Edward Rook during our voyage to the Icelands."

Stella couldn't help herself—she immediately made a face. "He doesn't seem like a very nice person to me," she said.

"Well," Felix replied, "you hardly know him. And we don't always show people our true selves on first meeting them, do we?"

"He's got a cold way of talking, and a sneering sort of face, and this nasty way of looking at you like he thinks you're less than him," Stella said.

"Give him a chance," Felix insisted. "It doesn't do to judge others too hastily. And sometimes people are fighting battles we know nothing about. What does it cost us to be kind?"

"Nothing," Stella dutifully supplied, although it seemed to her that it *did* cost something to be kind sometimes. Patience, for a start, and pride, and willpower. "But what did you mean about fighting battles? What battle is Ethan fighting?"

"How should I know?" Felix asked. "I only just met the boy."

"You do know something about it," Stella said, narrowing her eyes at him. "I can tell."

"Really, Stella, don't be such a nosy-boots," Felix replied mildly. "All you have to worry about is being kind to Ethan. It's not at all necessary for you to know his life story to do that."

"All right," Stella said, trying not to sigh. "Next time I see him I'll try to be nice."

"Good girl." Felix squeezed her shoulder and then continued walking down the corridor.

When they reached the president's office, Felix knocked firmly on the door and a voice called for them to enter. They walked into a large room dominated by a gigantic wooden desk at one end. Stella saw that it was intricately carved, with figures of snarling yetis serving as legs and holding up the large tabletop. Bookcases ran around the walls, filled with atlases and almanacs and travel journals, and a fire crackled and spat in a grand fireplace. Above it hung a huge painting of a polar bear, sitting on its haunches with its head thrown back, roaring into the frozen air and snow that swirled all around it.

"Ah, Mister Pearl," boomed a deep voice from the end of the room. "You found the girl, I see."

The president of the Polar Bear Explorers' Club stood

and walked around from behind his desk. Algernon Augustus Fogg was a large man with an extremely impressive mustache. It was twirled, curled, and waxed at the ends, and instantly made Stella think of walruses.

"Child, this is most irregular," the president barked. He even sounded a little bit like a walrus. "We have never had any lady explorers at the Polar Bear Explorers' Club, let alone *girl* ones. Goodness knows what the other clubs will make of us. Think us all a bunch of deranged mavericks, I don't doubt. Most irregular. Quite unheard of." He sighed, reached into his waistcoat pocket, and withdrew a circular tin of mustache wax, with which he proceeded to wax the ends of his impressive facial hair. Giving a final twisting flourish to its already pointy tips, he said, "But your, ah . . ." He hesitated and glanced at Felix, apparently unsure how to refer to him. "Your guardian—"

"Father," Felix said at once, slipping his hands into his pockets and developing a sudden interest in the polar bear painting above the fireplace.

"Yes, your father," President Fogg amended. "Your father has been most persuasive. Most persuasive." He scowled. "And since he is providing the lion's share of the funding for this expedition, I have decided to allow his request as a special favor—on this *one* occasion. You shall be admitted as a junior member of the Polar Bear Explorers' Club on a temporary basis. After that, we'll see." He

beckoned Stella forward. "I know you have a ship to catch, so let's not waste any more time."

Stella walked up to the desk and stared at a huge, glittering yeti paperweight that was cut entirely out of one massive piece of crystal and was holding down a pile of travel documents. She thought she had never seen such a magnificent paperweight in her life, and wondered whether she might be able to persuade Felix to get her one for her next birthday.

The president picked up a large leather-bound atlas, held it out toward Stella, and said, "Place your right hand over the atlas and repeat after me."

She dutifully did as he said and proceeded to recite the explorers' pledge, which went like this:

"*I, Stella Starflake Pearl, do solemnly swear that I will explore faraway lands, strange seas, exotic jungles, and forbidden deserts. That I will bravely face fierce monsters, bloodthirsty pirates, savage beasts, and ferocious weather. I will seek to extend the limits of human understanding, discover new wonders, and commit astonishing acts of derring-do. All my discoveries, scientific or otherwise, shall be made in the name of Queen, country, and the esteemed honor of the Polar Bear Explorers' Club. In wind, hail, sleet, or snow I shall keep a stiff upper lip, keep calm, and carry on regardless. I shall conduct myself in a gentlemanly manner at all times, ensuring that my collar is cleanly pressed and my mustache is well maintained, even when experiencing those narrow escapes and close shaves that are the unavoidable experience of intrepid gentleman explorers across the globe.*"

Stella thought he might have left out that last sentence on account of her being a girl, but went along with it anyway, while silently promising herself that one day, there would be a lady's pledge as well as a gentleman's one, and that it wouldn't once mention something as vain and useless as a well-groomed mustache. Instead, the lady's pledge would vow to fashion petticoats into sails for rafts, or bravely brandish parasols as weapons, or learn how to throw a fan so that it could knock a bandit down from fifty feet away. There was plenty of stuff, Stella was sure, that she could think of for the lady's pledge, which would be far more useful than collar pressing and mustache grooming.

"Here is your explorer's cloak," President Fogg said, handing Stella a smaller version of Felix's pale blue one, complete with tiny polar bear stitched onto the front. "And your explorer's bag." He handed her a blue satchel, also emblazoned with the club's polar bear motif. Then they shook hands and Felix said they must go or they would miss the ship.

Stella felt a great blazing glow of happiness as she slipped the warm explorer's cloak around her shoulders and followed Felix out to the waiting sleigh. Once settled inside, with the door closed and the brisk *clip-clop* of the unicorns' hooves filling the air, Stella lost no time in exploring the contents of her explorer's bag.

She was a little disappointed to find that it mostly contained mustache wax and beard oil, along with various other ointments, salves, and unguents, and a folding pocket mustache comb that was quite a handsome object, but regardless, not much good to Stella.

"Don't worry about that stuff," Felix said when Stella complained about it. "It's all quite useless. We'll sort you out with proper supplies once we're back on the ship."

CHAPTER SEVEN

THE NEXT COUPLE OF days on the *Bold Adventurer* seemed to race by in a flash. As soon as the ship set sail, Felix was crippled with seasickness once again, leaving Stella more or less to her own devices. She spent a fair amount of her time with Shay, helping him to look after the wolves, yaks, and unicorns, or watching him practice with his boomerang—a fantastic object that Stella coveted most ardently. Shay would stand on deck, Koa at his heels, and throw it out to sea, and somehow it always came back to his waiting hand. Stella asked if she could try but Shay told her, apologetically, that it took a lot of practice to get it right and if she were to throw it away from the ship, the odds were that it would fall into the waves and never be seen again.

On the morning of the third day, Felix was finally well enough to get out of bed without being in immediate danger of needing a bucket.

"What have you been up to the last couple of days?" he quizzed Stella, while standing in front of the mirror to carefully straighten his bow tie. "I've hardly seen you."

"Well, you could hardly expect me to sit around listening to you groaning all day," she replied. "It would be enough to drive anyone around the twist."

"Be that as it may," Felix replied, "you might have checked in with me from time to time."

"I *did* check in, but every time I came back you were asleep. Or in the bathroom. Or lying with your head under the pillow making that moaning sound."

Felix bent down to rummage under the bunk for his missing shoe, and Stella distinctly heard him mutter something about traveling by dirigible next time.

"I've always wanted to travel by dirigible," Stella said.

"Here it is." Felix straightened up with the missing shoe. "Come on. Let's go and have some breakfast."

Stella didn't see her friend Beanie until a few days into the voyage, when his uncle finally forced him to take a break from reading and made him go up on deck for some fresh air. Beanie was studying to be a medic and was so intensely interested in the subject that he could easily sit and read one of his textbooks for hours and hours. His uncle, Professor Benedict Boscombe Smith, wasn't too keen on reading, however, and felt that the best way to learn was by doing (even if you weren't completely sure what you were actually supposed to be doing). He was a booming, boisterous man, who, unfortunately, seemed to expect everyone else to be as booming and boisterous as he was. Stella had once heard him complaining about his nephew on a visit to Felix.

"He's just not like other children," he'd said. "He won't let anyone hug him, not even his mother. No doubt it's the elf blood in him, giving him all these strange ideas and fancies and whimsies. You saw the way he fussed over those carrots at the dinner table, lining them up in size-order before he would eat them. It's not *normal*."

"My dear Benedict, I'm sure I have no idea what 'normal' even means. And does it really matter how the boy chooses to eat his carrots in the grand scheme of things?" Felix asked.

"It's how he got that ridiculous nickname, you know," Professor Smith went on, as if Felix hadn't spoken. "He loves jelly beans—goes nuts over them—so his mother puts a packet in his lunchbox every day. But rather than just eating them, he has to separate the beans into color groups first. It's the most ridiculous thing you ever saw, and now they all call him Beanie."

"Well, there are worse things they could call him. Besides, I think you're really placing too much importance on—"

"Plus he has this crackbrained idea that he's going to be the first explorer to reach the other side of the Black

74

Ice Bridge," Professor Smith said. "Even though everyone knows it can't be done. Every explorer who's ever attempted it, including the boy's own father, has vanished without a trace. It's his mother's fault—elves *will* have these strange ideas—but she's convinced Benjamin that he can do anything a normal child can do."

"Sounds like a fine woman," Felix said.

Professor Smith scowled. "A deluded woman, more like. Aside from all his quirks, Benjamin is far too shy to be an explorer."

"Being shy is a personality trait," Felix replied with a touch of reproach. "Not a fault."

"Have you ever heard of a shy man being an explorer, Pearl?" Professor Smith boomed. "Of course you haven't. The very idea! Shy men twiddle their thumbs indoors."

"Thumb twiddling!" Felix exclaimed. "That's number one hundred and thirty-five for the list!"

"List?" Professor Smith snapped. "What list?"

"I'm drawing up a numbered list of ways I would rather choose to spend my time than mustache grooming and beard oiling—" Felix began to explain.

But Professor Smith shook his head impatiently and said, "Felix, please keep to the matter at hand! As I was saying, an explorer must be bold, brave, courageous, redoubtable—"

"'Brave' and 'courageous' mean the same thing," Felix

had said with a sigh. "And most of the redoubtable people I've met have also been insufferable. Quite insufferable, I'm afraid. No, I'm sorry, Benedict, but you're talking absolute balderdash, you know. A fearless man is far more likely to meet his death on an expedition than a thoughtful, careful one. Beanie is perfectly fine just as he is."

Now, on the ship, Stella came up on deck to find Beanie at the side of the railings, overlooking the icy ocean and holding a butterfly net. He was the same height as Stella, with dark hair that tended to stick out in all directions, as Beanie simply couldn't stand to have his hair combed. He didn't like having it cut, either, and he made the most gigantic fuss whenever his uncle dragged him to the barber, even when there were jelly bean bribes involved. His hair was always clean, though. Beanie rated personal hygiene very highly.

As Benedict Boscombe Smith had said, there was indeed elven blood in Beanie's family, and you could see this in his slender build, the way that the tips of his ears were slightly pointed, and the fact that his black hair had the odd bit of blue in it if you looked really closely.

There were three or four sea butterflies in Beanie's net, and it seemed as if they had been there for some time, because they all lay forlornly on their sides, their wings trembling slightly. As Stella watched, Beanie raised his free hand, and a glittery golden glow seemed to flow out of his fingertips, surrounding the butterflies. The next moment, they were fluttering about, their salt-tipped green wings sparkling in the sunshine. Beanie opened the net and released them, watching as they flew out across the water, dancing among the flecks of foam and sea spray.

Stella had first become aware of Beanie's healing ability when they'd attempted to climb the bagel tree in the backyard (as the poppy seed ones only grew right at the very top). When Stella fell and scraped her elbow, Beanie dropped out of the tree beside her, took her arm gently in his hand—the first time he'd ever touched her—and made that warm golden light shine from his fingers. Stella had gasped, delighted by her friend's magical power, and the next moment, there was no cut on her arm at all.

"Hi, Beanie," Stella said, joining him at the rails. She gestured at the butterfly net still clutched in his hand. "Will your uncle be terribly angry when he finds them gone?"

"I expect so. But he got the killing jar out this morning," her friend replied. "I had to do something."

Stella was glad that Beanie had saved the butterflies, and she would have liked to give him a pat on the back, only she knew that he would hate it, so instead she suggested that they build a family of snow penguins up on deck. The sea was as flat as a millpond today, but it had snowed during the night and there was plenty to spare for sculpting penguins.

"I'm glad you're here," Beanie said as they walked across

the frozen deck. "It's bound to make the expedition easier."

Stella noticed that he'd taken a little wooden carving of a narwhal from his pocket and was fiddling with it anxiously. "Oh, you brought Aubrey," she said. She wasn't surprised. Beanie's father had carved him the narwhal after seeing the strange animals—half seal, half unicorn—on his final expedition to the Black Ice Bridge. The bridge itself was a monstrously huge structure that stretched out over the sea and disappeared into freezing fog. No one knew how it came to be there, or where it led to, although many explorers had attempted to cross it.

Eight years ago, Beanie's father had set off on an expedition over the bridge and had not come back. They had never found out what had happened to him, and Stella understood that the not knowing haunted Beanie more than anything. His father had just . . . gone. And so had the rest of his team. Perhaps they'd frozen on the ice, or run out of food and starved, or been gobbled up by an enormous snow monster, or reached the end of the bridge and found something terrible on the other side.

The rescue party that went after them discovered the remains of their camp, the tents frozen and abandoned. There was no sign of any of the explorers, although they found Beanie's father's bag, which included the carved narwhal and also his journal. Several of the entries mentioned the fact that he was carving the animal as a gift for his son,

Benjamin. It quickly became Beanie's most precious possession, and he fiddled with it whenever he was feeling anxious—which was most of the time.

It probably didn't help that he knew far too much about the various ways explorers could perish or injure themselves. He'd become a bit obsessed with the topic since his father disappeared. He also, unfortunately, seemed to have an endless ability to recall gruesome facts, figures, and numbers. On their first day of school, Beanie had walked right up to Stella and said, "You can die from eating too many eels, you know."

"Oh," Stella had said. "Can you?"

Beanie had nodded. "Yes. Dr. Winston Wallaby Scott from the Ocean Squid Explorers' Club died thirty-one years ago after feasting on eels at Salty Ridge Harbor. I thought I'd better tell everyone. Mum says being nice to people is how you make friends."

Unfortunately, their classmates found Beanie odd rather than nice. And even though, in all honesty, Stella thought he was a bit odd too, Felix had told her many times that there was nothing at all wrong with being a bit odd. In fact, all the most interesting people had a little oddness about them, one way or another.

Stella and Beanie found a clear patch of deck, where there weren't too many sailors stomping about. The snow on the boards was white and crisp and sparkling, so they set to work and soon had a fine-looking family of snow penguins. Stella had just completed a particularly happy-looking penguin mother to go with Beanie's penguin baby when a familiar cold voice said, "What exactly are those things supposed to be?"

Stella turned and saw Ethan Edward Rook leaning against the rails, watching them. He wore his black Ocean Squid robe and had the same superior expression on his thin face as before. His pale hair was brushed straight back, his collar was pressed and starched, and even here on the ship he looked immaculate. Stella felt the same prickle of dislike she'd felt before, but remembering her promise to Felix, she said, "They're snow penguins. Do you want to join us?"

"Aren't you a bit old for building snow penguins? They look more like snow lumps, besides." He flicked a gloved hand toward Beanie and said, "Who's that?"

"This is my friend Beanie."

"You can't be serious?" Ethan replied, already curling his lip in disdain. "What's your real name?"

"Benjamin Sampson Smith," Beanie said, but the words came out so quietly they were practically snatched away on the wind, and Stella felt obliged to repeat them. Stella could tell Beanie was feeling anxious because he took Aubrey back out from his pocket and started to fiddle with the wooden narwhal.

"I'm Ethan Edward Rook," Ethan said, looking pleased with himself. "I'm a magician, you know."

"I like jelly beans," Beanie said, desperate to make a contribution to the conversation but not quite sure how he ought to go about it.

Ethan gave him a puzzled look. "Doesn't everyone?"

"My cousin Moira, doesn't," Beanie said. "But Stella says that's just because she's a snot."

Stella had met Moira only once, at Beanie's last birthday party. He'd optimistically invited the entire class from their school, and as usual, everyone had made excuses, or come up with a sudden change of plans, or else simply didn't bother to reply to the invitation at all. So when Beanie turned twelve, there were exactly two guests at his party: Stella and Moira. Moira turned her nose up at the jelly bean birthday cake, saying it was babyish and Beanie was weird and that she didn't even want to be there. So Stella called her a snot and said she and Beanie would eat the cake all by themselves. Which they did, although they both felt a little bit ill afterward.

"I've got some jelly beans somewhere," Beanie said, fumbling in the pockets of his grubby cloak. "My mum gave them to me before I left." He drew out a handful and held them out to Ethan. "Would you like some?"

The magician recoiled. "No! I don't know where they've been."

Beanie looked puzzled. "They've been in my pocket."

Stella was strongly tempted to tell Ethan to go away, but

felt she ought to make one last attempt to be nice, whether he wanted her kindness or not. She took a jelly bean from the pile in Beanie's cupped hand and said, "We should arrive at the Icelands in another week or so. Are you looking forward to the expedition?"

Ethan shrugged. "What's there to discover? The Icelands are just ice. They can't possibly compare with the secrets of the sea. Still, I suppose it will be dangerous enough, what with all the yetis stomping about. There's a good chance that many of us won't make it back at all. Even if you manage to escape being eaten by a yeti, many explorers before us have gotten lost in the snow and starved."

Beanie flinched and dropped the remaining jelly beans, which scattered into the snow at his feet. Stella knew he was thinking of his father, lost somewhere out on the Black Ice Bridge. "You shouldn't talk about starving at the start of an expedition," he said nervously. "Dad always said it was bad luck."

"I don't give two hoots what your father thinks," Ethan replied. "Magicians don't care about silly superstitions like that. Don't you know who you're talking to?"

Beanie frowned, even more confused. "Ethan Edward Rook," he said. "The magician. You told us that four and a half minutes ago. Don't you remember? Perhaps you've got a memory problem. That can happen sometimes, although usually not until you're very old and have to take your teeth out to put them in a little glass by the side of your bed at night." He looked at Ethan and said, "*Do* you have to take your teeth out and put them in a glass by the side of your bed at night? Because I might be able to help with that. I'm training to be a medic, you see."

"Good Lord," Ethan said, staring. He turned to Stella. "Is he an absolute freak, or just a plain idiot?"

Freak, idiot, weirdo, nutcase . . . Beanie had been called all of these things and worse at school, and it never failed to make Stella hot-blood furious. Beanie was easily the cleverest boy in their class—probably in the entire school—as well as one of the kindest people Stella knew. He was just different, and people never failed to say cruel things to him because of it.

She bent down and picked up the nearest snow penguin. It held together well enough as she straightened up and walked toward Ethan. The expression on her face made the magician feel suddenly alarmed, and he tried to take a step away, but was already pressed up against the side of the boat, the railings digging firmly into his back.

"What are you going to do with that?" he demanded.

Stella responded by dumping the snow penguin on his head.

It broke apart in a most satisfying way, and Ethan yelled as great clumps of ice slid down the back of his collar and soaked his hair. Stella saw, with immense satisfaction, that he didn't look anywhere near as immaculate with white snow streaking his black robe and icy water running down his face.

"I don't care what Felix says," Stella said, poking him hard in his thin chest. "You're no good, and I don't like you. If you're mean to Beanie again, I'll crush you."

"*You'll* crush *me*?" Ethan was almost spluttering with outrage. "*I'm* the magician here. Why, I ought to turn you into a little blind mole rat right now and toss you straight into the sea!"

He started to raise his hand and—for a horrible moment—Stella wondered whether he actually *would* turn her into a mole rat. She had a terrible vision of herself as a tiny blind pink thing, thrashing about in the waves as she watched the ship sail farther and farther away. Or perhaps he'd mess it up again and turn her into a tiny dancing polar bean, which would almost be worse, really.

"I'll teach you a lesson you'll never—" Ethan began.

"Say, this sounds interesting. Can anyone join the lesson?" a voice asked.

Stella turned and saw Shay just behind her. It was the first time she'd seen him wearing his blue Polar Bear explorer robes rather than the old shirt and trousers he wore to take care of the wolves. He had four of the expedition wolves with him—three gray ones and a brown one—and they were circling his feet, pressing up close to his legs.

"This has nothing to do with you!" Ethan said, pointing at him. "So get lost, whoever you are." One of the wolves instantly bared its teeth at him, and the magician hurriedly lowered his hand.

"Well, well," Shay said, looking him up and down. "Aren't you an uppity little prawn?"

"I'm taller than you are!" Ethan spluttered in outrage. "And no one calls me a prawn! I'm not uppity, either. I'm going straight to the captain to report a member of the Polar Bear Explorers' Club for assault!"

Stella's heart sank. Felix definitely wouldn't like that. He wouldn't like that at all.

"My name, if you care, is Shay Silverton Kipling, and I ought to call for the captain myself." Shay reached down to scratch one of the wolves behind the ears. "It's against maritime law to make magical threats against someone at sea, as you must already know."

"Oh, you lot aren't worth my time!" Ethan said before stamping off along the deck, leaving a wet trail of melting snow behind him.

"I didn't need your help," Stella said to Shay, although she wasn't sure that was entirely true. She really *hadn't* wanted to be turned into a mole rat, after all. "But thanks."

Shay inclined his head slightly. "Any time, Sparky."

Stella turned to Beanie to introduce him, but the boy's attention was firmly fixed on his narwhal and he barely glanced at Shay before mumbling, "Hello, I'm Beanie. I like jelly beans and narwhals, and now I'm going back to my cabin to study my medicine books and read about teeth." And with that, he turned and hurried away across the deck.

"Oh dear . . . he doesn't mean to be rude," Stella said. She really didn't want Shay to dislike Beanie too. "He just finds conversation difficult and needs to be alone sometimes, that's all."

"Seems fair," Shay said agreeably. "Wolves can be like that too. Sometimes they want to be part of the pack, other times they just want to be left in peace. Nothing wrong with that at all."

CHAPTER EIGHT

ON THE FINAL DAY of the voyage, Captain Fitzroy held a farewell dinner for the two explorer clubs in his private quarters. Even the junior members had been invited. The dinner was a tradition for explorers, who would have to rely on rations and foraging once they landed on the ice, and was always a lavish spread, laid out on a long table. Felix told Stella it was the last proper meal she would have for a while so she should absolutely be as greedy as possible.

The dinner was a strained affair from the very beginning. The problem was that the Polar Bear Explorers' Club and the Ocean Squid Explorers' Club each nurtured a grudge against the other because of the Snow Shark Expedition, which had taken place many years ago. Both clubs had been competing against each other then, too, and there had been accusations of cheating and foul play on both sides. At least one explorer was eaten by a snow shark, and others were seriously wounded on the ice. There had never been any formal apologies offered and the two clubs had been hostile toward each other ever since, each blaming the other for their losses and casualties, while both claimed the credit for discovering the existence of the snow shark.

The two clubs sat on opposite sides of the table, watching each other warily. The dinner started out politely enough, but it wasn't long before a quarrel broke out between the Polar Bear zoologist and the Ocean Squid hunter, both of whom wanted to be the first to kill a yeti and take it back as a trophy. It had never been done before, and both were keen to achieve a first for their clubs.

"Isn't it a little risky to go chasing after a yeti with a spear?" Felix asked, suddenly joining the conversation. "Seems like a guaranteed way to get yourself gobbled up."

"I wouldn't expect a fairyologist to know about such things," the hunter said with a curl of his lip. "But I intend to kill it with a rifle, not a spear."

"You'd never transport it back to the mainland," Captain Fitzroy broke in. "The average yeti is sixty feet tall. There's no ship built that can transport a beast of that size."

"I would cut off its head," the zoologist declared. "And take that back. There ought to be a yeti specimen at the Polar Bear Explorers' Club. It's shameful that there isn't one there already, quite frankly."

"I must admit I was surprised not to see any snow goblins or ice fairies," said a voice from the other end of the table. It was Ethan's father, the magician Zachary Vincent Rook. "We've got an entire cabinet of sea fairies on display at the Ocean Squid club. Their wings are pinned like butterflies. We keep the live ones in jars." He turned to Felix. "Really, I should have thought they'd be easy enough to catch. It doesn't even require a spear, merely a butterfly net. It's practically child's play."

Felix gave a thin smile. "The Polar Bear Explorers' Club used to have a fairy cabinet. At my urging they removed it a short while ago. Pinning fairies, or anything for that matter, is a barbaric practice that ought not to be encouraged. Or indeed, tolerated."

For a moment there was a chilly silence. Then Zachary Vincent Rook stood up. "Are you calling me a barbarian, sir?"

"What's a barbarian?" Beanie said to Stella, loud enough for the whole table to hear.

"An uncivilized person," Stella replied.

When Felix had taught Stella how to spell, he had made the task more fun by avoiding boring words like "obedience" and "cabbage" and "chalk" and favoring interesting words like "barbarian" and "tomfoolery" and "peregrinations." Once Stella learned how to spell a word, he would reward her by teaching her what it meant. She glanced at him across the captain's table and he gave her a small smile in acknowledgment of her correct description.

"'Uncivilized'!" the magician exclaimed. "If you *really* want to see something uncivilized, then I—"

"Don't be a bore, Zachary, sit down," said the captain of the Ocean Squid expedition with a yawn. "It's bad manners to quarrel at a captain's table. Besides which, you're spoiling my appetite. And it's too hot in here for squabbles."

He was right about it being hot. The number of people in the room, combined with all the hot plates they'd used to keep the food warm, had created an uncomfortably high temperature. Everyone had taken their jackets off and rolled up their shirtsleeves—everyone except Ethan, who looked as starched and smart and stuck-up as usual, with his sleeves buttoned at the wrist and his shirt done up right to the collar. Stella could tell he was hot, though, from the way he kept fanning his face with a napkin, and she thought he was very silly for not rolling up his sleeves along with everyone else.

Zachary Vincent Rook sat back down but didn't look happy about being told off in front of everyone. To make up for it, he turned to the hunter and said, "If I can assist you with the slaughter of this yeti, Jerome, do let me know. I quite agree that a yeti's head would make an excellent addition to our trophy room. It can hang right alongside the screeching red devil squid tentacle we brought back last time. Nothing more important than trophies when it comes to proving ourselves as explorers. Isn't that right, Ethan?"

Zachary thumped his son on the back, but Ethan didn't reply. In fact, Stella noticed that he actually looked rather unwell. The next moment he pushed away his plate and stood up.

"Please excuse me," he muttered, and then left the room without another word. Maybe he'd finally found it too hot in his long sleeves and gone to get some air. Or perhaps throw up over the side of the ship. Stella secretly hoped it was the latter, even if Felix would have chastised her for the uncharitable thought.

She glanced at Felix and was surprised to see him staring after Ethan with a frown on his face. Felix almost never frowned. It was all very strange.

Fortunately, just at that moment the cook brought out an ice cream cake in the shape of a yeti, which immediately cheered everyone up and cooled them all down quite considerably. The yeti's eyes were made from shards of chocolate mint, and the shaggy fur had been piped on with vanilla ice cream. Stella thought that the dead explorer clutched in one of the yeti's great fists was perhaps a little tactless, but he was made of sugared marzipan, so that made up for it to some extent. Stella adored sugared marzipan.

But the meal came to a sudden end when they heard a shout of *"Land ahoy!"* from somewhere up above. As one, the explorers all pushed back their chairs, almost falling

91

over each other in their rush to be the first out on deck.

When Stella stepped outside, she gasped in shock at the icy air. It had been cold at home, and at Coldgate, but that had been just a normal kind of cold—the kind that brings snow and frost. The cold here, though, was the type that brought snow goblins and ice storms—it was hard and sharp instead of soft and powdery. It was the kind of cold that could rip right through a person. The entire ship sparkled in a coat of frost, and it seemed like there were ten times as many stars as normal—hundreds of tiny little pinpricks of cold, white light, as if someone had scattered a great sack of glitter across the dark night sky. Stella's breath smoked out in front of her, and her teeth chattered, but she wasted no time in pushing her way to the railings with the others, where they all strained their eyes for their first moonlit glimpse of the Icelands.

Giant slabs of ice floated on the surface of the sea, and Stella could hear them bumping up against the ship and crashing into each other with such force that if anyone happened to fall into the water and get caught between two colliding pieces, they would surely be crushed into a messy pulp.

The snow-coated landscape ahead of them seemed to glow with a pale blue light all its own, and Stella wondered whether it was something to do with the great mass of stars twinkling above them. She could just make out the looming outlines of sharp, peaked mountains piercing the air like monstrous snow shark teeth. Something seemed to stir within her as she gazed at that view—some tingle of recognition, as if a deep-down part of her remembered the place where she had come from. For a moment, a memory felt within her grasp, but even as Stella reached for it, it drifted away like smoke.

There was a still, cold silence while the explorers stared at the vast, unknown landscape, dreaming of the adventures they might have and the stories—and yeti heads, in the hunter's case—that they would bring back with them.

Stella was the first to spot movement on land. The object was so big that she thought she was looking at a mountain. But then her eyes focused on an arm and a leg, and the full force of what she was seeing hit her. There was a great, humongous yeti lumbering across the ice.

"Yeti!" she cried, her voice cracking the frozen air as she pointed out across the ocean. "There's a yeti there!"

There were general cries of "Where?" and "I don't see it!" and then "Great Scott!" and "Extraordinary!" and "Behold the creature!" Then the explorers were all fumbling in their robes for a telescope to get a closer look. Stella quickly reached for her own telescope, which was made from solid brass and bound in soft, worn leather. Her hands were trembling with excitement as she focused the lens like Felix had taught her.

She gasped when she caught her first glimpse of the yeti's face, with its snow-crusted fur and white shining canines curved over its lips. The head alone must have been ten times Stella's height, and each one of those monstrous teeth was easily as tall as she was. She lowered the telescope—the brass surface freezing against her fingers—and gazed at the beast, hardly able to comprehend its size. It was a giant— far larger than any building Stella had ever seen, including the Polar Bear Explorers' Club itself.

The next moment, the yeti disappeared from sight as it passed beyond a cliff. It was too cold to stay out on deck any longer without their snow cloaks anyway, so the explorers returned to the warmth of the gramophone room, which was soon thick with the smell of brandy, and the fog of cigar smoke, and the thrill of excitement.

CHAPTER NINE

S TELLA WATCHED FROM THE deck the next day as some of the crew took a lifeboat over to the Icelands and proceeded to drive huge spikes into the snow. Sailors from the ship then threw across coils of rope as thick as Stella's arm, which were wound around the spikes to moor the ship.

It took the better part of an hour to unload the supplies, including the unicorns, wolves, and yaks. Stella checked and rechecked her pockets and her explorer's bag (which had since been emptied of mustache wax and beard oil) to make sure she had her telescope, compass, magnifying glass, pocket map, emergency mint cake, matches, and ball of string. Felix said you never knew when a ball of string might come in handy, and Stella had carried one almost for as long as she could remember. She'd also decided to keep the folding pocket mustache comb, because she'd discovered it made an excellent back scratcher.

There was a time and a place for dresses and petticoats, and exploring the Icelands definitely wasn't it, so Stella had changed into the same type of outfit that Felix and the other explorers all wore. This consisted of trousers tucked into a sturdy pair of snow boots, and a multilayer of vests, woolly pullovers stitched with polar bear emblems, and waterproof sweaters piled on beneath her explorer's cloak. Much as she loved skirts, Stella was rather fond of trousers, too, and often wore them at home when she wanted to go out riding on her unicorn. Finally, she'd tied her white hair back into a long plait to keep it out of her way and fastened it with a sparkly violet ribbon.

An hour after their arrival, the supplies had all been unloaded and it was the explorers' turn to walk down the gangplank, their snow boots crunching over the frost that had already formed into a fine sparkling coat across the thick wooden boards. The ship's captain came down to see them off, and one of the ship's flags was staked into the ice to mark the spot where the *Bold Adventurer* would return for them in two weeks' time, after enjoying a spot of whaling out on the open sea. Then the photographer set up the camera on its tripod, and the two teams gathered around the flag to have their picture taken.

They needed to stand still for quite a long time for the

camera to work. Stella wasn't very good at standing still and so she scratched her nose at just the wrong moment, causing her face to come out blurred in the black-and-white photo the camera printed out. She couldn't help thinking that the adult explorers all looked a bit like walruses, with their waxed mustaches and fussy beards and puffy sideburns. Stella didn't much care for mustaches and beards and sideburns, and was glad that Felix had none of those things.

"We'll be back here in twelve days' time at sunrise," Captain Fitzroy told them, once the business of the photograph was finished. "We'll wait one day and one night. After that we must set sail whether you have returned or not. Whale blubber doesn't keep for too long belowdecks, I'm afraid. A rescue boat will no doubt come back for any lost members of the expedition, but there's no telling how soon that will be organized or when it will arrive. So make sure you're here on time if you don't want an extended stay in an igloo."

He wished them all good luck and then returned to his ship, shaking his head as if he couldn't understand why anyone would be mad enough to willingly set off into a frozen wilderness in the first place.

The ship unfurled its auxiliary sails and set back the way it had come, leaving the explorers alone with the ice and yetis. Stella had hoped that the two clubs would take their leave of each other at this point, but instead it seemed they were

going to travel together as far as the giant ice bridge someone had spotted from the ship. Once there, one club would
travel across to explore the other side, while the second club
would explore the opposite side. The Icelands ought to be
big enough for two expeditions, after all, and both clubs
attempting to explore the same area would only lead to
brawls, squabbles, loud whining, and the inevitable duels.

To save time, it was decided that the sleds would set off
as they had been unloaded, and they would split up their
provisions and supplies once they reached the ice bridge.
Which was how Stella found herself sharing a sled with
Shay, Beanie, and—to her disgust—Ethan, who complained loudest of all about the arrangement.

Unfortunately, it seemed the children needed to ride
together in the same sled because of weight distribution, so
they piled in beneath a mountain of furs, and one of the
adult Ocean Squid explorers hopped on the back to control the wolves, all of whom were panting excitedly in the
freezing air, eager to be off. One of the unicorns was tethered to the back of the sled, and then the explorer gave the
command—and they were away, moving forward over
the snow, the other sleds following on behind them in an
orderly line.

Stella was so delighted that she forgot to be grouchy
about Ethan sitting next to her, his elbow wedged against
her ribs. She drew her furred hood up over her head to

protect her ears as the cold wind whistled past them. The wolves went faster than she'd been expecting, and she felt a fluttering of excited butterflies in her stomach, like having ten birthdays all come together. As the white landscape flashed past, there was no sound except for the singing of the sled's blades over the snow and the panting of the wolves around them.

It was just white, white, white as far as the eye could see. Stella thought it was enchanting and beautiful, but beside her Ethan grunted, "Ice. Absolutely nothing but ice."

Stella ignored him and let her thoughts soar with visions of snow sharks and woolly mammoths and abominable snowmen. She twisted in her seat and waved at Felix, who was traveling in the sled behind. He grinned at her and waved back, and Stella thanked her lucky stars that she had managed to come on the expedition after all. She vowed to herself then and there that she'd show everyone that a girl could be every bit as good an explorer as any boy. Probably better, in fact, as she didn't have a mustache to worry about.

The ice bridge, when they reached it about an hour later, was a mighty structure stretching the entire length between two sides of a deep, yawning chasm. It had looked large enough through the telescope, but now they were closer, it became immediately apparent that the bridge was too narrow to risk taking the expedition across. Barely four feet wide, it would only just have taken the wolf sleds—one wrong step and they'd all go flying over the edge, and that would be the end of that. It was quickly decided that the bridge was impassable and that the two clubs should split up to try to find their own way to the other side.

If everything had gone as planned, they would have divided their provisions and gone their separate ways at this point. Stella, Shay, and Beanie would have rejoined the members of the Polar Bear Explorers' Club, and Ethan would have gone back to Ocean Squid. It is a well-known rule, however, that intrepid expeditions into the unknown do not always go as planned. And it was pure bad luck that an entire herd of woolly mammoths chose to stampede in the valley below at the precise moment that the explorers decided to move on from the bridge.

The wolves of the Polar Bear Explorers' Club were all well-trained expedition wolves and did not react to the noisy tramping and trumpeting of the mammoths. The Ocean Squid wolves, on the other hand, had been acquired cheaply and in haste. They had not received the same extensive training, had never even been on a single expedition, and, inevitably, took fright at the sound of twenty six-ton woolly mammoths thundering beneath them. The wolves pulling four of the sleds—including Stella's—charged forward in a blind panic, forcing the unicorn tethered behind to come along as well. Most of the sleds turned and went back the way they had come, but Stella's kept going—right toward the ice bridge.

Seeing what was about to happen, the Ocean Squid explorer on the back of their sled threw himself off into the snow. Ethan scrambled up and made to do the same, but Shay grabbed his sleeve and dragged him back. "Don't!" he yelled. "It's too late for that."

He was right. The sled was already on the ice bridge and it was far too narrow to risk jumping. If the wolves put even one foot out of place, they would all go tumbling over the side to their certain deaths. A couple of bags from the back of the sled came loose and fell straight over the edge, turning over and over until they burst open upon the rocks below, cans of Spam smashing on impact.

Stella could hear the unicorn cantering along behind them and hoped that it wouldn't suddenly dig in its hooves and stop, causing them all to be pulled over the side. The four junior explorers could do nothing but try to remain absolutely still, and stared down in horror as the blades of the sled whisked perilously close to the edge of the bridge.

As they raced toward the middle, the wolves panting and drooling in panic, they had the perfect view of the mammoths below, their shaggy coats crusted in old snow, their great tusks curving upward, ready to impale anyone who fell on them. It sounded like a respectable and worthy enough death for an explorer—tumbling from an ice bridge to be impaled upon a mammoth tusk—but Stella really, really didn't want that to happen, just the same.

Beside her, Beanie screwed his eyes tightly shut and started muttering under his breath. Stella was horrified to realize that he was reciting explorers' deaths. Reciting facts was something he did to calm himself down sometimes, but Stella wished he could have perhaps listed the different types of sea cucumber, or various species of giant butterfly, or pretty much anything, in fact, other than sticky ends for adventurers.

"Captain James Conrad Copplestone," Beanie gasped beside her, "trampled to death by woolly mammoths in the Glacier Circle. Sergeant Arthur Primrose Poe, gored by a saber-toothed tiger in the Azurian Jungle. Sir Hamish Humphrey Smitt—"

"Shut up, shut up!" Ethan cried in a wild voice. "What's wrong with you? No one wants to hear that stuff right now!"

Then—above the panting of the wolves, the trumpeting of the mammoths, the thundering of the unicorn's hooves, Beanie's muttering, and the shouting of the explorers behind them—Stella heard a faint, dreadful sound. The quiet, deadly *crack* of ice breaking. She risked a glance behind, and saw hairline fractures crisscrossing out from the grooves left by the sled blades, a lethal spiderweb of cracks sending up little puffs of ice dust as the entire structure groaned.

"Sir Hamish Humphrey Smitt," Beanie groaned, his head in his hands, "ambushed by tiger poachers in the—"

But before he could even finish the sentence, part of

the bridge snapped away behind them. The ice shattered as it fell into the valley below, and Stella found she couldn't breathe. Surely they weren't actually going to die? Not on the very first day of her first expedition! It would be too awful if Aunt Agatha were to be proved right about exploring being too dangerous for girls, and she was sure to be extremely nasty to Felix about it too.

But then the racing wolves reached the other side of the bridge and the sled blades bit deep into snow—just as the last of the ice bridge collapsed. Stella looked behind her again and felt a numb sort of horror at the sight of a vast, empty space where the ice bridge had been—where *they* had been—mere seconds ago. The terrified unicorn breathed out icy puffs of air in agitated snorts, cantering to keep up with the sled. Past the unicorn's sweating flank Stella could see the explorers on the other side running around, waving their arms, chasing wolves, and yelling their heads off in a general state of unhelpful pandemonium. She searched desperately for Felix but couldn't pick him out in the crowd, although she thought she heard him shout out her name.

Then the wolves shot through a cave entrance carved deep into the mountainside, and the adult explorers were lost from sight as the sled entered the cold, eerily quiet world of a vast ice tunnel, taking them further and further away from the other members of their expeditions, and ever deeper into whatever perilous unknown lay ahead.

CHAPTER TEN

THE WOLVES WERE TERRIFIED, and although Shay kept shouting out the commands for them to stop, they completely ignored him and continued running at full pelt through the twisting, winding ice tunnels.

"We've got to do something!" Stella gasped. "We've got to stop them!"

If they had been on open snow, they could have let the wolves run until they burned all their fear and adrenaline away, but here in a narrow, twisting ice tunnel leading deeper and deeper into the side of a mountain, there could be anything up ahead. A gaping pit, a wall of rock, a hungry yeti. They had to get the wolves to stop, and quickly.

Shay chewed furiously at his lower lip. Suddenly his head snapped up. He looked at Stella and said, "Sparky, I've just thought of something! Can you skate?"

"I skate every day on the lake at home!"

He reached into the bottom of the sled and fished out a tangle of skates. "We have to get to the wolves at the front," he said. "It's the only way."

"You're mad!" Ethan exclaimed as Beanie continued muttering to himself under his breath. "You'll get yourselves killed! No one can skate faster than running wolves!"

Shay ignored Ethan and spoke to Stella. "We'll have to grab on to the harness to get to the lead wolves at the front. If we can calm them, the others will follow."

The skates were all too large for Stella, but she took the smallest pair she could find, stuffed some gloves into the toes, and tied up the laces as tight as she could. There wasn't time to think after that. She and Shay took opposite sides of the sled and scrambled out. Stella clung onto the side with all her strength, then grabbed the wolf harness and dragged herself along, hand over hand, making sure to keep her skates facing forward the whole time. On the other side she could see Shay doing the same thing.

They reached the front, and Stella knew Shay was whispering to the wolf on his side because she could see the flash of red from the open eyes of the whisperer's pendant at his throat. Stella spoke to the other wolf—which she saw was Kayko, the reddish female she had rescued from the storm—in a voice that she tried to make as low and soothing as possible. She saw a dark blur from the corner of her eye and realized that Shay's shadow wolf, Koa, had appeared, and was racing along, keeping pace with her. She felt comforted by Koa's presence, and the other wolves must have felt so too because their running slowed until it became a trot, then a walk, and then—finally—they stopped altogether, panting hard with their tongues hanging long from their mouths.

Stella's hands were trembling as she buried them in the lead wolf's fur. "Good girl," she said as the wolf tried to lick her face. "Good girl."

"Good girl?" Ethan repeated as he scrambled out of the sled. "They almost got us all killed!"

"And whose fault is that, I wonder?" Shay snapped. "They haven't been trained properly. These wolves aren't ready for polar exploration!"

Ethan glared at him. "How do you know they're Ocean Squid wolves?"

"Look at their harness, you fool."

Sure enough, the harness was black for Ocean Squid and had the club's squid insignia stamped in the leather.

Stella ignored their arguing, whispered her thanks to Koa—who'd sat back on her haunches and was regarding the explorers calmly—and then skated around to check on the unicorn at the back.

The unicorn was white from nose to tail, with a thick coat and feathered silky hair above her pearly hooves. She snorted at Stella in greeting and didn't seem too shaken up. The pale blue halter marked her as a Polar Bear unicorn, and therefore she would have been properly trained for expeditions like this. Her name—Glacier—was stitched in silver thread along the side of her harness. Stella fished in her pocket until she found some iced gems and then held them out on her flat palm. Glacier took them gently and munched happily, spraying multicolored crumbs on the ice below.

Beanie had stopped reciting morbid facts, but both his hands gripped the edge of the sled as if he'd never let it go. Stella skated around the side of the sled and looked at him. "Hey," she said. "Are you okay?"

He nodded at her wordlessly, but Stella couldn't help noticing that he'd turned an unhealthy shade of green. Stella skated over to where Shay and Ethan were still arguing over the wolves. "Would you two stop that bickering?" she said. "It's getting on my nerves. And we need to work out what we're going to do."

Beanie looked up. "We should turn around and go back to the others," he said.

"We can't," Shay replied. "The bridge collapsed."

Beanie now turned pale. With his eyes screwed up tight during the wolves' flight, he'd been blissfully ignorant of this important fact until now.

"We'll just have to stick to the plan," Stella said. "If

we head toward the coldest part of the Icelands, then we'll probably meet up with the others along the way anyway."

They all peered at the ice tunnel twisting around a corner in front of them. For the first time, Stella noticed that it wasn't as dark in the tunnel as it should have been. The entire place was filled with a cool, blue light, as if the sunlight from above was getting through somehow.

"I can't carry on with all of you!" Ethan exclaimed. "I'm not part of your club—I have my own!"

Shay clapped him on the back and said, "Well, I guess that's just tough luck for all of us, Prawn. First rule of exploring: Don't go wandering off by yourself. Not unless you want to fall into a ravine, or get washed over a raging waterfall or some such, and never be seen or heard from again. We're stuck with each other for now."

Ethan shook his head and kicked the side of the sled. "This is the worst expedition ever!"

"We're not exactly thrilled about it either," Stella told him.

"If we're the only explorers who made it across, then it's up to us to explore the area and see if there's anything worth discovering," Beanie said. "Mum told me I have to prove to Uncle Benedict that I can be an explorer, and that's exactly what I'm going to do."

"That's the spirit," Shay said cheerfully.

"I wish I was at sea," Ethan groaned.

"If it helps at all, we wish you were at sea too," Stella told him. "I wish you were at the *bottom* of the sea, actually."

Ethan's Ocean Squid cloak didn't help either. While the other three all wore pale blue cloaks that blended nicely with the ice and snow, Ethan's black one made him stick out like a sore thumb. Any passing yeti would spot them a mile away, and they'd probably all get eaten as a result.

Stella sighed and said, "Let's look and see what provisions we have."

Although they'd lost a couple of bags at the ice bridge, there was still a pile tied to the sled, and Glacier carried several more. The explorers emptied out their pockets, too, and counted up what they had between them. There was an assortment of telescopes, Stella's compass, some gloves and blankets, a travel journal, some mountain climbing rope, a tripod camera, a top hat box, and a nasty-smelling carton filled with round tins of Captain Filibuster's Expedition-Strength Mustache Wax.

They also had a sack of iced gems, some salted beef, a box of mint cake, some canned Spam, a cooking pot, and a small knife. And a gramophone, for what that was worth (explorers liked to listen to some music in the evening). There was also a magnificent wicker picnic basket filled with silver cutlery, fine china plates stamped with the Polar Bear Explorers' Club crest, a couple of bottles of champagne, and glass flutes. No doubt the champagne was for toasting a particularly fantastic find or amazing scientific discovery. But the weapons and most of the food had been with the other sleds, or in the two bags they'd lost. They found a long, thin bag strapped to the back of the sled that they thought might hold arrows but was, in fact, a map tube, filled with rolled-up maps.

"Maybe you can magic up some more of those polar beans," Stella suggested to Ethan glumly. She didn't think she'd care much for food that was giggling and cartwheeling about while she was trying to eat it, though.

"Maybe we should slaughter these useless wolves," Ethan replied. "At least they'd be some help to us then."

Shay suddenly went very still. "Touch a single hair on the head of any one of these wolves," he said in a dangerously quiet voice, "and I promise you will get to see my not-so-nice side. And you won't enjoy that one bit."

"Oh, calm down, I didn't mean it," Ethan snapped. "Who wants to eat wolf meat anyway? Gross! Still, I suppose it will fall to me to prevent us all from starving to death out here in this forsaken frozen wasteland. It's fortunate for you that I'm here or you'd all be dead within the hour."

"Oh, it takes longer than an hour to starve," Beanie hurried to reassure him. "Much longer."

The magician glanced at Beanie, then looked at Stella and said, "Perhaps you might come in handy with that compass of yours." He indicated Shay and said, "And he can look after the wolves he loves so much, I suppose. But what use is this one to anybody?" He pointed at Beanie. "What's he training to be? Bait?"

"A medic," Stella snapped. "As you well know. So you'd better start being nice to him because if a yeti bites your arm off during the expedition, then Beanie is the one who'll be sewing it back on."

"You can't sew an arm back on, Stella," Beanie said with a frown. "A finger, perhaps, but definitely not an arm. But if anyone loses any fingers or toes, then I'll sew them back on. Gladly."

Ethan shook his head. "You have to be extremely intelligent to be a medic; everyone knows that. If you're a medic, then I'm a ballerina!"

"Oh!" Beanie suddenly looked excited. If there was one thing he loved more than jelly beans and narwhals, it was the ballet. "That's wonderful! Although hasn't the dance academy tried to correct your slouching? You don't meet slouching ballerinas too often, and you slouch something terrible."

Stella inwardly sighed. Poor Beanie. It never occurred to him to say anything other than exactly what he thought, without pausing to make his words softer or more palatable first. "But that would be like lying," he'd said when Stella had tried to talk to him about it once. "It's not right to lie."

Ethan drew himself up to his full height. "I don't slouch, and I'm *not* a ballerina!"

Beanie looked more confused than ever. "But you just said—"

"You might as well be a ballerina for all the use you are," Stella cut in. "Beanie is a junior medic *and* he has healing magic, which is a lot more valuable than creating polar beans out of thin air. He helps his mum at the hospital all the time back home, and she says he's already more use than most of the doctors, *and* he can tie bandages as well as any of the nurses."

"I wouldn't trust him to tie his own shoelaces!" Ethan scoffed.

Stella tightened her hands into fists to stop herself from doing something she shouldn't. Poking the magician in the eye, for example. Or flicking his pointed nose as hard as she could.

Ethan pointed at Beanie's bag and said, "What have you got in there? If you're really training to be a medic, then your club would have given you a medical kit. Let's see it."

Beanie obligingly opened up his bag, which seemed to mostly contain jelly beans stored by color in glass jars. But after digging around, he produced the medical kit, which came in a pale blue pack, with the Polar Bear Explorers' Club crest stamped on the front. Stella peered forward curiously as Beanie unzipped it.

She wasn't quite sure what she expected to see. Rolls of bandages, perhaps, or various salves and ointments. Instead,

when Beanie pushed back the lid, the pack was empty except for what looked like two miniature dog kennels, about the size of Stella's hand. Everyone frowned down at them.

"What are they, for heaven's sake?" Ethan demanded.

Beanie tapped the roof of each kennel and instantly two miniature dogs, just a few inches long, came bounding out. They had thick, shaggy coats; pink tongues that lolled from their mouths in excitement; big, soppy faces; and little wooden barrels marked with a red cross tied around their collars.

"That's Murphy." Beanie pointed to one of the dogs. "And this is Maxwell. They're brandy rescue dogs. The Polar Bear Explorers' Club sends them out on expeditions because they say that a tot of brandy—that's what they have in the barrels—will warm you up if you get lost in the snow." He frowned and added, "Actually, my medicine books say that drinking alcohol is the worst thing you can do if you get stuck in the snow, but I didn't want the dogs to feel bad, so I thought I'd better take them along."

"But is that *all* you have?" Ethan demanded as Beanie zipped the dogs back up in their case.

"No, I have bandages too." Beanie held up a packet, and Stella was pleased to see that it was blue and had polar bears printed on it.

"Oh, good," the magician said. "If one of us *does* get an arm bitten off by a yeti, then I can see you'll be totally in control of the situation."

"Oh, well, actually, you know, a bandage would be no use at all if you were to get your arm bitten off—"

Before Beanie could finish, Ethan dramatically pointed a finger and cried, "Great Scott, what in the blazes is *that* devilish creature?"

They all turned to see Koa, sitting a little way off, regarding them with a cool, calm expression on her handsome face.

"That," Shay said, between gritted teeth, "is my shadow wolf, Koa."

"Is it rabid?" Ethan asked with an affronted air. "It looks rabid to me."

"Of course she's not rabid!" Shay snapped. "She's a shadow animal, you prize idiot."

"I thought shadow animals were a fairy tale made up to scare children," the magician replied dubiously.

"Well, guess again," Shay responded. "For there one sits before you." He shook his head, ran his hand through his long hair, and said, "We've wasted enough time squabbling. Let's load up and be on our way." He gave Ethan a look. "Before someone says something they might regret."

"We have to fix the flag first," the magician said, folding his arms over his chest stubbornly.

Stella hadn't even realized they were carrying the Polar Bear Explorers' Club flag until now. It had been attached to their sled as the one in front, and it still hung limply from the pole at the back.

"What do you mean, 'fix it'?" she demanded.

"That's a Polar Bear club flag," Ethan said, pointing at the explorers' crest. It showed the symbol for all four explorer clubs, but only the polar bear was picked out in gold thread. "Well, I'm a member of the Ocean Squid Explorers' Club." He pulled off his glove, snapped his fingers, and the black line around the many-tentacled squid turned slowly gold.

"The first joint expedition in history," Shay said, although he didn't sound too happy about it.

They repacked everything as best they could and Ethan, Beanie, and Stella piled into the sled, while Shay hopped onto the back to control the wolves. They set off—more slowly this time—deeper into the mountain.

A few hours later they reached the end of the tunnel, a moonlit snowy landscape stretching out beyond. Night had fallen while they'd been inside, so the explorers decided to make camp within the shelter of the tunnel for the night and get moving again first thing in the morning. They were all feeling a little unnerved, and Stella couldn't help wishing Felix was with them. There was a brief argument when Beanie emptied out one of his jars of jelly beans and tried to offer the empty container to Ethan for him to put his teeth into, but once Stella got Beanie to understand that the magician didn't really have false teeth, and once Ethan had stopped sulking at the suggestion that he did, the junior explorers bedded down in their blankets and sleeping bags and finally went to sleep.

CHAPTER ELEVEN

T HAT NIGHT, STELLA HAD the dream again.

She was sitting on a huge bed, playing with a beautiful tiara. It was covered in crystals and gems and ice-white stones that sparkled and shone in her hands. It was the prettiest thing she had ever seen.

But then the dream shifted, turning into a nightmare. The tiara disappeared and Stella was hiding underneath the bed, staring out at a pair of horribly burned feet that were slowly walking up and down the room, looking for her. The ruined feet were shriveled with blackened skin and red, open sores. Every shuffling footstep must have been agony. There were huge angry blisters and crusty old scabs where the toenails ought to be.

Don't cry, Stella told herself. *Don't cry. She'll hear you. . . .*

And then she was outside in the snow, and there were drops of blood all around, shockingly scarlet. Something bad had just happened. Something really, really bad. . . .

Stella sat up with a gasp and found herself face-to-face with Koa, who was peering at her in a concerned kind of way. Shay stood just behind the shadow wolf. "Wow," he said. "That must have been some dream. You were thrashing around hard enough to put your foot through the blanket."

Stella glanced down and realized that the blankets were indeed in a terrible tangle. Beanie and Ethan were still sound asleep in their own blanket piles, snoring contentedly.

"Are you all right?" Shay asked, still looking at her intently.

"Yes," Stella said quickly. "It was only a dream."

She couldn't help shivering as she remembered it. The burned feet had never been there before. That was new. And quite horrible. For some reason she couldn't put into words, she didn't want the others to know about her nightmare. She'd never mentioned it to anyone, not even to Felix. She wasn't sure why. Only that it felt like something she should keep to herself.

So she was relieved when Shay shrugged and said, "All right, Sparky. Whatever you say. Let's wake the others. We ought to be on our way anyway."

After a hasty and unsatisfying breakfast of tinned Spam, the four junior explorers emerged from the tunnel, only to squint and sneeze in the bright light that reflected blindingly off the snow all around them.

"Snow," Ethan complained. "Just nothing but snow as far as the eye can see. I knew polar exploration was a waste of time. We're not going to make any fantastic discoveries here. Absolutely none."

The others ignored him and proceeded to get out the maps strapped to the back of the sled. Unfortunately, it looked as if whoever had packed the map tube had done so in some haste, or perhaps they had just grabbed the first maps that had come to hand, but either way, most of them were completely useless.

"This one is a map of the Scorpion Jungle," Stella said, wrinkling her nose in disgust. "That's miles and miles from here. And this is a map for the Land of Pyramids, which is even further away."

By the time she'd pulled out maps for the Sapphire Desert, Volcano Island, and the Lost City of Muja-Muja, Stella was beginning to think that they had brought no maps of the Icelands with them at all. But then she found one, right at the bottom of the pile. The Polar Bear explorers' crest was stamped at the top of the map, and a snarling yeti drawing in the bottom right-hand corner held a box that contained the key to all the different symbols. Only a small proportion of the map had been filled in. The rest was left blank for the part that hadn't been discovered yet.

"Okay," Stella said, smoothing the map out on a box of mustache wax, enjoying the way the thick paper crinkled beneath her fingers. "So the *Bold Adventurer* dropped us off here." She pointed to the edge of the filled-in section. "And we set off north toward the ice bridge. Which means we're probably somewhere around here." She pointed at a blank spot and then passed the pencils from the map tube over to Beanie, who was very good at art and quickly drew the broken ice bridge and mountain onto the parchment.

There was then a brief delay while they tried to decide which direction they should head in next. They all agreed that their most important issue was food. The iced gems and salted beef were for the unicorn and wolves, which only left the Spam and mint cake for the young explorers. And as Ethan pointed out, those supplies wouldn't keep them going forever. Plus, no one wanted to eat Spam for breakfast, lunch, and dinner.

Stella set the explorer's compass to the Food heading and waited while the arrow spun around in circles a few times before finally pointing straight ahead. Ethan was obviously still sulking and refused to get back in the sled with them, saying he'd ride the unicorn instead, which suited Stella just fine as she'd had more than enough of the magician's bony elbows sticking into her ribs.

They set off across the snow, with the wolf sled following Stella's compass and leading the way and Ethan riding

Glacier a few yards behind. The cold air stung their faces as they moved along, forcing them to wrap their scarves up almost to their eyes. Stella pulled her hood back up over her head, and Beanie produced a striped knitted hat his mum had made for him, which he pulled down low over his pointed ears. It had a narwhal stitched on the front and a pom-pom on top, and it clashed horribly with everything else he wore, but it was his favorite hat in the world, and Beanie refused to be parted with it.

Ethan had been right about there being nothing to see. So far, at least, it really did look like there wasn't anything there but snow and ice. Stella hoped it was going to get more interesting up ahead. It would be pretty disappointing if she returned from her first solo expedition without making any fantastic discoveries or collecting any curiosities, grotesqueries, or rarities to put on display in the wooden cabinets Felix had had specially made for that purpose back home.

They'd been traveling for a while—and the frozen landscape racing by had started to seem like one endless white blur to Stella—when suddenly, Shay gave a shout of alarm and brought the wolves to such an abrupt halt that both Stella and Beanie slid right out of their seats and ended up sprawled on top of each other in the foot compartment.

"What did you do that for?" Stella complained, trying to disentangle herself from Beanie.

But Shay wasn't listening. He was looking back at Ethan

and yelling for him to stop. The magician was cantering straight toward them on the unicorn, a puzzled frown on his face. It didn't look like he was going to slow down any time soon. Stella heard Shay say a bad word under his breath and then scramble off the back of the sled, his boots crunching in the snow as he ran straight into the path of the oncoming unicorn. For a horrible moment Stella thought he was going to get run over and be trampled into the snow, which was bound to be a pretty messy affair, but Ethan dragged on the reins just in time, and the unicorn reared up on her hind legs, one pearly hoof narrowly missing Shay's head.

"Have you gone quite mad?" Ethan gasped, staring down with a shocked expression. "I might have bashed your brains in!"

Shay didn't reply but reached up for Ethan's cloak and dragged him from the saddle, ignoring his indignant cries of protest. "Look!" he snapped, forcing the magician around to face the direction they were traveling in.

"There's nothing there but ice, you fool!"

"Look *properly*!"

Stella gasped as she noticed what had been invisible to her before. Dozens and dozens of tiny igloos were spread out before them. Camouflaged as they were against the endless white snow, Stella hadn't seen them to begin with, but if the wolf sled and the unicorn had carried on, they would have surely smashed the miniature homes to pieces.

"Well, how was I to know?" Ethan said, shaking Shay off. "I'm a magician, not a psychic. And don't ever touch me again!"

Shay turned away from him, shaking his head in disgust, his long black hair brushing against the shoulders of his cloak as he returned to the wolf sled.

"What do you think could be living in them?" Stella asked. The igloos were a bit bigger than the penguin one Felix had given her, but still only a fraction of normal size.

"It could be snow goblins," Beanie said. "Or cold crabs. Or frost bats. Or ice scorpions. Or—"

"Surely ice scorpions don't live in igloos?" Stella replied.

"Uncle Benedict says they're fiendishly clever," Beanie said. "I bet they could build themselves some igloos if they wanted to."

"With pincers?" Stella asked dubiously.

"There's only one way to find out what's in there," Shay said. "Let's go and introduce ourselves." He fumbled in his cloak pockets and brought out a well-thumbed, rather battered book entitled *Captain Filibuster's Guide to Expeditions and Exploration*. Stella remembered that Shay's father was Captain Kipling, and she realized that Shay was probably training to be a captain too.

Stella and Beanie scrambled out of the sled and followed Shay, with Ethan slouching along behind. They stopped when they got to the nearest igloo and Shay crouched down in the snow. "Making first contact with the locals," he muttered to himself as he thumbed through the book's index. He opened the guide to the correct page and said, "Good day. We are members of the Polar Bear Explorers' Club—"

Ethan cleared his throat loudly behind him.

"*And* the Ocean Squid Explorers' Club," Shay said, rolling his eyes. "We have traveled a long way to make the acquaintance of the indigenous peoples of this land, and would like to formally introduce ourselves so that we may cultivate your friendship and esteem."

"Does it really need to be that verbose?" Ethan complained. "What's wrong with just asking them to come out of their igloos?"

"If they're ice scorpions, then they won't understand what you say anyway," Beanie pointed out. "I'm sure it's ice scorpions. There're one hundred and eighty-three types of poisonous scorpion in the discovered world. And I bet there's twice as many in the undiscovered world. Perhaps even three times as many."

"Put a stick through the front door and wriggle it about a bit," Ethan suggested, ignoring Beanie. "That will bring them out, whatever they are."

"Absolutely not!" Stella said, aghast. "We're guests here. We've got to be polite. And poking a stick into someone's house is definitely not polite."

She was about to suggest kneeling down and peering

into one of the igloos, but then it occurred to her that that was really every bit as rude, and besides, if there *were* snow goblins in there, then that was a certain way to get your eye poked out with a stick, or a claw, or some other pointy object.

But then Beanie suddenly said, "Stella, look—there's a butterfly on your shoulder!"

Stella glanced up at the beautiful blue wings, almost as large as the palm of her hand. "It's not a butterfly!" she exclaimed. "It's a . . ."

She was about to say "fairy" but trailed off unsure. Stella had grown up around fairies—they had lived at the far end of her backyard for as long as she could remember, tempted in by the beautiful fairy houses Felix built for them. But this was quite unlike any fairy she'd ever seen. Its blue wings were like lace, and its body looked like lots of ice shards stuck together. Its eyes were two chips of pale blue within its angular face, and it had long hair as white as Stella's own. The long hair made Stella think it must be a girl, but it was very difficult to tell otherwise. Stella was used to fairies with petticoats puffing out their dresses and flowers in their hair, but this creature wasn't wearing any clothes at all. And were those *claws* on the ends of its fingers? Stella had never heard of any fairy with claws before.

The next moment dozens of the winged creatures were coming out of the igloos, filling the air with fluttering blue

129

wings and glittering clouds of some kind of fairy dust. Stella heard Beanie sneeze behind her. Unfortunately, Beanie was allergic to fairy dust—as well as hamsters, daisies, ducks, horned frogs, spotted frogs, and blue frogs. Most types of frogs, really.

Soon Stella had them on both shoulders and arms, dangling from the ends of her fingers, and perched on top of her hood. The male ones, she noticed, sported waxed mustaches, very much like the men back home.

"Hello," Stella said to the creatures, who gazed up at her with their cold blue eyes. "Are you . . . are you some kind of fairy?"

"We're frosties," the frosty said. "Fairies are distant cousins of ours. It's a great pleasure to meet you and your intrepid explorer friends. Do you have time to pause your expedition long enough to take tea with us? We love throwing tea parties, but we don't get guests out here too often."

Stella thought that a frosty tea party in the middle of the snow was just about the best thing ever. So she was surprised, and quite annoyed, when Ethan said in a cold, unfriendly voice, "Why? What do you want in return?"

"Nothing at all!" the frosty exclaimed.

"So you're just trying to be nice?" Ethan said dubiously, as if he couldn't think of anything more unlikely or preposterous. "To total strangers who you've never even met?"

"Of course! Hospitality is very important to us. Please. Come this way."

"Are you deliberately trying to offend them?" Stella hissed at Ethan as the frosties moved away. "Haven't you ever heard of strangers being nice before?"

The magician crossed his arms over his chest. "It's just not my experience, that's all," he said. "And I *am* the only one of us who's ever been on an expedition before. You lot have got no idea. I could tell you some stories that would make your—"

"Perhaps the Icelands are just more polite than the South Seas, or wherever it is you went, Prawn," Shay said, before glancing down at Koa, who had suddenly appeared again at his side. The shadow wolf was staring at the retreating frosties with her ears flattened right back against her head. "Still," Shay said, frowning, "I guess it never hurts to be careful."

Ethan shrugged. "Don't say I didn't warn you," he muttered, but followed along behind them.

The frosties led the way past their igloos. Then they all fluttered down and brushed a layer of snow away to reveal a large door set into the ground. It was a bright, shining, golden color, with a glittering handle. It took five of the frosties to drag the door back with a thud. The explorers craned forward to see a set of steps disappearing into the darkness.

Perhaps it was Ethan putting doubts in her mind, but Stella suddenly felt unsure. After all, walking blindly into a hole in the ground did seem a bit on the risky side.

"What's down there?" Ethan said in a suspicious tone.

"A dungeon," the frosty replied.

"A *what*?"

"I'm joking!" the frosty said. "Really, there's no dungeon. Who ever heard of a dungeon with a golden door? The steps lead down to the goose garden."

"Is that a code word for dungeon?" Ethan said.

"No, it's where we keep our geese. You've got to see them. They're quite extraordinary."

"Extraordinary geese," Ethan repeated in a flat voice. He shook his head. "I'll be laughed out of the Ocean Squid Explorers' Club. Guffawed out, probably."

Privately, Stella also thought there was probably a limit to how extraordinary geese could be. When she'd dreamed about the kinds of discoveries she might make in the Icelands, she'd had marvels and wonders a little larger in mind. Like a giant dinosaur frozen in a block of ice, or a lost city, or a strange beast no one had ever heard of before. But sometimes an explorer just has to take whatever discoveries they can find, and Stella figured that a goose garden was better than nothing, and would at least give them something else to put in their Flag Report when they got back to the club. Besides, they'd already discovered a new type of fairy, which was sure to count in their favor, even if Stella didn't intend to take one back to be pinned to a board in a display case. She resolved to keep a close eye on Ethan—in case he tried to stuff one of the frosties into his pocket for the sea fairy cabinet back at the Ocean Squid Explorers' Club.

"Thank you very much for the offer. We would love to see your incredible geese," she said, and stepped down to the underground staircase.

CHAPTER TWELVE

THE FROSTIES LED THE way, followed by the explorers and the shadow wolf. Ethan was the last to step through the door, and he deliberately left it open behind him. No matter what the others said, he still had a bad feeling about this and wanted to be able to make a quick getaway if the frosties suddenly turned nasty.

The staircase curved around and around in a spiral that made the explorers feel dizzy after a little while. It was damp and very, very cold. When Stella put her gloved hand on the wall to steady herself, her fingertips left trails in the frost that coated the stones. Finally, the staircase came to an end, and Stella was surprised to step through an archway and find herself blinking in the sunlight once again.

"How have we ended up back aboveground?" she asked. "The stairs went down the whole way."

"Sometimes if you go down for long enough in the

Icelands, you start to go back up," one of the frosties said with a shrug.

The explorers squinted for a moment as their eyes adjusted to the light, and then Stella gasped as she took in the goose garden around her. They were in a walled space and there was no snow on the ground, but everything sparkled in a silver coat of frost. Colorful bunting hung from the branches of leafless trees, and a blue pond glittered in front of them. Geese paddled in the water, sunned themselves on the banks, and waddled among the trees—but they weren't entirely white like normal geese. They were covered in little gold spots.

"Aren't they fine?" one of the frosties said proudly. She might have been the frosty who first landed on Stella's shoulder, but they looked so much alike that it was hard to tell, especially without clothes to distinguish them. "We purchased them at the goose fair last year. They had all kinds of geese there: dragon geese, barking geese, hollow geese, raspberry geese—"

"There's no horned geese here, are there?" Beanie demanded. "Because, you know, they can be extremely dangerous. Extremely."

Beside him, Ethan snorted. "Doubtful."

"Seven explorers from the Jungle Cat Explorers' Club have been gored by horned geese in the last fifty years," Beanie said.

Ethan shrugged dismissively. "Jungle Cat explorers are buffoons," he said. "Most of them probably perish falling on their own spears."

"Twelve Jungle Cat explorers have died falling on their own spears in the last one hundred years," Beanie said promptly. "Another sixty-three have injured themselves, including Sir Hamish Humphrey Smitt, who lost an eye. And was later ambushed by tiger poachers—"

Ethan frowned at him. "How do you know all this stuff? It's not normal."

"I like facts," Beanie replied. "You know where you are with facts. Besides, if we don't take the trouble to learn about the mistakes of past explorers, then we're more likely to make the same mistakes ourselves."

"Sixty-three explorers poking their own eyes out with spears," Ethan said, shaking his head with a smirk. "What a hopeless bunch."

One of Stella's adopted cousins belonged to the Jungle Cat Explorers' Club, and feeling offended on his behalf, Stella said, "Beanie, why don't you tell us how many Ocean Squid explorers have died from eating too many eels in the last century?"

"Forty-three," Beanie replied promptly.

Ethan's smirk vanished. Stella stuck her tongue out at him.

"Excuse me for interrupting," one of the frosties cut in,

"but if we can get back to the subject at hand, I can assure you that we have no horned geese here. We only have spotted geese. They can't fly because their wings are too small, but they make up for that in other ways. Come along and we'll have tea."

The frosties fluttered off and the explorers followed them, their boots crunching on the winding white shingle path. The geese were quite a noisy bunch and kept up a continuous honking in the background. The children walked through the trees to where several tables were set with crisp white tablecloths and china teacups. The tables were all different sizes, ranging from human-size to fairy-size.

"I thought you said you didn't get many visitors?" Stella said.

"We don't, but we like to be prepared just in case," the frosty replied. She gestured toward the largest table. "Please do sit down."

The explorers took their seats and Koa settled herself at Shay's feet. Stella peered at the nearby trees and decided that they were quite odd looking, with their leafless branches, and trunks as smooth and white as bleached bone. Multicolored glass jars hung from the branches, and Stella thought they were lanterns at first, but then some of the frosties fluttered up, pulled eggcups out of them, and set them on the table before the explorers.

They were, without doubt, beautiful eggcups, fit for a

king in gold and royal blue, with intricate scrollwork and embedded crystals that put Stella in mind of the jeweled egg Felix had brought back with him from the Exotic East. But even so, she couldn't help being a little disappointed. When the frosties had mentioned a tea party, she had imagined tiny cupcakes, and iced buns, and jelly dragons, and sticky jam roly-polies. Perhaps even some cream éclairs and purple macaroons. Stella had a weakness for purple macaroons. But instead, the frosties announced that they were to be having goose eggs for tea.

Stella didn't want to seem ungrateful for the goose eggs, so she made sure to thank the frosties again for their hospitality before asking if they knew of anywhere nearby where they might be able to find more food.

"We lost most of our supplies when we were split up from the rest of our expedition," she explained, "so we're going to need to stock up on provisions."

A male frosty sat on one of the overturned teacups, twirled his mustache, and said, "You'll get food and other supplies at the Yak and Yeti."

"The Yak and Yeti?"

"It's a luxurious hotel," the male frosty said. "The most luxurious hotel you've ever seen. They're very friendly there. And helpful."

One of the frosties perched in the tree above giggled and was quickly shushed.

"How do we find it?" Stella asked.

"It's on the other side of the rainbow."

Ethan narrowed his eyes suspiciously. "Is that a riddle? I hate riddles."

"It's not a riddle. Just follow the rainbow and you can't go wrong," the frosty said.

The others returned with the goose eggs, and Stella immediately saw that these were no ordinary eggs: The eggshells were completely gold, and spotted with shiny silver freckles. The explorers each received an egg, and then a basket of cutlery was put in the center of the table. Instead of the teaspoons Stella had expected, she saw that there was a total jumble of utensils—everything from steak knives to oyster forks to honey stirrers. She also saw a set of wooden chopsticks, as well as a popcorn fork, cookie dipper, and pickle spoon.

"What does this one do?" Ethan asked, reaching for one of the utensils. "Remove warts?"

"That's an artichoke scraper," the mustached frosty said politely.

"When do you need scissors to eat your food?" Beanie asked, holding up a silver pair and frowning at them.

"Sounds like another riddle," Stella said.

"Those are grape scissors," the frosty replied. "And before you ask, these other ones are a marrow scoop, aspara-gus tongs, cake breakers, pita bread opener, lobster cracker,

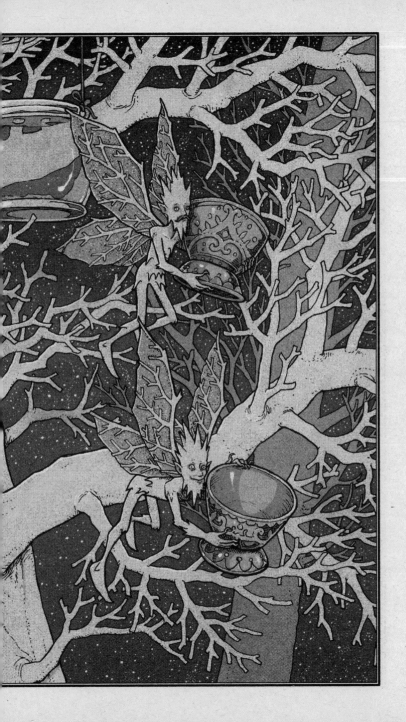

crab pick, folding fruit knife, and, of course, that one there is a mustache spoon."

"A *mustache spoon*?" Stella snatched it up curiously. "But what's it for?"

"To protect a gentleman's mustache when drinking soup, of course," the frosty said. "Really, don't you have fine dining where you come from?"

"Do you really need all this stuff for eating goose eggs, though?" Ethan said, poking at the cutlery with his finger. "I mean, are there any egg spoons in that lot or is it all just crazy stuff like banana forks and parsnip shears and bacon prongs?"

A female frosty walked out onto the middle of the table, smiling. "These are magic eggs, my young friends," she said. "All you have to do is think really hard of what food you would most like to eat, and the egg will provide it for you."

They all gaped at her.

"Are you serious?" Stella said at last.

"Quite serious," the frosty replied. "Each egg will provide you with one savory course and one dessert course. You just have to picture it inside your head. Imagine it so hard you can almost smell it in the air or taste it on your tongue. Then use a spoon to crack it open, just like you would with a normal egg."

Stella stared down at the egg in front of her. After going

through the various options in her mind she finally decided on soup, mostly because she wanted to use the mustache spoon, but also because it would help warm her up. She closed her eyes and thought as hard as she could of the hot, fresh, creamy tomato soup that she and Felix enjoyed at home, with little croutons floating on top. When she could practically taste it, she opened her eyes and used the mustache spoon to break off the top of the egg.

The gold shell came away easily and tendrils of steam rose up, along with the delicious smell of piping hot tomato soup. Stella exclaimed in delight, and having seen her success, the others were quick to grab utensils from the basket and conjure up meals of their own.

Beanie had a fish finger sandwich, Shay had barbecued chicken, and Ethan had oysters, which the others all thought smelled terrible and looked like snot. The magician pointedly ignored their remarks and picked them neatly, and rather elegantly, from the egg using the silver oyster fork. Once they'd finished their savory course, they all thought of a dessert, which magically appeared in the egg. Stella had jam roly-poly, Shay had some kind of fried banana pancake, Ethan had chocolate cake, and Beanie had jelly beans, which, of course, he had to separate into various colored piles before he could eat.

Stella was feeling satisfyingly full, and was just thinking that it was a really good thing that they had trusted the frosties, and not listened to Ethan when he'd been all sus-picious before—when one of the frosties said, "We've made up your beds in the guesthouse."

"Beds?" Stella repeated. "Oh, well, thank you but we can't stay. We're explorers, you see—we need to get going."

"But didn't you say that you'd lost all your supplies?" the frosty persisted. "Wouldn't it be better to spend the night here in a warm bed and leave in the morning?"

"Exploring isn't really about spending the night in a warm bed," Shay said. "Besides, it's far too early to go to sleep just yet. Thank you very much for your hospitality, but I'm afraid we really must be on our way. We have a lot of adventuring still to do."

Shay stood up. Despite his relaxed tone, he had a wary expression on his face. The frosties seemed too still, too silent. All of a sudden, Koa was on her feet, her lips pulled back in a snarl. Stella could hear a low growl rumbling in the back of the shadow wolf's throat. She and Ethan both stood up quickly, and Stella nudged Beanie, who was tidy-ing his last pile of jelly beans.

"Come on, Beanie," she whispered. "We're going."

"We can't," he replied. "I haven't finished organizing my jelly beans."

"We've already made the beds," the female frosty said again, suddenly sounding far less friendly. "It would be very rude of you to go without sleeping in them."

Stella was suddenly very aware of the rows of silent frosties standing on the branches of the trees above them, staring down with a look that seemed almost . . . hungry.

"Sorry to disappoint you, but we really can't stay," Shay said. "Places to go, things to see, and all that."

"That is a pity," the female frosty said slowly. "Because it would have been far less painful if you'd been asleep."

"What would have?" Beanie asked, suddenly looking up from his jelly bean pile.

The frosty smiled—smiled properly for the first time since they'd arrived—and Stella was horrified to see that her mouth was full of row upon row of glittering, needle-sharp teeth. "Frostbite," the frosty said.

Stella had, of course, heard of frostbite. It was hard to live with a polar explorer for ten years and not do so. She knew that sometimes explorers came back from expeditions to the Icelands having lost entire fingers and toes to frostbite, and that it could be very dangerous. If it was left untreated and led to hypothermia, it could even kill you.

"But frostbite isn't an actual *bite*," she protested. "It's caused by exposure to extreme cold."

The frosty grinned even wider, exposing another set of teeth. "Is it?" she said.

And then, quick as a flash, the frosty flew at Ethan, who happened to be the nearest explorer—or perhaps the frosty simply found him the most irritating of the four children.

The magician threw up his hands and a blast of magic flashed blue. Stella wasn't sure what Ethan had intended to do, but she was fairly sure it hadn't been to create another polar bean.

The bean's shrill giggle turned into a shriek as the frosty's fangs impaled it, and Stella watched as lines of ice spread out from the bite. The bean froze solid in seconds. The frosty withdrew her teeth and threw the bean on the floor in disgust, whereupon it promptly shattered into hundreds of frozen, broken pieces.

Stella saw Shay's eyes widen in shock. Beside him, Koa was snarling ferociously, but having no substance, she was no threat to the frosties. The whisperer's wolf at Shay's throat opened its gleaming red eyes, and Stella really hoped that meant he was calling the wolves. They had to get out of there. Right now.

Then everything happened at once. The frosties from the tree all came swooping down at them, claws curled, teeth bared. The geese ran about, honking and flapping in panic and generally getting in everyone's way. Shay whipped the boomerang out of his cloak and threw it through the cloud of frosties, knocking them from the air like stones. Ethan threw more magic at them: a mixture of tiny arrows, which were quite effective at stopping the frosties; and more polar beans, which were less so. Beanie hastily started moving all the red jelly beans as far away as possible from the blue ones, because he simply couldn't bear for the red and blue ones to touch, and he was rather concerned that that might happen if someone were to bash into the table during the fracas.

Meanwhile, Stella snatched up the only weapon within her reach, which happened to be the mustache spoon. It was actually quite an effective object for smacking any frosty who came near, and the thud they made when they hit the spoon was extremely satisfying. There must have been a hundred frosties, though, and it was a difficult thing for three young explorers armed only with a mustache spoon, a boomerang, and unreliable bean-and-arrow magic to fend them off.

As Shay reached up to catch the returning boomerang, Stella noticed, to her horror, that there was a frosty heading directly for him, mouth open and teeth gleaming, moments away from biting.

Fortunately, Ethan saw it too. "Watch out!" he cried, shoving Shay out of the way. The frosty missed him, but it got Ethan instead, clamping its fangs firmly into his finger. The magician yelled and dragged the frosty from his hand, flinging it away from him—but the damage had already been done.

Stella was so horrified that she didn't notice the frosty flying toward her until Beanie—who'd finally finished organizing his jelly beans—shouted out a warning. She tried to raise the mustache spoon but could already see that she wasn't going to manage it in time. The frosty was almost on her, fangs bared—but then the strangest thing happened.

When the frosty reached her, it didn't sink its pointy teeth into her arm, like she'd expected. Instead it gasped and gave Stella a frightened look, as if she'd just done something particularly fearsome. Then it clamped its jaws firmly shut and flew away from Stella as fast as it could.

She didn't have much time to puzzle over its odd behavior because just then the wolves arrived. Stella heard them before she saw them: a ferocious mixture of howling, snarling, and barking that made the hairs on her arms stand on end. The whisperer's wolf around Shay's throat still had its eyes open, gleaming blood red, so Stella guessed that he must be talking to the wolves and telling them to attack the frosties. The wolves did so with a vengeance, snatching the horrible creatures from the air and crunching them up between their teeth. They were still attached to the sled's harness, and had in fact brought the sled down with them, but it didn't seem to hinder them much.

The frosties sought the safety of the trees, gathering together on the highest branches and staring in terror at the snapping wolves below. The explorers raced for the staircase—all except Ethan, who was hunched over his injured hand and groaning. Shay grabbed his arm and dragged him along after them, and Stella took the opportunity to snatch up one of the golden-spotted geese as she ran past the pond.

Stella didn't normally agree with stealing, of course, but if someone bit a member of her expedition and tried to freeze his finger off, then surely that left her perfectly free to steal their magic goose and mustache spoon in return.

The four of them tumbled out of the golden door and into the snow, the wolves and sled close on their heels. With the honking goose still tucked under one arm, Stella grabbed Beanie, despite his protests, and dragged him into the sled with her. Shay shoved Ethan in too and then leapt onto the back, yelling for the wolves to run as fast as they could. They sped across the snow, with Glacier galloping alongside, the frosty igloos growing smaller and smaller behind them.

CHAPTER THIRTEEN

I T STARTED TO SNOW as they raced away from the
frosty igloos, and soon the air was thick with swirl-
ing flakes that made it hard for them to see where
they were going. After the initial panic wore off and they
managed to put some distance between themselves and the
frosties, Shay slowed the wolves down before they could all
go tumbling off the edge of a cliff.

It was just in time, too, because all of a sudden a giant
wall of colors loomed up out of the snow before them,
soaring straight up into the sky. Stella saw orange and red,
yellow and green, blue, indigo, and violet, and suddenly
realized what they were looking at. "It's a rainbow!" she
cried. "A frozen one!"

"Didn't the frosties say that the Yak and Yeti hotel was
at the end of the rainbow?" Shay asked, hopping off the
back of the sled and coming around the side to join them.

"Why should we believe a word they said?" Ethan groaned. His already pale face had gone white as chalk and Stella could see beads of sweat forming at his blond hairline as he hunched protectively over his hand. "I *told* you we shouldn't trust them! I *told* you that something wasn't right. But no, no, you had to go and see the incredible magic geese and put all of our lives at risk!"

The goose in Stella's arms honked importantly and Stella quickly shushed her. "How's your hand?" she said to Ethan.

"How do you think?" the magician snarled. "It's frozen! It hurts more than you can possibly imagine!"

"Let me see," Shay said.

Ethan carefully drew his hand out from the folds of his cloak, and the others gasped. His index finger had frozen solid. It had turned completely blue and was locked rigidly in place, with frost sparkling across the skin. And worse than that, the finger next to it had started to go blue as well.

"It's spreading!" Stella cried.

"That's what frostbite does," Ethan said, through teeth that had started to chatter. "I'm going to end up losing all my fingers to frostbite thanks to you lot. Probably my toes as well."

"Captain Kieran Caspian Carter," Beanie said, "succumbed to frostbite in—"

"Beanie, not now!" Stella said sharply.

"Sorry. Let me see if I can help." Beanie pulled off a glove, raised his hand, and placed it just over Ethan's. Sparkling gold light shone from his fingertips and washed over Ethan's frozen skin.

"Can you cure it?" Shay asked.

"There's no known cure for frostbite," Beanie replied. "All I can do is slow down the spread of it."

"What use is healing magic if it doesn't cure anything?" Ethan complained.

"Magic is useful but it only takes you so far. Science has to take you the rest of the way." Beanie drew back his hand and replaced his glove. "Besides, healing magic is unpredictable. Sometimes it becomes unstitched. I've slowed the frostbite down for now, but it's vicious, and there's no telling how long the magic will hold."

"We've got to get help," Shay said, running his hands through his long dark hair. "Let's follow the rainbow to the Yak and Yeti. There might be someone there who knows what to do."

"We don't even know if there is such a place," Beanie said. "The frosties might have been lying."

Stella took her compass from her pocket and set it to Food and then Shelter. Both pointed in the direction of the frozen rainbow.

"The compass says to go this way," she said, holding it up. "And it's not like anyone's got any better ideas."

And so, with the lack of any better ideas, they piled all the blankets they had on top of Ethan—because that rather seemed the thing to do for someone with frostbite—then Shay hopped onto the back of the sled and they set off in the direction of the frozen rainbow. Ethan's black Ocean Squid cloak didn't have a furred hood like the Polar Bear ones did, so Beanie tried to offer him his striped pom-pom hat, but Ethan sneered at the offending article with such a look of disgust that Beanie hurriedly replaced it on his own head.

The snow eased a little as they went, and Stella was able to see the rainbow properly. It soared high in the sky, its many colors sparkling in the sunlight that had started to shine through the snow. Stella was pretty sure that she'd read somewhere—probably in one of the scientific journals Felix left lying around at home—that a rainbow was not a physical object at all, but an illusion that could not be reached or touched. And yet here they were traveling below a solid, frozen rainbow that definitely *could* be reached and, presumably, touched. Stella made a mental note to try. It would, she felt, be a very fine thing to return from an expedition having touched an actual rainbow.

When the last snowflakes ceased to fall and the sunlight shone stronger, the snow all around them changed color, from blue to pink to green and back again. Stella thought the rainbow had to be one of the most magnificent, beautiful things in the whole world, and she probably would have been quite excited about it if she hadn't been so worried about Ethan. She really would feel terrible—and at least partly to blame—if he lost all his fingers and toes. Plus, his lips were turning blue, and that couldn't be a good sign at all, even if he was too vain to wear Beanie's narwhal hat.

They continued traveling for the rest of the afternoon, until the sky began to turn a dusky shade of purple velvet. Stella could clearly see the end of the rainbow diving down into the ground, but she couldn't spot the Yak and Yeti, and for a moment, she felt a deep panic that perhaps there was no such place at all. Perhaps the frosties really had been making it up. After all, who ever heard of a luxurious hotel in the middle of the Icelands? The more she thought of it, the less likely it seemed.

But then she spotted a little hut, huddled in the frozen landscape. An orange sign was lit up against the darkening sky, clearly spelling out the words YAK AND YETI—only the bulb in the *K* and *I* had gone, so in fact it read: YA AND YET. It was not a large place but it did at least look inhabited—there were several sleighs and sleds parked outside it, light spilling from the windows and smoke puffing from the chimneys.

"It's there, look!" Stella said, pointing it out to Shay.

"That's not a hotel," Shay replied. He squinted at it dubiously. "Looks more like a shack."

"Well, there's obviously people in there, so it'll do." Stella nudged Ethan, who was huddled in the corner with his eyes closed. Stella really hoped he wasn't dead or anything. "Ethan, we're here," she said, giving him a poke and trying to sound cheerful and reassuring and not at all scared. "We're here."

The magician groaned and pushed her hand away. "Quit p-p-poking m-me," he stuttered through frozen lips.

Stella scrambled out of the sled the moment it stopped, and hurried around to the side. Ethan stood up but he was slow and unsteady on his feet, and when he tried to get out of the sled he staggered forward and would have fallen face-first into the snow if Shay hadn't caught him.

"I c-c-can't f-feel my t-t-toes." Ethan struggled out the words through his chattering teeth.

"Let's get you inside, Prawn," Shay replied, draping one of the magician's arms around his shoulders. Stella took the other arm and they half carried, half dragged him along, with Beanie hurrying behind them.

Stella kicked the door to the Yak and Yeti open with her boot, and for a moment the four of them stood framed in the doorway of what was clearly some kind of tavern. A fire blazed in a large fireplace that took up most of one wall, and there were candles placed on rickety wooden tables, but no electric lights like back home. A smell of pine needles, woodsmoke, and spilled beer hung about the place—but it was dry and warm, and that alone made it inviting.

The occupants of the tables went instantly silent at the

sight of the explorers, and with just the crackle and pop of the fire in the background, you could have heard a pin drop. Or a goose honk. Stella had forgotten about her, but not wanting to be left behind, the goose had followed them into the tavern, and now promptly waddled across the room and settled herself quite happily in front of the fire, fluffing her feathers and making herself comfortable.

There were perhaps ten or fifteen men sitting at the tables in the Yak and Yeti, and they all looked rather terrifying. Stella saw a lot of facial scars, glass eyes, and grim tattoos. She gulped, and then winced at how loud that noise sounded in the silent room. She tried to compensate by glaring at the men instead.

"Are you outlaws?" one of them asked. He had a great big black beard and a tattoo of a skull on his right cheek.

"What?" Shay said. "No, of course not! We're explorers."

"Then go away," Skullface said. "This here is an outlaw hideout. Bandits and outlaws only."

Stella silently groaned. She'd known that a luxurious hotel out here was too good to be true. It should really have come as no surprise that the frosties had sent them straight to an outlaw hideout.

"Please, we need help," Shay said, and Stella could clearly hear the desperation in his voice. "Our friend is hurt."

One of the bandits glanced at Ethan. "Frostbitten," he said. "He's a goner."

"What?" Shay was aghast. "Are you saying he'll *die*?"

The bandit shrugged. "Chop off his fingers and toes and maybe he'll live. Then again, maybe he won't. It's his best chance, anyway."

"I've got an axe you can borrow," Skullface put in helpfully. "It's a bit blunt but it should do the job all right, if you keep hacking."

"You've *g-g-got* to be *j-j-joking*!" Ethan gasped. Stella could feel that he was trembling from head to foot. Or was that her? It was quite hard to tell.

"I use it for chopping wood mostly," Skullface continued with a shrug. "But you're welcome to it. As long as you clean it afterward, of course. I don't want blood all over the blade and staining the handle. Even frostbitten fingers bleed quite a lot when you chop 'em off. And it's a bit blunt, like I say, so you'll have to put some muscle into it, otherwise you won't cut through the bone. Do it outside, though, eh? We don't want all that gore and mess and screaming in here." He produced from beneath the table a most gigantic axe, which he held out to them.

Ethan fainted dead away, almost dragging Shay and Stella down to the floor with him. They tightened their grip around the unconscious magician, and Stella could feel her shoulders burning with the effort of holding him up.

A chair over in the corner of the room suddenly scraped back, and a huge man walked toward them. He must have only recently come in from outside because Stella could see ice glinting in his reddish-colored beard. A jagged scar ran down the right side of his face, but when he spoke his voice was a friendly, lazy drawl.

"Hey," he said. "Have you kids got any mustache wax? Explorers normally carry mustache wax."

"What?" Shay gave him an incredulous look. "Can't you see that we're dealing with an emergency here, man?"

"Sure. That's why I—"

"Go away!" Stella snapped. "We've got more important things to deal with right now."

"Do I look like the kind of guy who waxes his mustache or oils his beard?"

Stella had to admit that he did not. In fact, he looked more like the kind of person who had strange things living in his beard, or saved bits of food in there for later.

"You don't look like you wax your mustache, but it would probably improve your appearance enormously if you did," Beanie said, trying to be helpful. "I've got some mustache wax. Here, you can have it."

Stella didn't know why Beanie had even bothered to bring the foul-smelling stuff, but she was too horrified at the prospect of having to chop off all Ethan's fingers and toes to worry too much about it just then.

"'Captain Filibuster's Expedition-Strength Mustache Wax,'" the man read off the tin. "Yep, that'll do the job just fine." He snapped his fingers and said, "Get your friend up on the table. I'll put him to rights."

Stella tightened her grip around Ethan. This could not be happening. This simply could not. She had not signed up for blood everywhere and chopped-off fingers. She had not signed up for that *at all*.

"There's got to be some other way," Shay said desperately. "We can't let you chop all his fingers off! I mean, we just can't!"

"I ain't gonna chop his fingers off," Redbeard replied. "Keep your shirt on. I'm talking about another way. One that don't involve blood and gore and screaming. It's the most effective cure for frostbite I know. And I'll share it with you on one condition." He pointed a stern finger at them. "You gotta promise to leave all mention of the Yak and Yeti out of your Flag Report. Yep, I know all about them," he said at their surprised expressions. "Carried enough explorers on my ship in me day before switching to carrying convicts."

Stella frowned. "Are you saying that you're a ship's captain?"

"Used to be," Redbeard replied. "Captain Ajay Ajax, at your service." He gave them a little bow. "Got stranded here during my last voyage trying to take this lot"—he gestured to the other men—"to the prison colonies on the other side of the world. Darned ship got trapped in the ice and that was that. We've been here ever since. And it ain't a bad spot when all's said and done, so the last thing we want is a bunch of lawmakers chasing after us because you kids yapped about our hideout in your report. This lot don't want to be hauled away in chains again, and I don't want to go back to being a ship's captain sailing on an ocean full of dangerous sea monsters. Not when I can be warm and safe here in the tavern that I always dreamed of owning, ever since I were a boy—"

"Okay, okay, we get it," Stella said. "We won't tell anyone about you. Please just tell us how we can help our friend *without* using an axe!"

Captain Ajax held up the tin of mustache wax and said, "This heals frostbite as well as anything. Not what it was made for, right enough, and I only discovered it meself by accident when we got stranded here. You just need to apply it to the first bite, and any bits that have turned blue, and he'll be right as rain by morning."

Stella wasn't really sure she believed that mustache wax could cure frostbite, but she was willing to try anything if it meant they didn't have to start chopping off fingers in the snow outside.

The outlaws at the nearest table removed their drink tankards and then helped the explorers to heave Ethan up onto the table. Perhaps there were a few too many of them trying to do it all at once, because in the confusion Ethan thumped down on the table pretty hard, and Stella winced as the back of his head whacked against the wood with a solid-sounding *clunk*. If there was a lump there when he woke up, he was bound to think they'd dropped him on purpose.

"All right, get his gloves off," Captain Ajax said. "Carefully, mind! You'll snap any frozen fingers clean off if you yank at 'em."

Stella, Shay, and Beanie proceeded to slide the gloves off with as much delicacy as if they'd been performing a surgical operation. Stella couldn't help flinching at the sight of the magician's hands. The frostbite had gotten a lot worse while they'd been traveling to the Yak and Yeti—all Ethan's fingers were frozen in a solid coating of ice that looked extremely painful, and there was a blue twinge creeping up his wrists as well. She dreaded to think what would have happened without Beanie's magic slowing it down.

"Just in time," Captain Ajax declared, and Stella prayed he was right.

He unscrewed the lid of the mustache wax, and Stella wrinkled her nose at the overpowering combination of sandalwood and black pepper.

They spent the next ten minutes or so carefully dabbing the mustache wax onto Ethan's frozen fingers, and Stella was delighted to see that it started to work instantly. Perhaps it was one of the many ingredients in the mustache wax—or the combination of all of them—but something in the powerful-smelling stuff seemed to penetrate right through the ice, causing it to crackle and melt away, leaving the skin beneath perfectly unharmed.

Next they pulled off Ethan's boots and went through the same thing with his feet. Normally Stella would have been quite squeamish about having to deal with a boy's feet, but compared to the alternative—the axe and the blood and the snow and the screaming and the sawing—this was a piece of cake, really. And Ethan's feet were extremely clean and tidy.

"All right," Captain Ajax said. "Only the wrists left and then we're done. Get that cloak off and roll his sleeves up to the elbow, just to be safe."

Because Ethan was, like the rest of them, wearing layers and layers of clothing, it took a while to get all his sleeves rolled up. When they'd finally done so, Stella was so intent on his frozen blue skin that she didn't notice the scars at first— not until Captain Ajax came out with a harsh, shocked swear. It was very interesting and colorful, and Stella made a mental note to write it down so she wouldn't forget it later.

Beside her, Shay gasped, and Stella finally saw what the others had already noticed. Both of Ethan's forearms were covered in angry-looking scars. They were all perfectly circular, and they stood out stark and white against his skin.

"Are those . . . *squid* scars?" Shay said, peering at them.

"Aye," Captain Ajax said in a grim voice. "The screeching red devil squid. They only live in the Bone Current of the Poison Tentacle Sea—one of the most dangerous monsters in one of the most dangerous oceans in all the world." He shook his head. "Explorers," he muttered. "Only explorers would be crazy enough to go somewhere like that *willingly*. Stark raving mad, the lot of yers. That's why I stopped carrying expeditions in the end," he went on. "Too many burials at sea. Too many creatures trying to eat the ship. Too much mayhem all around."

They applied mustache wax to the last of Ethan's frozen skin, then Captain Ajax said there was a couch in the kitchen they could put Ethan on until he woke up.

"Can't have unconscious magicians lying around the place, using up the tables, cluttering up the décor," he said.

"What décor?" Stella asked, staring around the bare wooden room with its rickety old tables.

Captain Ajax ignored her. "I got a business to run, y'know," he said. "You can stay till he wakes up but then you'll have to go."

They carried Ethan through to the kitchen at the back and put him down on the threadbare couch. Stella noticed as they did so that a couple of buttons at the top of his cloak had come undone, and that there were squid scars on his throat as well. She wondered whether that was why he'd always worn his shirt buttoned all the way up to the collar, even on the ship when it was hot and stuffy and everyone else had had their sleeves rolled up.

Stella realized it was pretty ironic that the mustache wax she and Felix had assumed was useless had actually been so vital to them. Felix would have said something about how that just goes to show you should never be too absolutely sure that you're in the right and the other fellow is in the wrong. Sometimes you're the silly fool who needs to learn something.

Stella couldn't help wondering whether the beard oil she and Felix had given away to the crew of the *Bold Adventurer* might also have had any secretly useful properties. Perhaps a drop of beard oil in your hot chocolate cured hiccups, or allowed you to speak another language, or gave you the ability to become invisible.

"You kids like a drink?" Captain Ajax said, turning to the kitchen cupboards. "All we got is grog. One-Eyed Bill out there made it himself. It tastes terrible but it'll warm you up some."

Stella felt she could do with something warming, even if it did taste terrible. The frosty attack and then that scare with the axe had released an awful lot of adrenaline, and her hands were still shaking a little.

They sat down around the kitchen table and Captain Ajax handed out chipped mugs of grog. He was right about it tasting terrible, but he was also right about it warming them up. Soon they were even able to remove their cloaks and one or two of their top sweaters. Stella was particularly pleased to get down to her third sweater because it was one of her favorites—Beanie's mum had made it for her and it was powder blue in color with a big polar bear stitched on the front. Stella noticed that Beanie too wore one of his mum's creations—a bright green sweater with a stitched narwhal.

"So, you came across a frosty camp, eh?" the captain said cheerfully. "I s'pose they lured you in with promises of tea and cake and whatnot and then wanted you to go off to bed?"

"Yes. But why would they do that? Why go to all that trouble to be friendly just to turn on us a few minutes later?" Shay asked.

Captain Ajax shook his head. "Don't you know nothin'? Frosties bite people when they're asleep because they don't feel it then. Come morning they've got full on frostbite and it won't be long before the fingers fall off. And that's what the frosties want."

"But why?" Stella said, flipping her long white plait over her shoulder. "What do they want fingers for?"

Captain Ajax looked surprised. "To eat, of course. Fingers is food to them."

Stella was horrified. "Can't they just get the magic eggs to conjure up fingers?" she asked. "The frosties said it would create any food we wanted."

Captain Ajax shrugged. "Perhaps fingers ain't food to a magic egg, neither."

"Well," Shay eventually said. "That thing Ethan did with the tiny arrows came in pretty handy, didn't it? I mean, the polar bean thing was a bit weird, but the arrows were excellent. Maybe we should take him along with us on our next expedition after all. If he can learn to stop moaning all the time, that is."

"Seems like he must be pretty good at exploring, if you ask me," Captain Ajax put in. "I never heard of anyone tangling with a screeching red devil squid and living to tell the tale. Biggest monster that roams the Poison Tentacle Sea, that is. Biggest one I ever saw was a twenty-foot whopper! Snatches sailors straight off the deck of ships when they stand too close to the edge. Once it's got you in its tentacles, that's that. You're toast." He snapped his fingers.

The sudden sound jerked Ethan awake and he sat up on the couch with a cry. "Don't chop them!"

He lifted his hands up in front of his face and sighed in relief at the sight of his fingers, all still there, all still intact. But then he turned his head to look at the others, and the expressions on their faces made him panic all over again.

"What's the matter? Why are you staring at me like that? It's my toes, isn't it? Oh gods, they're all gone! You've chopped them off!"

"Settle down, kid. No one's chopped nothing," Captain Ajax said.

Ethan narrowed his eyes. "That's a double negative," he said. "So do you mean that you *have* chopped all my toes off, or do you just have terrible grammar? Because technically, 'no one's chopped nothing' actually means that everyone has chopped everything. So—"

"For goodness' sake, Ethan, we never even touched the axe!" Stella said.

Ethan visibly paled at the word. "Please," he said. "Let's not talk about that axe. Ever again."

"We used the mustache wax," Stella said. "Turns out it cures frostbite. Luckily for you, Beanie had some on him and was the only one of us who listened to the captain."

"Just remember your promise," Captain Ajax said. "Not a word in the Flag Report. Say you found out about the mustache wax by accident. I ain't never going back to that way of life." He shuddered. "Wouldn't have been so bad if I could've just transported the thieves, but the Crown wanted me to return all the stolen loot as well. I mean, *all* of it! Had to travel halfway around the world, most times, across every one of the Seventeen Seas. And just you try returning a stolen treasure map to a heat-crazed captain of a pirate galleon. More likely to threaten you with a cutlass than say a nice civilized thank-you." He frowned at Ethan. "But there's some folk you just can't do favors for."

"Why does my head hurt?" the magician said, wincing.

"Oh," Stella sighed. "We might have dropped you on the table. But it was an accident, a *real* accident. It definitely wasn't accidentally on purpose."

Stella felt she was somehow making it worse because

Ethan gave her a suspicious look, but he rubbed his head and kept his mouth shut for once.

"It's time for you lot to be on your way," Captain Ajax said, collecting their mugs. "I said you could stay till the skinny one woke up. Well, now he's awake—talking and charming us all with his endless gratitude—so that means you gotta go. I can only keep that lot outside in check for so long. They're not a bad bunch, really, but there's only so much temptation they can resist, and they'll have the shirts off your backs if you stay much longer."

The explorers hurriedly stood up and reached for their cloaks. They'd already lost half their provisions—the last thing they needed now was to have the rest of their stuff stolen by a motley crew of bandits and outlaws.

"So how *did* you get away from that screeching red devil squid?" Captain Ajax asked as they walked out.

Ethan stiffened. "How do you know about that?"

"I've got eyes, haven't I? We can see the scars."

Ethan scowled and yanked his sleeves back down to his wrists. "My scars are none of your business."

"The way I figure it," the captain went on, quite unperturbed, "is that to escape a monster like that, either you're the luckiest fella alive or the most fearsome magician who ever lived. Personally, my money's on the first one."

"If you must know," Ethan said in an ice-cold voice, "my brother saved my life."

Stella glanced at the magician, surprised. She'd never heard him mention a brother before.

"How?" Captain Ajax asked.

Ethan hesitated for a moment. Then he said, "He cut off the squid's tentacle. Now it hangs in the entrance hall of the Ocean Squid Explorers' Club."

Captain Ajax gave a low whistle but didn't say anything more. They walked back out into the tavern and everyone looked around at them expectantly.

"Well, what do you know—the mustache wax works after all!" Skullface said when he spotted Ethan. He glanced at one of his tablemates. "Looks like you lost the bet."

"The explorers need to get back to their exploring," Captain Ajax said. "So give them back their goose, and they'll be on their way."

"What goose?" Skullface said innocently.

Captain Ajax pointed a stern finger at him. "The one I can see wriggling around under your coat. Give it back to 'em. Now."

Skullface sighed and grumbled but he opened his coat and allowed the goose to scramble free. Some of her feathers were a little ruffled but otherwise she looked no worse for wear. Skullface set her down on the floor, and she ran over to Stella, stared up at her, and honked to be picked up.

Stella hurriedly scooped her into her arms and they followed Captain Ajax out from the warmth of the Yak and

Yeti and into the frozen landscape. It was properly dark now and the moon and stars gave the snow a ghostly blue sheen. It all seemed very inhospitable after the log fires and glowing orange light of the candles they'd just left. Felix had told Stella once that even though exploring was the most fantastic, wonderful thing in the whole entire world, there were still times when you wished you were warm and safe and dry and back at home in your own bed. Stella supposed this was one of those times.

But there were still adventures to be had. Now that the panic with Ethan was over, Stella went straight up to the frozen rainbow and placed her hand on it. It tingled and fizzed like sherbet beneath her touch. She grinned, delighted. She could go home and say that she had actually *touched* a rainbow, and that it had felt just like fizzy sherbet. Already, the urge to explore was coming back, and she suddenly found herself eager to be off and find out what they would discover next.

"Well, then," Captain Ajax said. "My advice, if you want it, is to head that way." He pointed out across the blue snow. "My ship, the *Snow Queen*, is still there, trapped in the ice. It ain't much—it's rotting, it smells something fierce, and there are probably rats and all—but it'll provide shelter for the night."

Stella wasn't sure she liked the idea of spending the night on a smelly, rat-infested, doomed ship trapped in the ice, but there was such a thing as "any port in a storm," after all, and the simple fact was that they didn't have enough tents with them. And after one close shave with the frosties, Stella didn't fancy the rest of them ending up with frostbite during the night too.

So they said their good-byes and their thanks to Captain Ajax and piled back into the sled. As they pulled away across the blue snow, beneath the glittering night sky, Captain Ajax suddenly called out after them, "Just make sure you don't wake up the cabbages!"

Stella frowned, thinking she must have heard him wrong. She glanced at Ethan beside her but he just rolled his eyes.

Nuts, he mouthed. *Totally nuts.*

Stella felt rather inclined to agree with him. Useful though he may have been, perhaps Captain Ajax had had a bit more of One-Eyed Bill's terrible grog than was really good for him.

CHAPTER FOURTEEN

THE SHIP WASN'T FAR away and it didn't take long to find it. It was frozen at an angle in the ice, looking pale and ghostly in the moonlight with the prow rising up into the sky, its shredded sails hanging in tatters, and gaping holes showing through the rotted, crumbling wood. Cold and still in the starlight, it seemed like a dead thing, a husk, a ghost ship.

"Wow," Shay said. "That is extraordinary." He turned to grin at the others. "Isn't being an explorer just the best thing in the whole world, ever?"

Everyone agreed that the ship was magnificent, but the problem was that it wasn't stuck in the middle of a vast, flat expanse of ice as they had expected. At first, Stella thought it was perched on the edge of a cliff, but then she saw that this was no cliff—it was a wave that had frozen right at its highest peak. A ladder ran all the way up its hull but the steps sparkled with ice, and the whole thing looked a bit precarious.

"Do you think it's safe?" Ethan asked, peering at it suspiciously.

"The wave is frozen solid," Shay replied. "It'll be fine. Besides, it looks like this is our only option."

They quickly put up their one tent, which was only just large enough to shelter the animals, and then the four explorers took one of the mountain climbing ropes and tied it around their waists to form a chain. Shay was in the front, then Stella, followed by Ethan and finally Beanie.

"Beanie, put Aubrey away," Stella said, noticing that he had the wooden narwhal clutched in his hand. "You can't climb the ladder if you're holding that."

After checking that the knots were all securely tied, they took hold of the frozen rungs and carefully made their way up the side of the ship. It hadn't seemed so high from the ground, but now that Stella was up there, she thought it seemed very high indeed—dizzyingly high, in fact—and she had to force herself not to look down as she climbed, one hand over the other, and she prayed she wouldn't slip on a frozen rung and break her neck.

After what seemed like forever, Shay reached the top of the ship and scrambled up over the side. Stella heard a thud as his snow boots hit the frozen deck, and then his hand was reaching over to help her on board. She didn't think

she'd ever felt so glad to feel a solid surface beneath her feet. Together, she and Shay helped Ethan up over the side.

"Well, that was a long—" he began, but that was as far as he got before the rope suddenly went taut as Beanie slipped off the ladder behind him. Beanie's weight dragged the magician back into the railings with a thump, and then flipped him backward right over the edge. The force of their combined weight dragged Shay and Stella across the deck, and they both slammed hard into the railings. Stella braced her boots against them and gritted her teeth against the strain in her arms as she grabbed hold of a rail. Shay did the same and they just managed to avoid being dragged over the side with the others. Stella could hear Ethan and Beanie both kicking up a tremendous fuss as they swung to and fro at the end of the rope, dangling helplessly above the vast drop spread beneath them.

"Lord Rupert Randolph Rutledge," Beanie gasped, "plunged to his death after his teammate cut the rope in order to—"

"I'll cut the rope on you if you don't shut up!" Ethan snapped, before yelling to the others, "For goodness' sake, pull us *up*!"

"Give us a chance!" Shay shouted back.

Together, he and Stella carefully got to their feet, gripped the rope, and pulled it until Ethan reached the top once again. Shay grabbed his cloak and hauled him over the side before doing the same for Beanie. The four of them gasped for breath as the wooden deck creaked beneath their boots.

Ethan rounded on Beanie at once. "What's the matter with you?" he snarled. "What kind of explorer can't even climb a ladder?"

"I'm sorry," Beanie said. He had the wooden narwhal clutched tightly in his hand. "Aubrey started to slip out of my pocket, so I had to let go of the ladder to—"

"You're joking." Ethan fixed him with a cold, gray stare. "You must be. You're not seriously telling me that you endangered your life, and mine, over a *wooden toy*?"

"He's not just a toy," Beanie protested. "He's—"

But he never got to finish his sentence, because Ethan snatched the narwhal from his hand and, before anyone could stop him, tossed it over the side of the ship. One moment it was there, and the next it was gone, swallowed up by the vast drop below.

There was a moment of total silence. Beanie stared numbly in the direction of the vanished narwhal—then he untied the rope around his waist, turned without a word to anyone, and walked off to the covered bridge, closing the door quietly behind him.

The next moment, Stella flew at Ethan. She simply couldn't help herself. Using her hands and her feet, she kicked and punched at him mercilessly. The magician tried to fend her off but the rope tying them together made it impossible to get away from her. Finally, Shay grabbed her around the waist and dragged her bodily away.

"Stella, calm *down*!" he said.

"You're crazy!" Ethan gasped. "You know that, right? You're absolutely crazy!"

"You're the most horrible person I've ever met!" she yelled.

"I almost just fell to my death because of your idiot friend and his stupid toy," Ethan replied, looking outraged.

"Beanie's father made him that narwhal," Stella said.

Ethan shrugged. "So he can make him another one. Big deal."

"His father has been missing for eight years!" Stella said. "He went on an expedition across the Black Ice Bridge and never came back. That narwhal was Beanie's most precious possession!"

Ethan looked taken aback for a moment. Then he scowled and said, "Well, only a complete lunatic would attempt to cross the Black Ice Bridge. Everyone knows that no one ever returns from there. And only a total halfwit would bring their most precious possession with them on an expedition. How was I supposed to know? I'm not—"

"You're the worst teammate ever!" Stella cut him off. "You're selfish and cruel. I bet that's why your brother didn't come on this expedition. I bet even he can't stand to be around you!"

All the color drained from Ethan's already pale face, and for a moment Stella thought he wasn't going to speak at all. But finally he said in a low voice, "My brother isn't here because he died in the Poison Tentacle Sea."

Stella couldn't have felt any worse in that moment than if he had slapped her. Guilt raged all the way through her body, hot and awful. Felix had known about Ethan's brother, she realized. That was why he'd asked her to be nice to him; that was why he'd talked of battles she knew nothing about. He'd be so ashamed of her if he heard what she'd just said. Stella hated herself and wished she could take the words back.

"Ethan, I didn't mean—" she began.

But the magician turned away from her, clutching at his head. "Gods, I really do have the most *insane* headache thanks to you lot!"

"Are you all right?" Shay asked quietly.

"'All right'?" Ethan repeated in an incredulous voice. He dropped his hands and Stella distinctly saw his nostrils flare. "How can I possibly be *all right*, you utter moron? Didn't you just hear me say that my brother is dead? Would *you* be all right if you were in my place? Nothing will ever be all right for me or my family ever again."

"I'm sorry—" Shay began. He reached out a hand as if to grip Ethan's shoulder but the magician pushed him away.

"Don't you *dare* feel sorry for me!" His eyes flashed in

the cold moonlight. He looked livid. "I don't want your pity! And I don't want your friendship, either! I just want to live long enough to get through this expedition and return to my own team. That's it!"

He untied the rope around his waist, turned away, and started walking toward the shelter of the bridge. Stella hurried after him. She really felt she needed to say something, to make some effort to soften the harsh words she had spoken before.

"Ethan, look—" she began.

"*Will* you leave me alone?" he snapped. "You're right, okay? I *am* selfish. And it's cost me more than you can ever imagine."

He stormed off. There seemed to be nothing more to say, and nothing more to do, other than follow Ethan across the deck to the bridge. Stella glanced at the night sky, which was now thick with falling snowflakes, and knew that fresh snow meant there was practically zero chance of finding Beanie's narwhal in the morning. It would be buried deep by then, and they'd have no way of knowing where to look for it. Stella knew Ethan was right—Beanie should never have brought such a special thing on the expedition with him—but she felt terrible for her friend anyway. And she felt terrible for Ethan, too.

The magician opened the door to the bridge and the three of them joined Beanie inside. He had settled himself in the corner and was calmly organizing a jar of green jelly beans into identical piles. There was a big brass navigational wheel in the center, which was covered in red flakes of rust, and there were maps on the walls that had almost completely crumbled away. The room had a damp, shut-up smell about it, but at least it had four walls and a roof, and they'd be able to stay dry for the night.

Shay unzipped his bag and handed around blankets, which everyone took in silence. Stella was just about to turn away, when Shay held something else out to her. It was a little bird made from dozens of tiny beads and gemstones, shimmering in jade and green.

"Oh, it's a hummingbird!" Stella exclaimed, taking it from Shay.

"Actually, it's a dream snatcher," Shay replied. He tapped it once, firmly, on the head, and the little bird suddenly came to life, rapidly flapping its wings and flitting around Stella. Lowering his voice so that only Stella could hear, he said, "I thought it might help with that nightmare of yours."

Stella thought about denying she'd ever had a nightmare, but she could tell from the expression on Shay's face that there would be no point.

"It's all right, Sparky," he said softly. "The night is full of good and bad dreams for each of us. I had terrible nightmares when I was little, so my grandmother made me this. Dream snatchers don't like the taste of good dreams—they're too sugary for them—but they go mad for nightmares. Gobble them up the second they arrive, which means they never even have a chance to reach you."

Stella looked up at the little dream snatcher, which was beating its wings so fast that it hovered in the air right over her head, just like a hummingbird. Stella returned her gaze to Shay. "What were your bad dreams about?" she asked, then immediately wished she hadn't in case Shay thought she was being nosy.

He didn't seem to mind, though, and said, "I dreamed I was a wolf caught in a trap. There was trouble, you see, between the wild wolves and the village where I grew up. Being a wolf whisperer isn't always fun. In fact, sometimes it's just no fun at all. Hang it up near where you're sleeping. That way you'll be protected."

Stella whispered her thanks, then went to join Beanie in the corner. He wordlessly pushed one of the piles of jelly beans over to her and they sat and ate them together in silence. Then Stella hung the dream snatcher from the nearby navigational wheel before lying down next to her friend.

The Polar Bear explorers all drew up the hoods of their cloaks, and the fur linings felt snug and warm against their ears. Looking at Ethan's bare, blond head, Stella wondered if he regretted not taking Beanie up on his offer to lend him his hat. But if he did, he didn't say anything. In fact, no one was in much of a chatting mood at all. It had been a long day. Without another word to each other, the explorers bedded down and went to sleep.

CHAPTER FIFTEEN

THAT NIGHT, STELLA HAD one of the nicest dreams she could ever remember having. She was tucked up in bed, and someone was reading her a bedtime story. At first Stella assumed it was Felix, but then she realized that it wasn't his voice, and that the hands holding the enormous book that masked the reader's face were actually a woman's. She could tell by the delicate silver charm bracelet dangling from her wrist. There was a unicorn charm, along with other charms Stella couldn't make out properly, and they made a tinkling noise every time the woman moved her hand to turn the page.

"'When the first unicorn came to the Icelands,'" she read, "'it searched high and low for a home of its own where it would be safe from the yetis.'"

She snapped her fingers, and out of thin air, a tiny unicorn made of snow appeared on Stella's bed, prancing excitedly up and down the covers, leaving little frosted hoof-marks in its wake. Stella clapped her hands together, delighted.

"'The unicorn soon found itself in a beautiful ice garden . . . ,'" the voice went on, and Stella watched as snow flowers and ice trees began growing up from her blanket, filling the air with the scent of magic and petals. . . .

But then, all of a sudden, something went wrong. Stella heard another voice, raised in anger. The book dropped from the woman's hands, and the snow unicorn and trees and flowers disappeared instantly.

"Quick!" the woman's voice gasped. "Hide under the bed, dear! Don't make a sound!"

Stella found herself out of her soft warm blankets and lying on the cold hard floor beneath her bed. Her hands were spread flat against the polished wood, so she felt the exact moment when the floorboards started to tremble.

That angry voice came from downstairs again, and Stella stared down at the floorboards, dreading whatever it was that was lurking just out of sight below. There was something evil down there, and it was looking for her. She could feel its rage beating up through the floor, thumping like the pounding of a black, shriveled-up heart. Stella felt a wail of fear bubble up in her throat, but knew that she absolutely must not make a sound. Suddenly, there was a crash from the hallway, and Stella watched in breathless terror as the door handle on the other side of the room slowly started to turn—

A hand clamped down on Stella's arm and she sat up with a shriek—only to see that the fingers gripping her were Shay's. She realized she was still inside the ship, and the darkness pressing up against the windows told her that it was still the middle of the night. Beanie and Ethan were tucked up asleep in their blankets, but Shay was staring down at her, his long hair messed up from sleep, a shocked expression on his face.

"Are you okay?" he said.

Stella nodded. "I'm sorry if I woke you."

"Never mind that," Shay replied. "Stella, what the heck were you dreaming about?"

"It's . . . it's just that nightmare I have sometimes."

Shay lifted his hand, and Stella realized the dream snatcher lay curled on his palm, its wings fluttering feebly. Its beaded feathers were choked full of writhing dark shapes, long snakes of shadowy smoke that twisted and tangled, until suddenly they ripped free, breaking the dream snatcher apart in the process. The broken pieces fell through Shay's fingers, and the green beads flew over the floorboards. The nightmare shadows melted away like fog.

Shay and Stella looked at each other.

"No normal dream should be able to do that," Shay said.

He was looking at her as if she might be able to explain

what had just happened, but Stella didn't know what to say. At that moment, Koa padded out from the shadows and lay down close beside her. Stella wished Koa were a real wolf so that she could throw her arms around her and be comforted by the warmth and softness of her fur.

"I'm really sorry about your grandmother's dream snatcher," she said.

Shay shook his head. "It's not your fault." He glanced out the window. "We should try to get back to sleep." He paused, then added, "Koa will watch over you tonight if you like."

Stella looked at the shadow wolf and felt comforted by the steady dark eyes gazing back at her. But even so, as she settled back down in her blankets, she felt scared to go back to sleep in case the dream returned.

Thankfully, there were no more nightmares that night, and when Stella woke the next morning Koa had gone, along with Shay and Ethan. Stella sat up, and the movement woke Beanie beside her. He propped himself up on his elbows, his dark hair sticking out in all directions. He blinked a few times and then frowned. "Was that there last night?" he asked.

"What?" Stella replied.

"That chair." Beanie pointed into the corner of the room.

Stella turned to look, and then gasped. "That's no chair," she said. "It's a throne."

They both stared at it. It was indeed a magnificent throne, made entirely from snow, with images of frosties, yetis, and polar bears engraved on the back of it.

"Who could have built it?" Beanie wondered.

Stella stood up. She knew it was silly, but she had the distinct feeling that her dream had somehow built the throne. She had the almost overpowering urge to touch it.

She felt it was calling out to her to sit in it. She started to walk forward, but suddenly Beanie was beside her.

"I don't think we should touch it," he said.

"Why not?" Stella replied. "It's only a chair."

"I don't know. I have a bad feeling about it," Beanie said.

Stella felt so drawn to the throne. It seemed almost familiar. She reached out to run her finger along the top of the seat, but the next moment the throne melted away, and the two children were left staring at a puddle that quickly froze as it spread across the icy floor.

"I told you we shouldn't touch it," Beanie said. "Where have the others gone, anyway?"

Stella couldn't help feeling irritated with Beanie for preventing her from touching the chair, but she tried to push the feeling away. And moments later she felt a little bit ashamed. Beanie was right to be cautious, wasn't he?

Stella shook herself. "I don't know." She went back to her bag and pulled out the folding pocket mustache comb. "I hope they're not having a duel or anything." She undid her long hair from its plait, tugged the comb through its tangles, and quickly plaited it again. "Right," she said, stuffing the comb back in her bag, "we'd better go find them."

They stepped out onto the deck, where it was brilliantly sunny but still bitterly cold. Stella was glad of the fresh air. The two explorers hugged their thick blue cloaks tighter around themselves, shivering as they fumbled to do up the buttons with their gloved fingers.

They spotted Shay at once. The wolf whisperer had tied his dark hair back with a piece of leather cord and was building a fire in the middle of the deck using some broken pieces of wood he must have found inside the ship. Koa lay on the deck at his side, her head lifted to sniff at the early morning air. The smoke from the fire was a little salty and dank, but the warmth of the flames more than made up for that, and Stella and Beanie hurried to settle themselves beside it.

"Hi, folks." Shay greeted them. "I went down to feed the animals and found us some breakfast."

He gestured at the little pile of speckled goose eggs on the deck beside him. "Thank you, magic goose," he said, handing them around.

"Where's Ethan?" Stella asked.

Shay shrugged. "He wasn't here when I woke up. That was about an hour ago. I was going to look for him but I haven't had time."

Stella couldn't help feeling a little bit worried, despite the fact that she was still angry with the magician—but then a scraping sound made them all turn around in time to see Ethan scrambling over the side of the ship. He looked rather like he'd been rolling around in the snow. His black sleeves were wet, the front of his explorer's cloak was all dusted with white, and there were even clumps of it in his pale blond hair.

"We thought you'd gone," Shay remarked. "Taken yourself off to die in peace and quiet somewhere."

Ethan ignored him and walked straight up to Beanie. "I'm sorry for throwing your narwhal away. And for calling you bait. That was . . . unnecessary. And cruel. I am cruel sometimes. I'm sorry."

They all stared at him for a moment. Ethan had not struck any of them as the apologizing type. Fortunately, though, Beanie was definitely the forgiving type, so Stella wasn't surprised when he said, "That's okay. You're right, anyway; I should never have let go of the ladder and dragged you off in the first place." He paused, then added, "Look, I know I'm not like other people. I know I do odd things. Uncle Benedict says I'm enough to drive anyone around the twist, and that it's no wonder I only have one friend in all the world, and that no one ever wants to come to my birthday parties. Even my cousin Moira said she would never come again, no matter what her parents said, because I'm a weirdo, and she doesn't like me, and she wishes we weren't even related."

"Moira really is such a snot!" Stella said, hating Beanie's cousin all over again. "It's her loss, anyway. More cake for us, Beanie."

At the mention of that cake, they both immediately

winced at the memory of how many jelly beans they'd eaten.

Ethan looked taken aback. "Well," he said. "Be that as it may. I shouldn't have done what I did. Perhaps this will help make up for it."

He reached out his hand and opened his gloved fingers to reveal a wooden narwhal—frozen solid, but otherwise quite unharmed.

"Oh!" Beanie scrambled to his feet and snatched the narwhal from Ethan's hand. "Oh, you found him!"

He stared down at the narwhal for a moment before carefully putting it in his pocket and placing his hand on Ethan's arm—which surprised Stella, because it was highly unusual for Beanie to touch another person of his own free will. "Thank you so very much," Beanie said.

"Forget it."

Beanie removed his hand, looking puzzled. "How can I forget it? It only just happened."

Ethan sighed. "I mean, you're welcome."

He peeled off his wet gloves and turned away to shake them out over the deck, but before he could finish doing so, Stella had gotten to her feet and thrown her arms around the magician.

"Oh, please don't hug me," Ethan groaned, trying to disentangle himself from her embrace.

Stella let him go with a grin. "How did you find it?" she asked.

"I tried to use a locator spell," Ethan replied. "Only it didn't work. So I just had to dig in the snow."

"But that must have taken hours!" Shay said.

"Most of the night," Ethan agreed. He looked at Beanie. "Look, my brother, Julian . . . well . . . he's gone too," he said. "So I know what it's like to lose someone on an expedition. And I am sorry about your father. The Black Ice Bridge has claimed many good explorers."

Beanie nodded. "Thank you. I'm sorry about your brother."

"Me too," Stella said. "You should have told us about him before."

"Why?" Ethan said. "You never knew him. It doesn't matter to you."

"But we know *you*," Stella said. "So it does matter. Plus, we would have, you know, made allowances for you whenever you were being obnoxious."

"Obnoxious" was another one of the words Felix had taught her how to spell, and Stella was rather fond of it and enjoyed using it whenever possible. She remembered Felix telling her once that grief could make people a bit obnoxious sometimes. Why, Aunt Agatha had been particularly obnoxious for practically an entire year after their father died. Stella didn't want Ethan to think she was being horrible to him again, though, so she threw her arms around him in another hug.

"Would you please stop doing that?" Ethan said.

Stella gave him a final squeeze and then let go. She couldn't help noticing that he looked pink and embarrassed, and maybe just a little bit pleased as well.

"Ethan—" Shay began.

The magician pointed a warning finger at the wolf whisperer. "Don't. Don't even think about hugging me. Nothing's changed. I'm still obnoxious."

Shay grinned. "Don't worry," he said. "I still think you're uppity. And a prawn, come to that. I was just going to say, 'catch.'"

He threw one of the goose eggs at him. Unfortunately, Ethan wasn't very good at catching flying objects and ended up fumbling with the egg for a moment before dropping it on the deck, and then he had to scrabble around for it in an undignified kind of way. It didn't break, though, and he soon scooped it back up again.

"Stop messing about with that egg and sit down," Shay said. "Have some breakfast."

Ethan sat and the four of them concentrated on what breakfast they'd like to find in their eggs. Before long, the smells of porridge, toast, and bacon filled the air, and the explorers enjoyed their first breakfast on the ice in companionable silence.

CHAPTER SIXTEEN

WE SHOULD EXPLORE THE ship before we go," Stella said once breakfast was finished.

"Definitely," Shay said. "There could be supplies down there. We still need another tent. And some weapons."

"Does anyone here even know how to use a weapon?" Ethan asked.

Stella shrugged. "How hard can it be with a spear? You just point the pointy end at the enemy and jab them with it. Or if it's a heavy thing—like that mustache spoon—you whack them with it. It made quite a good weapon, actually." She patted her pockets to make sure that the mustache spoon was still there, just in case she came across anything else that tried to give her any trouble.

"Captain Ajax and the outlaws probably didn't leave something on the ship worth having," Shay said. "But we might as well have a quick poke around while we're here."

The four of them quickly located a trapdoor with a ladder and made their way down into the murky belly of the ship. Captain Ajax had been right—it stank something dreadful down below: a horrible mixture of rot and mildew and slimy, seaweedy things.

Stella noticed the crest for the Royal Crown Steam Navigation Company on one of the walls and realized that the *Snow Queen* had been built by the same company that had made the *Bold Adventurer*. But the ship that had brought them to the Icelands had been plush with rugs and lamps and fine silverware. The *Snow Queen*, on the other hand, was a dark, damp, hollowed-out shell. The corridors were long and narrow and full of shadows, and the wood groaned in a most disconcerting way beneath their feet. The planks were covered in a film of salty dust, and the explorers had to lift the hems of their cloaks to stop them getting sticky with it.

Stella was a little worried that they might come across a skeleton at some point, but they never did, which made her feel half relieved and half disappointed. They did spot one or two rats, though, scampering about in the corners, running over old chains in the dark. They were surprisingly large, no doubt having grown fat from feasting on whatever stocks of inedible ship's biscuits had been left behind.

Between the rats and the crew, the ship seemed to have

been stripped of anything even remotely useful. There was no food left in the kitchen, no books in the library, no tents or blankets or rope in the old convict cells. Only endless coils of rusty chain.

"We should get back to the animals and push on," Shay said. "There's nothing here to get excited about."

"Let's just go down this last corridor," Stella said, pointing. "And if there's nothing there, then we'll leave."

It didn't seem right that they should venture into the dark, deserted ship without discovering *something* for their trouble. To make all this effort and not even see so much as a skeleton seemed like the most dreadful letdown.

So they ventured into the final corridor, which got darker and darker as they walked down it. There were portholes in the wall, but they weren't letting any light in, and Stella guessed they must be near the bottom of the ship and that the windows had been covered up with snow. Shay took a lantern from his bag and lit it to guide their way down to the door at the end of the corridor. There were words carved into the wood, and Shay lifted the lantern up a little higher to illuminate them. Stella grinned when she saw what they said. This was definitely more like it.

Do Not Open This Door Under ANY Circumstances!

Ordinary children would certainly have turned and walked away from that door at once and never looked back, but these were junior explorers, and a warning like that was impossible for them to resist.

"Perhaps we shouldn't open it," Beanie said, trying to be sensible. "They must have carved that there for a reason."

"There can't be anything dangerous in there now," Stella replied. "The ship must have been stranded here in the ice for years."

"There could be crates of pirate gold in there!" Ethan said.

"Or the skeletons of fascinating beasts and monsters," Shay suggested.

"Or an entire crate of exotic-flavored jelly beans!" Beanie said.

"Or forbidden maps to forbidden places." Stella rubbed her hands together with glee. "Let's find out."

A heavy chain was wrapped around the handle of the door, but the lock had rusted away and it sprang open. All they had to do was unwind the chain.

Together they dragged it free and it fell to the ground in a long, heavy coil. Then, with one last glance at each other, they threw open the door.

CHAPTER SEVENTEEN

STELLA DIDN'T QUITE KNOW what she was expecting in the locked room, but when Shay lifted the lantern, it illuminated a large storage area filled with cabinets, trunks, and boxes, all coated with a thick layer of dust. The words "Dangerous Cargo" and "Swag" and "Stolen Loot" were stamped all over everything.

The explorers walked cautiously into the room and peered into the cabinets. They were organized into categories, with the first one being dedicated to "Cursed Objects." Stella saw a little jade truth god, a grotesque painting of a deranged-looking child holding a knife, and a stuffed hyena that looked like it was about to start cackling at any moment. Each item had a small card attached to it, naming the object and who had stolen it. Stella examined the nearest label and saw that it said: "Laughing Hyena—stolen by Leeroy Livingston from the Lost City of Muja-Muja."

Noticing a dark shape out of the corner of her eye, Stella glanced down and saw that Koa had appeared beside her. The shadow wolf was staring intently at the stuffed hyena.

"I don't like the look of it either," Stella told her.

"This must be what Captain Ajax was talking about before," Shay said, gazing into one of the cabinets. "He said the convict ship took the thieves to the prisoner colonies and then sailed around returning all the stolen loot."

"I guess he decided to just leave it all here when the ship got trapped in the ice," Stella said. "Most of this stuff doesn't look like it would be much use in the Icelands. It's no wonder this ship was doomed—I've never seen so many cursed objects in one place before." There was even a tiny mummy wrapped in dirty bandages inside a broken sarcophagus. It was far too small to be human—only a few inches long.

"Hey, look at this!" Shay exclaimed.

Stella turned and joined the others. They were bending over what appeared to be the most impossibly tiny volcano.

"It's a baby volcano from Volcano Island!" Shay said. "We should take this with us—it'll be far easier than trying to make a fire out of wet logs. All you do is shake it."

It looked extremely heavy, but Shay just managed to pick up the mini volcano with both hands, and then he gave it a good shake. He set it back down on the floor and it instantly glowed red hot, little trickles of lava spilling out over the top and tiny red sparks shooting out like miniature fireworks.

"But do you think we ought to take anything?" Beanie said. "Isn't it stealing?"

"Not really," Ethan replied. "This stuff has been abandoned. It can't be returned to its owners now anyway. I say if there's anything that might come in handy on the expedition, we nab it."

"But no cursed objects," Stella said. She didn't like the snarling expression on that hyena and wouldn't trust it not to bite her in her sleep.

"No, definitely no cursed objects," Shay agreed. "Nobody wants to wake up to find a stuffed hyena trying to gnaw through their boots."

They poked around the rest of the room and found a single book chained to a table, a gigantic diamond, and even a trunk filled with teeth.

"Why would anyone steal teeth?" Beanie peered into the trunk, bemused.

"Perhaps they stole money from the tooth fairy and it all turned back into teeth?" Stella said.

Ethan halfheartedly suggested that they take the diamond with them, since it really was massive and would make a fine addition to either of their clubs. But Shay pointed out that it would be impossible for the two clubs to share the diamond and, more importantly, it was housed in the Cursed Objects cabinet, which probably meant that they shouldn't even so much as look at it. Everyone knew that precious jewels like diamonds were among the most deadly of cursed objects, so they left the sparkling thing where it was. It was time to be on their way.

"Come on, Beanie," Stella called to her friend, who for some reason was rummaging around in a chest of clothes over in the corner. "We're leaving."

Beanie straightened up and turned around with a dress in his hands. It was the most fiendishly ugly garment—a weird shade of brown with awful-looking giant flowers printed all over it. "Do you think Moira would like this?" he asked.

"Your cousin?" Stella pulled a face. "Who cares?"

"Mum says it's nice to bring family members presents when you go adventuring," Beanie said. "I thought if I picked a nice party dress for Moira, then she might change her mind about coming to my next birthday party."

"Beanie, forget about Moira. She's really mean, and you're better off not having her at your party anyway."

"Oh." Beanie frowned but put the dress back. Then he grabbed something else from the chest and tapped Ethan on the shoulder. He held up a pair of pink satin ballet slippers. "Would you like these?" he asked.

The magician stared at him. "What would I want with a pair of ballet slippers?"

"I just thought you might like to practice your pirouettes and things," Beanie said. "That's what ballerinas do, isn't it?"

Ethan groaned. "For the last time," he said, "I am not a ballerina."

"Why did you say you were, then?" Beanie asked, genuinely puzzled. "Back in the tunnel you said—"

"I was being sarcastic!"

"Oh. I don't really understand sarcasm. Mum says it's something people do when they're not as clever as they think they are." He looked from Ethan to the slippers and back again. "So do you want these or not?" he asked.

"No!" Ethan snatched the slippers from Beanie's hand and tossed them into the corner. Unfortunately, this upset a teetering pile of jewelry boxes, which went tumbling to the floor, where they burst open. There was quite a din as precious rings, bracelets, tiaras, and trinkets rolled across the floor, sending white sparkles of light shooting out all over the place. One of the boxes was also a music box, and it began playing a tinkling, highly irritating tune the moment it opened. A tiny princess spun around and around inside until Stella shut the lid with a snap. Everyone looked at Ethan.

"What?" he said defensively.

"Come on." Shay turned away, Koa at his heels. "Let's get out of here."

They set off toward the door. And then froze. There had been nothing there just a moment before, but now a long, strange, stringy sort of plant sat there in a pot, blocking the way.

"What the heck is that?" Ethan said.

"It wasn't there before, was it?" Beanie asked.

"It must have been," Stella replied. "Potted plants can't move around on their own, can they?"

They cautiously took a few steps closer to it. A low growl started in the back of Koa's throat.

"I've just remembered something Dad told me about once," Shay said slowly. "Has anyone ever heard of the Valley of Carnivorous Plants? The carnivorous plants there, they, um . . . they're supposed to be able to move about on their own. And eat people."

There was silence as they all stared warily at the plant. It was completely motionless as it sat innocently in its pot. Now that they were closer, they could see that its leaves were a strange, dark color, and that little clusters of fruit— about the size of oranges—hung from its branches.

"What kind of fruit is that?" Stella asked.

"That isn't fruit," Ethan replied. His eyes met Stella's. "They're cabbages."

"Cabbages aren't carnivorous," Beanie said at once.

"Didn't Captain Ajax say not to wake up the—" Shay began, but that was as far as he got. The plant suddenly snapped out a long, hairy vine and wrapped itself all the way up Shay's arm, causing him to drop the baby volcano, and then started dragging him slowly forward. At the same time, the leaves around all the little cabbages spread out to reveal sharp, pointed, glistening teeth, all drooling with saliva, and the plant started making a horrible hissing sound.

The explorers all screamed at once, although Shay screamed loudest of all, which was only fair since he was the one being attacked by the carnivorous plant. His free hand clawed at the vine but it was clamped firmly around his skin and he couldn't loosen it at all.

"Do something!" he cried. "Do something *now*!"

Koa was barking and snarling at the plant, but being a shadow wolf, she couldn't do much to help. Ethan threw up his hand, and some tiny miniature arrows—like the ones he'd used against the frosties—sailed toward the plant. But instead of piercing it, the arrows turned around in midair and bounced back toward the explorers, which meant they all had to duck to avoid being shot in the eyeball.

"It's got some kind of anti-magic protection spell on it," Ethan said.

Stella grabbed the vine and the other two quickly joined her, but they couldn't pull it free either, and they were definitely losing the tug-of-war with the cabbage plant: Shay's boots were sliding ever closer toward those glistening fangs buried within the cabbages.

"Find a knife or something!" Shay gasped. "You need to chop off the vine!"

Stella, Ethan, and Beanie scattered across the room,

tearing around the cabinets in search of something sharp. Finally, Beanie located an axe in the iron grip of a suit of armor. Ethan managed to wrestle it free and they raced back to Shay, who was now only inches away from the teeth of the plant.

"Don't move!" Ethan yelled as he raised the axe high over his head.

The axe came whistling down and sliced cleanly through the vine. Black sap splattered out like blood and the plant made a horrible squealing sound that made Stella want to clap her hands over her ears. Shay grabbed the vine still twisted around his arm and flung it to the floor, while Koa ran around his legs excitedly. More vines quickly came shooting out toward them but the explorers leapt out of reach just in time, retreating to the safety of the far end of the room.

"Well, what are we going to do now?" Ethan asked, still clutching the axe. "It's blocking our only way out."

The plant rustled its leaves at them in a threatening way, and the black sap dripping from its chopped branch gave off an unpleasant, dank stink.

"Why don't you look in Captain Filibuster's guide?" Stella said. "Maybe there's some advice in there."

Shay pulled his battered copy of *Captain Filibuster's Guide to Expeditions and Exploration* from his pocket and thumbed to the index. "There's nothing in here about cabbage trees that want to eat you," he said. "I don't think Captain Filibuster ever went to the Valley of Carnivorous Plants."

"Why would *anyone* go to the Valley of Carnivorous Plants?" Beanie groaned, tugging at his pom-pom hat in agitation.

Stella snatched the book from Shay's hand and found the chapter on confronting enemies.

"'When confronting ferocious monsters in a hostile environment,'" she read, "'it is important to keep calm and in control at all times. The monster is probably more afraid of you than you are of it—'"

"I don't think that's true in this case," Ethan said.

"Oh, this is no use at all," Stella said, thrusting the book back at Shay. "We're just going to have to work it out for ourselves. Why doesn't one of us chop it up with the axe? Give it to me—I'll have a crack at it."

"Where's it gone now?" Beanie said.

The explorers looked back at the door and realized, to their horror, that the plant had moved again. The pot was still there, and a trail of soil led around one of the cabinets, but there was no sign of the plant at all.

"Never mind, let's just get out of here while we still have the chance!" Shay said.

They started toward the door but had gone only a few steps before vines shot toward them—and this time they came from above. Before they knew what was happening, Stella and Shay were both plucked from the ground and drawn up toward the hissing plant, which had attached itself to the ceiling.

"Oh, yuck—it's all hairy!" Stella exclaimed, clawing at the vine wrapped around her arm, while Koa howled beneath them.

"Throw me the axe!" Shay yelled down to Ethan, then hurriedly added, "But don't throw it at my head! Do *not* throw it at my head!"

"I'm not going to throw it at your head! I'm not an idiot!" Ethan yelled back.

He threw the axe up handle first but it sailed past Shay and went to Stella instead, who caught it and then swiped at the vine that was holding Shay, slicing it clean off and splattering herself with more of the black stuff. Shay fell to the ground and managed to land on his feet with a loud thump. Stella lost no time in slicing at the vine wrapped around her arm, and then she tumbled through the air, away from the squealing, hissing plant.

Unfortunately, she wasn't quite as agile as Shay and landed on her back rather than her feet. She supposed she ought to count herself lucky that she hadn't landed on the axe, which was still gripped in her hand—but even so, landing from that height really, seriously *hurt*! She groaned, gasping for breath, but before she had time to work out if she'd broken any bones, Shay was taking the axe from her grip and Ethan was dragging her to her feet.

"Come on, come on," the magician was saying, hurrying her up.

Beanie grabbed the baby volcano Shay had dropped and they all ran toward the door. Stella heard a thumping, rolling sound behind her and glanced back. Some of the cabbages had fallen from the plant and were rolling across the floor toward them, gnashing their teeth and leaving wet trails of drool and saliva in their wake.

"The cabbages are following us!" she yelled, which wasn't a sentence she'd ever thought she'd speak unless she was seriously ill and suffering from the most appalling hallucinations.

Shay reached the door first and kicked the plant pot away before dragging open the door and turning back around to brandish the axe at the cabbages. Beanie raced through the door first, closely followed by Koa and Stella. She heard a *thump, thump* behind her as Shay chopped at the hissing, rolling vegetables. But there were too many of them, and Stella heard the rip of boot leather and then Ethan yell as he tumbled out into the corridor. Shay was right behind him, slamming the door firmly closed, and they all heard the thuds of a dozen cabbages slamming into the wood only seconds later.

One of them had made it out, though—and it had its teeth firmly clamped on Ethan's ankle.

CHAPTER EIGHTEEN

I T WAS SO OBVIOUSLY going to be *me* who got bitten by the cabbage!" Ethan moaned. "I mean, it was just never going to be anyone else, was it?"

He bent down, intending to grab the slobbering vegetable and yank it out of his ankle, but Shay stopped him. "Wait," he said. "We should probably find something to put it in first. Otherwise it'll only start snapping at us all the moment it's free."

"He's right. We should leave it where it is for now," Stella said.

"That's easy for you to say!" Ethan exclaimed. "It's not *your* ankle it's got its fangs sunk into! We don't need anything to put it in because I'm going to stamp on it as soon as it's off."

"You can't!" Beanie said. "We should take it with us."

"Oh, good idea! Perhaps we can make a salad out of it," Ethan suggested sarcastically.

"Gross and horrible though it may be, it's still a scientific find," Shay said. He slapped the magician on the back. "Good job, Prawn. You captured it."

"I didn't capture it," Ethan replied. "It captured me."

"Well, we should still take it back to the club as a specimen," Shay said.

"I am *not* traveling all the way back to Coldgate with a cabbage embedded in my foot." Ethan crossed his arms over his chest. "I won't do it."

"Don't talk nonsense," Shay replied. "We'll stick it in the top hat box once we get back to the sled."

Ethan groaned. "You're giving me a headache again," he said. But he accepted that the cabbage—which seemed to have gotten its teeth stuck in the leather of the magician's boot, as well as his actual ankle—would stay where it was until they returned to the sled.

The four of them made their way back through the ship and up to the deck, where Ethan forced Beanie to hand over his wooden narwhal before he would agree to be tied to him again. Beanie fussed a little, but Ethan was adamant.

"I have already been bitten by a cabbage today—I refuse to be dragged off a ladder as well," he said. "I promise I'll look after it, but I'm not going to be tied to you again unless that narwhal is in my pocket instead of yours."

Beanie was finally persuaded to hand it over.

"Have you got any other prized possessions about your

person you want to declare?" Ethan inquired. "Any precious jewels or sacred icons you'd like me to take charge of?"

"No," Beanie said, "there's just Aubrey."

They slowly climbed down the ladder single file as before, except this time they made Ethan go first since no one wanted to have their head near his feet, in case the cabbage managed to get itself free from Ethan's boot and needed to find something else to clamp its teeth into.

As soon as they reached the bottom, the goose came flapping out of the tent toward them and honked at Stella until she picked her up. Stella stroked her head and felt the goose begin to settle.

"Here," Ethan said, handing the narwhal back to Beanie. "Do us all a favor and put it somewhere safe, for goodness' sake."

The wolves, too, were very pleased to see them, flocking around Shay and fidgeting, eager to be off once again. First, though, they had to deal with the cabbage. The top hat box was fetched from the sled and opened up in preparation. The cabbage had wedged itself in deep, and it took all four of the explorers to prize it off. It turned on them the moment it was free, snapping its awful teeth in an extremely menacing way, but they managed to wrestle it into the box without any further mishap and firmly fasten the buckles behind it. Unfortunately, though, it left a few rather large fangs embedded through Ethan's boot and into his ankle.

"I knew I might get bitten by a snow shark when I came to the Icelands, but I never thought I'd be savaged by a cabbage!" Ethan exclaimed. "I have all the bad luck."

"You have all the fun," Stella said, and sighed.

"If you really think so, then why don't you stick your hand in the box?" Ethan said, offering it to her pointedly. "Better still, poke your head in there and get a real thrill!"

Stella frowned. "It's not the same if you get bitten on purpose," she said. "That's just plain weird."

"So is wanting to be bitten by a cabbage in the first place!"

It wasn't that Stella wanted to be bitten by a cabbage, really; it was just that it would have made such an interesting story to tell once she got home—the kind of interesting story that explorers were supposed to return from expeditions with. But poking about on the ship hadn't been a total loss. She may not have been bitten by a cabbage, but at least she'd been attacked by a vine and dangled from a ceiling for a little while.

"Let's not argue anymore about who's going to be savaged by a cabbage in a hat box," Shay said, rolling his eyes. "It's ridiculous. The pair of you are ridiculous. We need to deal with *this* problem next." He pointed to the fangs still sticking out of Ethan's ankle.

"They'll have to come out," Beanie said. "The foot will get infected otherwise."

"I guess we're just going to have to pull them out one by one," Stella sighed.

Ethan sat down on the sled seat and stuck his leg over the side. There were three teeth left embedded, and Shay, Beanie, and Stella each gripped one while Ethan gritted his teeth and grabbed onto the side of the sled. They had to pull the teeth out slowly and carefully, so as to avoid any of them snapping off and getting stuck like gigantic splinters. The teeth were much longer than they had imagined—several inches long from root to tip, glistening and needle sharp—so Stella really couldn't blame Ethan for whimpering a bit as they were removed.

"These will make excellent specimens for the club too," Stella said, examining them with satisfaction.

"Goodness knows what kind of a mess it's made of my foot," Ethan groaned. He scrambled out of the sled and yanked off his boot, only for blood to immediately pour out of it. His sock was dark and wet and sticky with it too.

"Oh," Ethan said, dropping the boot in the snow. He'd instantly gone pale.

"Oh dear, you're not going to faint again, are you?" Stella said, rushing forward to support him.

"Of course not." Ethan batted her away. Then he swayed on his feet and said, "I don't know. Maybe. I don't . . . I really don't like the sight of blood."

Stella wasn't too keen on it herself. And the fact that it stained the snow pink made it worse somehow. Or perhaps it was simply that it brought back memories of her nightmare—the tiara, the blood on the snow, the burned feet....

"I don't mind blood," Beanie said. "I've seen much worse at the hospital. I'll take care of it for you, if you like."

"I'm going to sit down," Ethan said, before abruptly half sitting, half falling in the snow.

Beanie knelt beside him and peeled Ethan's sock from his foot. "Don't worry," he said. "It looks worse than it is."

He held his hand out, and healing magic shimmered from his fingers. They all went quiet and watched in fascination. Afterward, Beanie washed the blood off with snow and took the packet of bandages out of his bag. He was about to stick the first one on Ethan's ankle, but the magician waved it away. "I don't want a unicorn bandage!" he said indignantly. "Unicorns are for girls."

"What do you want, then?" Beanie replied. "I've got polar bears, penguins, yaks, and—"

"I want a penguin one."

After Beanie had patched up Ethan's ankle, Stella and Shay clapped, and even Ethan looked impressed. Beanie blushed and tried to wave their praise away, but Stella could tell he was pleased.

They decided to have lunch before continuing. They'd spent longer than they'd thought inside the ship and although they were eager to be on their way and discover whatever might lie ahead, they were also very hungry.

Unfortunately, they had to make do with some Spam and mint cake since Dora—as Stella had decided to name the goose—hadn't yet laid any more eggs for them. Stella was starting to regret not snatching up two of the geese when she had had the chance.

Beanie suggested naming the carnivorous cabbage Pepe and feeding it little scraps of Spam—a notion that was quietly ignored by the others, who thought it best to pretend he had never spoken at all, although Ethan did come fairly close to taking off his glove and slapping Beanie with it.

After a quick consultation of the map and Stella's compass, which she'd set to the Cold heading, they were ready to continue on toward the coldest part of the Icelands. Stella and Beanie piled into the sled, Shay hopped on the back, and Ethan rode Glacier the unicorn. Stella didn't think she'd ever get tired of the magical feeling of not knowing what might be in front of them. It was a bit disappointing, therefore, when they traveled all afternoon without making a single interesting find, or a single scientific discovery. She told herself she was being greedy—after all, they *had* discovered the cabbage just that morning.

After a few hours, they decided they ought to start looking for a place to spend the night. They still had only one tent, and all of the landscape they'd passed so far had been flat and white and filled with snow. They paused to consult the compass, set it in the direction of Shelter, and then changed course in the hope of finding somewhere to make camp.

Thankfully, Stella's compass didn't let them down, and just as it was getting dark, they emerged from a heavy snowfall to find a mountain looming up before them. Cut into the side of the rock were some caves that would at least provide shelter from the ice and wind. They chose the largest one—a gigantic circular space with impressive stalactites reaching down from the ceiling.

After hours spent traveling in the sled, it was a relief to stretch their legs, and everyone helped to get settled in for the night. Shay saw to the animals while Ethan got the baby volcano hot and molten in the center, and Beanie and Stella set out the dinner.

"What about Pepe?" Beanie asked. "Shouldn't we feed him, too?"

"Please don't call the cabbage Pepe," Stella groaned. "And anyway, it's not a 'he,' it's an 'it.'"

"You've named the goose," Beanie said. "How is this any different?"

"It just is, Beanie."

He didn't argue with her, but Stella noticed him slipping a couple of pieces of Spam into the hat box when he thought she wasn't looking.

Dora had laid only two speckled eggs since that morning so they would have to share, but they put out some Spam and mint cake to bulk out the meal. Stella decided they might as well do things properly, so she got out the china plates stamped with the Polar Bear Explorers' Club crest, set the gramophone going with a scratchy jazz record, and found the champagne. Ethan knew a spell to turn it into ginger ale (which, miraculously, really did turn it into actual ginger ale rather than swamp slime, or some such), and finally, they all stood around the fiery heat of the bubbling volcano and raised their glasses in a toast.

"What shall we drink to, gang?" Shay asked.

"The discovery of the cabbage?" Stella suggested. "If an angry cabbage with teeth isn't a curiosity worth taking back home, then I don't know what is."

"To the cabbage!" Ethan said, only half sarcastically, as he raised his glass.

The others did the same and they all took a sip of the ginger ale—which tasted a little too gingery and burned the back of their throats as it went down, but no one said anything so as not to hurt Ethan's feelings.

"We should toast Dora, too," Beanie said, indicating the goose, who had settled herself close to the warmth of the volcano and was fluffing her feathers contentedly. "She's a good discovery. And she provided the dinner tonight."

"To Dora, the goose," Stella said, raising her glass.

They drank to the goose and were about to sit down to eat, when Ethan said, "Hang on. I've thought of one more."

"We haven't discovered anything else, have we?" Stella asked.

"Just one other thing," Ethan said. He raised his glass, hesitated for a moment, then said, "Beanie, you mentioned earlier that you only have one friend in the world. Well, I just wanted to tell you that's not true."

"Yes, it is," Beanie replied. He glanced at Stella and said, "You're still my friend, aren't you? I haven't done anything to spoil it, have I?"

"Beanie, you could never do anything to spoil it," Stella said. "We'll always be friends."

"No, no, that's not what I meant!" Ethan said. "I meant that you don't just have one friend anymore." He tapped himself on the chest. "You've got two."

"Make that three," Shay added.

Beanie flushed right down to the roots of his hair. "*Three?*" he finally said. "Does that mean . . . will you come to my birthday party?"

"Naturally," Ethan replied. "Magicians always go to their friends' birthday parties."

"Wouldn't miss it," Shay agreed.

"So that's the last discovery I think we should toast," Ethan said. He raised his glass. "To friendship."

The other explorers raised their glasses, grinning. "To friendship," they echoed.

They sat down around the volcano and ate until they were full. The top hat from the box served as a useful holder for the bottle of ginger beer, especially after they filled it up with snow.

"Can you pull a rabbit out of a hat?" Stella asked Ethan, nudging the hat with her boot.

"Pulled a mongoose out of a hat once," he replied.

Beanie frowned. "What's a mongoose?"

"Not something you want to be pulling out of a hat," Ethan said. "Dratted thing almost took my eye out. After I gave it life and magicked it into existence from nothing. That's gratitude for you."

"I used to know a mongoose whisperer," Shay said. "He was a bit odd. Twitchy."

"I don't think I'd care to be a mongoose whisperer," Stella said. "It must be much nicer being a wolf whisperer."

"Speaking of which," Shay said, standing up, "I think I'll go and spend some time with them. They're probably feeling a bit neglected."

He wandered off to go and chat to the wolves. Beanie pulled his father's travel journal out of his bag and settled down to reread it for the hundredth time. Dora made herself comfortable in Stella's lap, draping her long neck around Stella's arm.

"She's taken quite a fancy to you, hasn't she?" Ethan said.

He reached over to stroke the goose's feathers but she immediately pecked his hand and hissed at him.

"Why am I always getting bitten by things?" the magician complained, snatching his hand back. Without looking up, Beanie threw over another bandage (a polar bear one) and Ethan stuck it onto his hand with bad grace. "First a frosty, then a cabbage, and now a goose. I suppose I'll be savaged by a penguin next. It's practically inevitable."

"Oh dear, the penguins!" Stella exclaimed. In all the excitement of the expedition, and running away from various things, she had forgotten about her Polar Pets. Although Felix had said they didn't need feeding, she still felt guilty for not at least checking on them, and she quickly rummaged around in her bag.

"You haven't really got penguins in there, have you?" Ethan asked, raising an eyebrow.

"They were a birthday present from Felix," Stella said.

Her hand finally closed around the cold little igloo; she drew it out and peered through the door. The penguin family were tucked up in tiny beds, wearing nightcaps with little tassels on the end. It looked rather cozy in there, actually. There was even a tiny igloo nightlight on a bedside table next to one of them, emitting a soft, golden glow.

"Can I see it?" Ethan asked.

Stella handed it over to him, and the magician examined it carefully. "Fascinating," he said. "Julian loved penguins."

"Was he older than you?" Stella asked.

Ethan nodded. "Four years older. He was sixteen when we went on that expedition last year. He'd been on several with Dad before but it was my first one."

"What happened?" Stella asked quietly.

She wasn't sure whether she should have asked or not, but Ethan just shrugged and said, "Dad wanted to hunt a screeching red devil squid. It's one of the most dangerous monsters in the Poison Tentacle Sea so he thought it would make a fantastic trophy to bring back to the Ocean Squid Explorers' Club. Julian tried to talk him out of it. He said it was too dangerous, that it was too big a monster for us to chase after on my first expedition. He said I wasn't experienced enough." He sighed and handed Stella back the igloo. "I wanted to prove him wrong. So when the squid attacked the ship I didn't go belowdecks like he told me to.

I picked up the harpoon gun and ran to the starboard netting and tried to shoot it myself. The tentacle came up out of nowhere—a huge, monstrous thing. It curled around me and dragged me right off the ship."

Stella shivered at the thought of suddenly being in the cold ocean with a huge squid. Beanie also flinched, momentarily distracted from his father's travel journal.

"Julian jumped in after me," Ethan went on, shaking his head. "He just jumped straight in with no hesitation at all. He must have known he'd probably die trying to save me, but he did it anyway."

Stella thought of Felix and knew that she would definitely risk her life if he was in danger and needed saving, even though she knew he'd be very angry with her if she were to put herself in harm's way. She glanced toward the mouth of the cave, the frozen landscape stretching beyond it, and hoped that Felix was okay out there.

"That's what family does," she said.

Ethan glanced at her and said, "It's not what all family does. Julian jumped in, but Dad didn't. When Julian sliced off the squid's tentacle, it floated up to the surface and Dad dragged it onto the deck. It was still wrapped around me so I came up with it, but part of me always wonders whether it was the tentacle he was after or me."

Stella was shocked to hear him speak in such a way about his own father. "I'm sure it was you," she said. "No one could care more about a trophy than their own son!"

"Well, then he should have been trying to help Julian," Ethan said. "I know he's upset that he died—that's why we came on a polar expedition rather than going back to sea—but he never talks about him. And he didn't come into the water after us. He didn't try to help. Maybe things would have been different if he had. But instead, the squid got away. It went down to the bottom of the ocean, and it took Julian with it. Mum says she'll never forgive Dad for what happened. They argue all the time whenever Dad's home now. It's horrible. She didn't even want me to come on this expedition, but luckily Dad insisted. She'll be even more angry with him now, I expect."

Stella thought of Felix again and it struck her how lucky she was that he was the one who found her in the snow that day. She could have been discovered by anyone, or no one at all, but she'd been found by the kindest man she knew. Someone who loved her and had taught her what it meant to be part of a family, even if they were only a family of two.

"Felix says it's always better to give people the benefit of the doubt," Stella said. "Maybe your father doesn't talk about Julian because he finds it too painful."

"Who knows?" Ethan replied. Then he looked at her and said, "Felix isn't your real father, is he?"

"He *is* my real father," Stella said. "But not my biological one, if that's what you mean. I never met my mum or dad. Felix found me one day on an expedition. I'm a snow orphan. I don't know where I came from. Maybe my parents didn't want me." Stella thought of Felix, and Gruff, and Magic, and Buster, and all the other pygmy dinosaurs at home in the orangery, and said, "But it doesn't matter, because I found a family anyway."

Ethan nodded and said, "I think that anyone who won't let you down, who'll be there for you no matter what, counts as family."

"I think you're right."

Stella gazed around at their little expedition, and the thought occurred to her that the four of them had become rather like a family since they had set out together. She looked at Ethan, who was staring thoughtfully into the flames of the volcano, and wondered whether he was thinking the same thing. She was about to ask him, when the magician glanced over at Beanie and said, "What are you reading there?"

Beanie looked up. "This? It's my dad's journal. They found it at his abandoned camp on the Black Ice Bridge."

Ethan shuddered and said, "I'd rather return to the Poison Tentacle Sea and swim with the squid again than venture onto that bridge. Don't they say that it's cursed?"

Beanie nodded. "Dad wrote in his journal that the men said they could sense an evil presence that got stronger and stronger the further they crossed. You can't see the water because of the fog, but Dad wrote that they could hear strange splashing noises from below, like there were terrible monsters down there, trying to leap up at them."

"The sea is full of terrible monsters," Ethan agreed.

Shay wandered back to join them and flopped down by the fire next to Ethan. Two of the wolves came too and curled up beside him with their heads in his lap.

"There's an awful lot of ghost stories and rumors concerning the Black Ice Bridge," Shay said. "Talk like that doesn't come out of nowhere. It's not a good place. Dad says there are some lands so forgotten and forsaken and forbidden that even explorers shouldn't venture there."

"I'm going some day," Beanie said. "I'm going to be the first explorer to reach the other side of the Black Ice Bridge."

Stella already knew that Beanie hoped to do this, of course, but his ambition was news to the others, and for a moment there was a stunned silence.

Finally, Ethan said, "I'm honestly not trying to be mean, but that's like a mouse saying it's going to eat a walrus. No one comes back alive from the Black Ice Bridge. No one."

"I will," Beanie said. "I'm going to complete my father's unfinished expedition."

"It can't be done, Beanie," Shay said gently. "And if you were to perish on the Black Ice Bridge yourself, then that's no way to honor your father, is it?"

"I don't care what anyone says or who tries to stop me," Beanie said, perfectly calmly. "I am going to find out what's on the other side of that bridge."

Shay glanced at Stella, who shrugged. If she was perfectly honest, she wasn't sure whether Beanie should, or could, try to cross the bridge either, but she wasn't about to risk knocking his confidence by telling him that.

Before anyone could say anything else about it, a low wailing sound started up beyond the cave, making them all jump.

"What's that?" Beanie asked.

The four junior explorers turned and squinted into the darkness. Stella thought it was the most mournful sound she had ever heard. Although it didn't seem quite human, it reminded her somehow of crying children. All the hairs on her arms stood up, and she felt a cold, prickly feeling at the back of her neck.

"Cold spirits," Shay said.

"How do you know that?" Ethan demanded.

"The wolves told me. They've been sensing them for a while now. It's all right; the wolves say they can't hurt us." Stella wasn't sure whether he was speaking to them or to the wolves at his side, who had started to cower. "It just means we're getting closer to the coldest part of the Icelands. The wolves say that's where they come from."

"But what are they?" Beanie asked, frowning.

"Who knows?" Shay said. "The wolves seem to think

they're the lost souls of all the men and women who've died out in the cold."

The explorers looked back at the mouth of the cave once more. Koa had appeared there and stood staring out, completely motionless from the end of her snout to the tip of her tail. It was impossible to see anything beyond the cave except for the snow and ice. But suddenly, what had seemed like unintelligible moaning began to sound to Stella like whispered voices.

Pity the cold ones, Your Highness, they said. *Pity the cold ones.*

"Who are they talking to?" Stella asked Shay.

He gave her a strange look. "I don't hear any talking."

"Me neither," Beanie said.

"Ethan?" Stella asked. Surely if anyone else was hearing magical voices, it was the magician. But he shook his head and said, "It's just noise, Stella."

"The wolves say the spirits won't come into the cave as long as we keep the fire burning," Shay told them. He glanced over at the other wolves, who'd all become agitated since the voices started up.

The moaning voices disappeared after only a few minutes, but they kept the fire going all night, just in case they came back.

CHAPTER NINETEEN

THE EXPLORERS SPENT A restless night in the cave and were glad to be on their way bright and early the next morning. Stella had taken some time to examine the map and consult the compass, and had calculated that they were no more than two days away from the coldest part of the Icelands.

"We're going to do it, aren't we?" Shay said excitedly. "We're actually going to get there."

"I hope we're the first," Ethan said. "It would be such a worthy achievement to go back with." He glanced at Beanie beside him and said, "Might even shut your uncle up for a bit, don't you think?"

"I doubt it," Beanie replied. "Mum says Uncle Benedict could talk the hind legs off a polar bear—which isn't possible, of course, but I think it just means that he really likes to talk."

"No, I meant that it might make him think you can be an explorer."

"Oh." Beanie frowned. "Yes, it might. Why didn't you say that to begin with?"

"Come on," Stella cut in, because she could tell that Ethan was rapidly losing patience. "There's no time to lose if we want to be the first ones there."

They spent all that day sledding across the ice, making no discoveries other than a rather worrying number of yeti footprints stamped into the snow. They stopped at a couple to photograph them and take some measurements, and found that even Ethan—who was the tallest member of their group—could lie down in the middle of the yeti footprint with room to spare.

"Do we have any kind of battle plan in case we stumble upon a yeti?" Ethan inquired, lying in the footprint while Beanie took the photograph. "I mean, we don't have any weapons other than that axe we got at the *Snow Queen*, so—"

"I don't think one axe will be much good against a yeti," Stella said. "Felix says the best thing is to remain completely still and hope it doesn't see you. Yeti eyesight is supposed to be really bad, isn't it?"

"Yes, but they have a very good sense of smell," Ethan pointed out as he stood up and dusted snow from his black cloak. "And none of us have washed since leaving the *Bold Adventurer*."

Stella had to admit that he had a point. They probably were smelling a bit ripe by now. The lack of washing and toilet facilities was definitely Stella's least favorite part of the expedition so far.

They found another cave to spend the night in, and although there were no cold spirits this time, Stella was once again troubled by that horrible dream—with the burned feet wandering around, looking for her, and then the blood-splattered snow.

Shay woke her up when she was only partway through the dream, and she could tell from his face that something strange had happened again. When she asked, he said, "It was snowing all around you, right here inside the cave. Look." He pointed and Stella saw that flakes of snow still clung to her clothes. "Aren't you cold?" Shay asked.

Stella shook her head. She wasn't cold at all. She decided she would tell Shay about her dream, as she felt obliged to give some kind of explanation now that he'd had to wake her up from it three times—but he couldn't make any sense out of it either.

"One thing's for sure," he said. "It's no normal dream. It means something."

He didn't add: *Something bad*, but Stella felt as if those words were hovering right on the tip of his tongue.

• • •

The next day they set off again, only hours away from the coldest part of the Icelands, according to the map. Stella found herself wondering once more whether any of the other members of the Polar Bear or Ocean Squid expeditions had already beaten them there, or whether the four of them would be the first.

"How will we know when we get to the coldest part of the Icelands?" Beanie asked.

"The compass arrow should just go around in circles instead of pointing anywhere," Stella said. "If I had Felix's sextant I could take a reading as well, but that's with him. I think we'll just know, though, once we arrive. For one thing it'll be really, really cold."

It was a bright, sunny day, but as they traveled through the morning and into the afternoon, the air around them became colder and colder. Frost formed in the furry linings of their hoods, and ice glinted all around the surface of the sled. Even Shay's wolf-fang earring froze solid. It felt more and more like they were breathing knives, and the four explorers couldn't help thinking with longing about the warm beds and hot chocolate waiting for them at home.

And then, all of a sudden, the sled rose up over the crest of a hill—and they came face to face with a white, glittering, magnificent castle. Countless spires and turrets rose up high into the sky, the frozen windows reflected back the sunlight, and the frost icing the turret roofs sparkled at them like hundreds of tiny diamonds.

For a moment, they all just stared at it. Then Shay said, "Do you think it belongs to a snow queen?"

"It looks like the kind of castle a snow queen would have," Beanie replied.

"We should stay away from it," Ethan said quickly. "Snow queens have frozen hearts. It could be dangerous."

"But the compass is pointing straight toward it," Stella said. "Perhaps the castle marks the coldest part of the Icelands? We should get a bit closer. We need to put our flag in the snow outside at least."

"Won't the snow queen think that's rude?" Beanie asked.

"There might not even *be* a snow queen," Stella said. She glanced around at the others. "We're explorers, aren't we? We've come all this way. We can't leave without at least taking a look."

To Stella's relief, Shay agreed with her that they ought to get closer, and so they continued on across the snow. She suddenly had the strongest feeling that she was *supposed* to go to that castle. Something about those thin white spires, pointing up into the air like fingers, was strangely familiar to her, as if she had seen the place before, a very long time ago. Felix had found her in the Icelands, after all. Perhaps she had been here before.

They couldn't see any other explorer flags in the snow around the castle as they approached.

"We're the first!" Stella said as the sled pulled up to the huge front doors. "This is it, look!" She showed the others her compass. She'd set it to Cold but the arrow wasn't pointing anywhere—it was just spinning around and around. "We're the first explorers to reach the coldest part of the Icelands!"

There is no greater thrill for an explorer than to be the first to do something incredible, and they were all extremely excited as they piled out of the sled and staked their flag in the snow. It had frozen solid so it didn't flutter and flap so much as swing stiffly back and forth, but it was still a flag and it was still a first, so everyone felt pretty happy about it.

"They'll have to let you stay in the Polar Bear Explorers' Club now, won't they?" Beanie said to Stella. "Now that you're one of the first explorers to reach the coldest part of the Icelands!"

Stella hadn't thought of it like that, but she sincerely hoped Beanie was right. She hugged her cloak tighter around her, almost bubbling over with happiness at the thought of being able to stay in the explorers' club on a permanent basis. There were so many other places she wanted to visit. Why, she could spend her whole entire life exploring and it still wouldn't be enough time to see the world.

"We should take a photo," Shay said. "So that there's some kind of record to take back to our clubs."

The tripod was duly unloaded from the back of the sled and they set it up on a timer. The four of them gathered in front of the sled and were all trying to hold as still as possible, when suddenly, sparkly silvery things started to drift down from the sky. At first, Stella thought it had started to snow again, but then she saw that these flakes were not made from snow at all. They were cold to the touch, but smooth and solid. And they gave out a soft, silver light of their own that twinkled all around them. Stella thought it was the prettiest, most lovely thing she had ever seen.

"What kind of weird snow is this?" Ethan complained. "It's messing up our photo."

"This isn't snow," Shay said. "It looks more like—"

"Stars," Stella said. She put out her hand and one of the flakes landed in the middle of her gloved palm, where it sparkled and shone. "Perhaps these are starflakes? Maybe you only find them at the coldest part of the Icelands. They're falling right here and nowhere else."

The others glanced around and saw she was right. The starflakes only drifted down around the castle, making a faint ringing noise when they knocked into each other, rather like wind chimes.

"That must be why the fairies gave you your second name," Beanie said to Stella. "Because you come from the same place as the starflakes."

In another moment, the starflakes had stopped falling,

and lay twinkling in a shining silver carpet. Once the photo had been taken, Beanie produced some bottles of beard oil, which they emptied to fill up with starflakes to take back with them. The silvery flakes didn't melt or break underfoot but clinked together like tiny diamonds.

After storing the starflakes away on the sled, the junior explorers finally turned their attention to the double doors of the castle looming above them. They were made of white marble, shot through with sparkling veins of silver and gold, and they had intricate pictures carved into them: Icicles and crowns and snowflakes ran all the way around the edge, and in the center stood a tall, beautiful woman in a fur-lined dress, with a glittering crown upon her head.

"This is definitely a snow queen's castle," Ethan said nervously. "We should leave. It's not safe here."

Stella walked over to the nearest window, her boots crunching on the twinkling starflakes beneath her feet. She lifted her hand and squinted through dirty glass at a deserted room. It looked like it had once been some kind of dining room, with a hugely long table taking up most of the space, and ornate candelabras placed along its length all covered in cobwebs. The tapestries hanging on the walls were frozen stiff, and there was a puddle of what looked like spilled wine on the flagstones by the fireplace, frozen solid.

"The castle is deserted," Stella said, looking back at the others. "There's no one here."

Shay walked over to the doors and tried the handle, but it wouldn't budge.

"Locked," he said.

"Perhaps there's another way in around the back," Stella said.

"I really think we should leave," Ethan said. "I have a bad feeling about this place."

Stella reached her hand out toward the door, wanting to see for herself that it really was locked. But before her fingers could make contact with the marble, there was a soft *click*, the handle moved down a fraction, and the door swung open just slightly, exposing a sliver of darkness that led into the hallway beyond.

Stella looked back at the others, almost beside herself with excitement. She therefore couldn't help feeling a bit annoyed with Ethan when he decided to put a damper on things by grabbing her sleeve and saying, "Stella, please, let's turn back. I can sense magic in there and it's . . . I don't know . . . it's dark, somehow—it feels bitter."

"The frosties and the carnivorous cabbage tree were pretty dark and bitter too, but we still faced them," Stella said.

"Yes, and *I* was the one who got bitten both times—" Ethan began, gesturing pointedly at the bandage on his hand.

"Oh, I'm sure nothing's going to bite you in here," Stella

interrupted impatiently. "Besides, that bandage is from Dora pecking you. What's gotten into everyone? What kind of an explorer just walks away from an abandoned castle without at least having a look inside first? I'm going in. You can all stay outside if you want to."

And with that, she reached her gloved hands forward and pushed both doors open wide. The sunlight behind them spilled into the front entrance, illuminating the dusty flagstones nearest their feet and allowing them to pick out the massive chandelier suspended above them and the vast curved staircase leading up to the next floor. Much of the room was still in shadows, however, so Stella took a step inside to take a closer look at everything.

The moment her snow boot crossed the threshold, something happened. The half-burned candles in the chandelier above her burst into life, as did the sconces on the walls, casting out a golden, flickering light that illuminated the entrance hall. Stella saw that there were tapestries frozen onto the walls here, too, and a couple of stone trolls guarded the staircase.

But most astonishingly of all, the air around Stella began to sparkle and glitter. The hood of her cloak fell back, as if pushed by an invisible hand—and then a tiara formed on her hair right before their eyes, curling tendrils of white gold twisting around ice gems and pale crystals and cold chips of cut diamond.

Stella reached up to snatch the tiara from her head and stared at it in astonishment.

"This . . . I . . . I remember this. I've seen it before, in my dreams," she said.

The others stared back at her, all equally gobsmacked, and then a whispery female voice spoke, seeming to come from all around them: "Welcome home, Princess. We've been waiting for you for a very long time."

CHAPTER TWENTY

WHO SAID THAT?" STELLA asked, looking all around.

"To your right," the voice said.

Stella turned and found herself staring straight into her own reflection in a huge, ornate mirror. The tiara, she noticed, was no longer in her hand but somehow back on her head again. She snatched it off hurriedly. The white gold felt cold, even through her glove. "I can't see you," she said.

The voice came again: "Look closer."

She looked back into the mirror, and this time, she saw a pale face gazing back at her. It was a woman's face, as beautiful and perfect as a porcelain doll's. Her skin was white and smooth, her eyes were blue, and tendrils of silvery hair waved gently around her head as if she were underwater.

"What . . . what are you?" Stella asked, taking a step closer.

"A magic mirror, of course," the mirror replied. "We

are hung all over the castle. We watched as you took your first steps, Princess."

"There's been a mistake," Stella said. "I'm not a princess—"

"These castle doors would only open for a snow queen or an ice princess," the mirror said. "And the tiara would appear only for you, Morwenna."

"My name isn't Morwenna," Stella said, wrinkling her nose. "Thank goodness. It's Stella. Stella Starflake Pearl."

"That may be your name now, but it's not the one your parents gave you when you were crowned," the mirror said. It blinked its large eyes and said in a sad voice, "Do you really remember nothing of your life here at all?"

Stella frowned, not knowing what to say. The castle *did* feel familiar somehow.

"You must explore," the mirror said. "Perhaps it will come back to you."

Stella glanced behind her at the others. Ethan frowned and shook his head, just slightly. But the magician always suspected the worst of everything and there didn't appear to be anything dangerous about the castle. Stella had always wanted to know where she'd come from, and this could be her one chance to get some of the answers she'd been waiting for her whole life.

"I'm going to explore," she said. "But you can wait outside if you want."

Ethan scowled and shook his head. "I'm not waiting outside," he said.

"I'm sure there are no carnivorous cabbages here," Stella said. She glanced at the mirror and said, "Are there?"

"Certainly not, Your Highness," the mirror said, sounding shocked.

"Well, then," Stella said. "That settles it."

She walked further into the castle, and as she did so, the most extraordinary thing happened: The abandoned, run-down place began to come to life all around her. The candles in the chandeliers blazed even brighter as the ice fell from the tapestries in sheets, the dust melted away from the floor, the dirt smearing the windows vanished, letting in the sunlight, and everything became bright and white and sparkling.

"You're waking up the castle," the mirror said happily. "It recognizes you. It wants to welcome you home!"

As the mirror spoke, one of the stone trolls by the stair-case moved, startling the explorers. It was an extremely ugly creature—short and round, with a helmet that almost covered its eyes and a bushy beard that hid its mouth. Its companion—which also began to move and stretch—didn't have a beard, and its too-small helmet perched precariously on top of its bat-like ears. One eye was higher in its face than the other, but the troll grinned delightedly at the sight of Stella and gave her a low, scraping bow. "We'll show you around, Princess," it said eagerly. "We'll show you around."

The stone trolls led the way up the staircase and the explorers followed. A rug ran down the steps, and Stella had taken it for gray before, but as she walked up it, all the dirt and grime fell away to reveal a royal red rug, edged in golden braid.

The castle had dozens and dozens of rooms, and every time they walked into one, the room lost its dust before their eyes and became clean and bright once again. A few more stone trolls came to life, and soon they had quite a group of them fussing around.

All the rooms were lavishly decorated with plush rugs, chandeliers, and exquisite tapestries in golden thread, depicting snowy mountain scenes, and yetis, and mammoths, and grand castles. There was one room filled entirely with musical instruments, some of which Stella had never even heard of before, including a singing harp that started to serenade them the moment they walked in. It was quite annoying, actually, but Stella felt obliged to applaud afterward, out of politeness. Aunt Agatha insisted on singing for them at home sometimes, and Felix had taught Stella that she must always enthusiastically applaud a singer once they've performed, even if their voice was absolutely dreadful. She felt a pang of homesickness at the thought of Felix, and wished he could be here to explore the enchanted castle with her.

They went on to another room filled with jeweled eggs, dazzling in their coats of white diamonds and blue sapphires and green emeralds. Stella picked one up, opened it at its hinges, and found a little jeweled yeti nestled inside.

"These were your mother's," the mirror on the wall said. Most of the castle's rooms seemed to have a mirror, and they were all magical talking ones with the same beautiful face appearing in each. "She loved to collect pretty things. You'll find an exquisite collection of music boxes in the next room."

They went through and did indeed find an extensive music box collection. Some were small and some were large, but they were all incredibly beautiful, with painted lids, and golden clasps, and tiny clawed feet. Stella picked up one with a painting of two birds on the lid, with diamonds for eyes, and when she opened it two mechanical birds flew right out of the box, fluttering their blue wings and filling the room with the sweet sound of birdsong.

"Did all this really belong to my mother?" Stella asked, watching the pair of mechanical birds fly around the ceiling.

"Oh, yes," one of the trolls said. "She was a fair and beautiful queen."

"But what happened to her?" Stella asked. "What happened to my father? Why is the castle shut up and abandoned like this?"

The trolls suddenly went quiet, shuffling their feet and scratching at their beards and looking anywhere other than at Stella.

"A witch killed your parents," the mirror said at last.

Stella thought of the burned feet from her dream and shivered. "But why?" she asked.

"She was a witch," the mirror replied. "Witches are evil. She would have killed you too if faithful servants hadn't smuggled you from the castle." The mirror turned its lovely face to the trolls then and said, "Why don't you take the princess to her old nursery?"

Stella followed the trolls up to a circular room at the top of one of the turrets. Like the others, the room came to life before her, and she stared around in amazement. The walls were painted with delicate white snowflakes and there were dozens of the prettiest toys, including a unicorn rocking horse, a plush white yeti, and a magnificent dollhouse that was a perfect replica of the castle itself. When Stella opened the doors to expose the inside, she saw that all the rooms were decorated just as they were in the real castle, right down to the room filled with jeweled eggs and the other with music boxes. When she ran her finger over the tiny harp in the music room, it even started to sing, just like the one in the actual music room had.

Stella felt a sudden sense of loss for her parents then, and mourned the fact that she had never gotten the chance to know them. They must have loved her very much to have gone to all this trouble with the nursery and to fill it with such beautiful toys.

"There's a painting of your parents in the red dining room if you'd like to see it," the mirror said.

"Yes, please."

One of the trolls slipped its stone hand into Stella's and led the way back downstairs into the dining room that they had glimpsed from outside. As the candles lit themselves and the dust fell away, Stella saw that there was a gigantic painting hung over the fireplace. She walked slowly up to it, hardly able to believe that this was her real mother and father. They were both so grand looking, so regal, so royal.

They had the same pale skin, white hair, and light blue eyes as Stella and were dressed in fur-lined robes and wore sparkling crowns. Stella thought that her mother was incredibly beautiful, even though she wasn't smiling in the painting. Her dress was the same light blue as her eyes, lined in white fur, and her long, pale-fingered hands rested loosely in her lap as she gazed out of the painting, almost as if she could see Stella standing there.

Stella turned her attention to her father next and thought that he couldn't have been any more different from Felix. He had a tall, proud, noble look, a square jaw, and a smart dress robe that he wore with easy grace, looking every inch the king.

"Since they've been gone the whole castle has been trapped in sleep," the mirror said beside her.

Stella glanced into the mirror and saw that the tiara was on her head again. No matter how many times she took it off, it somehow always seemed to appear on her hair.

"What's going on with this tiara?" she asked. "I keep trying to take it off but it—"

"It probably wants you to do some magic," the mirror replied. "It's been waiting for you for such a long time."

Stella stared at the mirror. "I can do magic?"

"Of course," the mirror replied. "You're an ice princess."

Stella suddenly felt excited. She had always wanted to be able to do something magical or to have some kind of special ability. After all, Shay had his wolf whispering, Beanie had his elfin healing, and Ethan had his magician's powers. It would be the best thing in the world if Stella could have something special like that too. "What kind of magic?" she asked eagerly.

"Ice magic," the mirror replied. "Naturally. All ice princesses can perform ice magic if they're wearing their magic tiara. You can make anything you like out of ice, or freeze anything into ice. You just have to imagine it happening in your mind."

Stella quickly thought of something and was about to try it out when Ethan caught her arm and said, "Careful. You don't understand this magic. It could be dangerous."

Stella shook him off impatiently—she was really getting pretty irritated by his constant doubts. She turned away from him and concentrated very hard before pointing her finger at the dining room table. To her delight, a burst of ice shot from her fingertip, and right before her eyes there appeared a glorious ice sculpture of a unicorn rearing up on its hind legs, its pearly hooves glinting in the sunlight streaming in through the windows. Stella felt a sudden chill race up her arms, but she rubbed at them quickly and

pointed her finger at another spot on the table. Within seconds, an ice castle appeared there, complete with sparkling spires and turrets. This time a chill ran down her back, as if someone had just dropped an ice cube down her cloak.

Stella ignored the strange sensation and turned her attention to one of the candelabras. She pointed at it, and ice shot from her finger once again and froze the object solid. Stella looked at the others and said, "It's too bad I didn't have this tiara when we faced that carnivorous cabbage tree."

"I'm not sure about this, Sparky," Shay replied, frowning.

Stella scowled at him and said, "I suppose you're jealous!" She felt a sudden strong flare of dislike for Shay that took her by surprise. She almost felt like she wanted to shove him. . . . But then the feeling melted away and she was left puzzled as to where it had come from.

Shay ignored her remark, pointed at the fireplace, and said to the mirror, "What are those?"

Stella followed the direction he was pointing in and saw that there was an object among the cold ashes of the fireplace. They looked like shoes, only these were no ordinary shoes. They were made from bands of iron and had heavy-looking padlocks on them, as if the wearer's feet would be locked inside.

"Those are iron slippers, of course," the magic mirror replied.

"What are they for?" Shay asked.

The expression on the face in the mirror never seemed to change, but she sounded confused as she said, "Don't you know?"

"I guess I wouldn't have asked if I already knew," Shay replied.

"Well, the iron slippers are heated in the fire until

they're red hot," the mirror explained. "And then they're put onto the feet of any person who refuses to dance."

It took Stella a moment to work out what the mirror meant, but then she gasped and her hand flew to her mouth. "But that . . . that would burn them horribly. It would be agony!" She thought of her dream and said, "The witch wore the iron slippers, didn't she? That's why her feet were burned."

"Your parents wanted the witch to dance at their wedding," the mirror replied. "She refused."

Stella tore the tiara from her head with shaking hands. "That . . . that's the cruelest thing I ever heard," she said, blinking back tears. She looked back at the painting of her parents, and although their features hadn't changed, they didn't look quite so beautiful to her anymore. In fact, they really didn't look beautiful at all.

Suddenly she wished that Felix were there beside her. She wished she were far away from this castle and back in the orangery, eating ice cream for breakfast and throwing twigs for Buster.

"It only seems cruel to you because your heart hasn't frozen yet," the mirror said. "Too much time spent away from your own kind. After the wedding feast, the witch crawled away into the snow and we all thought she had died. When she attacked the castle three years later she took everyone by surprise. The servants who took you away knew that you needed to be sent far from the Icelands or the witch would find you, too, so they left you in the path of that oncoming explorer. He kept you safe, as we hoped he would, but no doubt he filled your head up with lots of silly ideas that you will have to unlearn, as it seems your heart didn't freeze the way it was supposed to. But every time you use the magic in the tiara your heart will freeze a little more, until the change is irreversible, and then all will be as it should be."

The tiara was on her head again so Stella dragged it off and flung it into the fireplace. "Then I'll never use its magic again!"

"You are an ice princess," the mirror said in a stern voice.

Stella clenched her hands into fists. "I don't want to be a princess—I want to be an explorer!"

"No one can change what they were born to be," the mirror replied.

"Of course they can," Stella said crossly. "No one is *born* to be anything! You decide for yourself."

"That is not the way it works here," the mirror said patiently, as if talking to someone who was very stupid.

"Well, we're leaving now anyway," Stella said. "Thank you for showing us around and explaining what happened to my parents, but now we really have to go."

"Go?" the mirror replied. "But you can't go. It is forbidden. You will stay here, Princess, and you will rule your kingdom as you were meant to do all along. This castle has had enough of being asleep."

And then the room went dark as the shutters over the windows slammed closed, the doors shut with a bang, and the stone trolls gathered all around them, cutting off their only route of escape.

CHAPTER TWENTY-ONE

THREE DAYS LATER, STELLA was pacing the nursery at the top of the tower, fuming.

She hadn't seen the others since the trolls had dragged them off to the dungeons beneath the castle. Shay had made a decent attempt to bring the trolls down with his boomerang, and Ethan had brought out the magic arrows again, but none of that seemed to have any effect on stone. Koa had howled piteously as the explorers were taken away. And now three whole days had passed and Stella was starting to get seriously worried. If they didn't leave today, then they wouldn't be able to get back in time to be picked up by the *Bold Adventurer*. Stella knew Felix would never give up on her and that he'd come back to the Icelands with a rescue party, but that could take weeks, probably months.

The trolls brought meals on trays to the nursery for Stella, but the magic mirror was refusing to allow her out unless she agreed to use her magic and stay at the castle forever. Koa appeared in the nursery from time to time and Stella felt comforted by her presence, but there wasn't much the shadow wolf could do to help her escape.

Stella felt particularly annoyed that she was missing out on the dungeon. She'd never been in a dungeon before and was certain there must be all kinds of interesting things down there. Ethan had probably been bitten by several different creatures already. There were probably bats and skeletons, and trapdoors and fire pits, and secret passages and big iron spikes, and all kinds of fascinating stuff.

After searching through her bag and deciding there was nothing dangerous in there, the trolls had let her keep it. Stella had gone through it again herself to see if there might be anything useful, but she had to admit that the chances of her bringing down a stone troll with a mustache spoon seemed slim.

She'd poked into every corner of the nursery too, but had found nothing that might help her escape. She'd gotten quite excited when she discovered a secret compartment, right at the back of the wardrobe, but the only thing it contained was a witch puppet. It was a beautifully made thing, carved entirely from pale gold wood, with real clothes and frizzy gray hair puffing out from beneath the pointed witch's hat glued to its head. Stella was horrified to notice that the witch puppet had burned feet, and she realized that

258

it must be a replica of the witch who had killed her parents, and who had tried to kill her, too. But why was there a puppet of her in the nursery? It didn't make any sense.

Stella found herself constantly coming back to the puppet, staring at it and frowning hard. She had the weirdest feeling about it. Almost as if there was something she was supposed to remember about the witch, something important. For some reason that she couldn't quite explain, she didn't put the puppet back in the secret drawer, but tucked it into her bag instead.

Having failed to find anything that might help her escape, Stella thought about freezing the trolls who brought her meals and then making a run for it down to the dungeon to find her friends—but she was afraid of doing too much magic and permanently turning her heart into ice. She remembered the chill she'd gotten in the dining room before and that strange feeling of dislike she had felt for Shay. She didn't want to run the risk of freezing her heart, but she didn't want to remain stuck in the nursery either. And somebody needed to do something about rescuing the others, after all.

In the end, it was the dollhouse version of the castle that gave Stella the idea. As it seemed to be an exact replica of the real castle, right down to the items inside the various rooms, Stella decided to study it to get an idea of the layout. If an opportunity for escape were to arise, the last thing she wanted was to go charging down a corridor into a dead end, or find herself trapped in the pantry, or wasting time strumming at lutes in the music room.

She got quite excited when she spotted a little room with a plaque that said ARMORY on the door, imagining that it would be full of swords and maces and axes that might help them escape. But when she peered into the room, she found only spinning wheels, and shiny red apples, and jeweled hair combs—ideal weapons for evil queens to use but not much use to a junior explorer.

The dolls' castle even had its own dungeon, hidden beneath the floor, and Stella spent some time working out the quickest way to get down there, even managing to work out a route that would avoid going past any of the magic mirrors.

At the top of the staircase that led down to the dungeon was a huge library. Stella peered at the minute books on the bookshelves and saw that they all seemed to be fairy tales. With the edge of her thumbnail, she pulled out one of the books to see if it had actual writing inside, but when she removed the book, the entire bookcase swung open to reveal a secret passage hidden behind. Stella was delighted. All castles ought to have secret passages, and this could provide them with their means of escape.

On the morning of the third day, Stella decided she couldn't wait any longer and would have to risk using her

ice powers. When the two trolls came to deliver her breakfast, she concentrated really hard on turning them into ice,
and to her relief it worked exactly the same as it had with
the candelabra. The trolls were quite a bit larger than the
candelabra, though, and Stella felt even more of a chill this
time, as if a bucket of icy water had been thrown in her face.

She shivered, shook it off, and concentrated her thoughts on what she needed to do: Get down to the dungeon, find her friends, escape.

She tried to tiptoe along the corridor, but chunky snow boots aren't designed for tiptoeing, and so she was forced to take them off and carry them in her hand as she went along the corridor and down the stairs. Following the route she'd memorized from the dollhouse castle, Stella swiftly made her way down to the dungeon, taking care to avoid any corridors with magic mirrors hanging in them. This meant she had to take a rather roundabout kind of route, which led her past a vast fish tank that took up an entire wall and was filled with drifting pink jellyfish, and also through rooms that stored some more of her mother's collections, only these objects were not as nice as the jeweled eggs and music boxes she'd seen upstairs. The huge collection of iron slippers was particularly horrible. They were all sizes and shapes, to suit all different types of creatures, including—from the look of some of them—frosties and even yetis.

Finally, Stella reached the staircase that led down to the dungeons and dove into it quickly to avoid two trolls who were clumping down along the corridor toward her. She put her boots back on then, because the steps were wet with condensation and she wanted to be able to run away very fast if she needed to.

The stairs were lit by flickering sconces, but as Stella

went further down, it started to feel darker and darker. She hoped her friends were all right down here and that they hadn't been chained to the wall or anything uncivilized like that. Stella knew from studying the dolls' castle that the dungeon was a warren of cells, and she expected to have some difficulty locating the right one. But in fact, she heard Ethan's loud, carrying voice the moment she reached the bottom of the staircase.

"—is nothing to do with any of us," he was saying. "*We're* not ice princesses, for heaven's sake!"

Stella peered around the corner and saw a troll holding up a mirror and facing it toward a cell. She could make out Ethan, Shay, and Beanie on the other side of the bars, and was just about to wave to try to catch their attention, when the magic mirror spoke. "So you'll go?" it said. "You'll agree to return to your own people and leave the ice princess behind?"

"We can't leave Stella behind," Beanie said. "We just can't."

Stella felt a surge of affection for Beanie, but the next moment, Ethan grabbed the front of his cloak and slammed him up against the wall of the cell. "We *can* leave her behind, and we're going to!" he said—in fact, he almost snarled the words at the smaller boy. "I am not going to spend the rest of my life locked up in this foul place for anyone—not for *anyone*, do you understand?"

263

Beanie shoved the magician away and turned to Shay. "You don't agree with him, do you?"

Shay shook his head and said, "Look, I don't want to leave Stella here any more than you do. But we have a responsibility to our clubs. And there's no point in *all* of us staying locked up. That isn't going to help anyone, including Stella."

Stella could hardly believe what she was hearing. She supposed Ethan and Shay were right, in a way, but she'd never thought that they would agree to abandon her so easily, especially when she was on her way to rescue them. Had they even *tried* to escape? Had they at least considered a rescue attempt before deciding to leave her to her fate?

Beanie tried to argue with them a little more, but it was a bit halfhearted and he was outnumbered. In no time at all, it had been agreed that the three explorers would be set free, taking with them the sled and wolves and unicorn.

Stella turned and raced back up the stairs the way she'd come. If she wasn't on that sled when it left, then she'd have no way of getting home and no way of surviving out in the frozen wilderness by herself. She would be trapped here, maybe forever. No doubt Felix would try to rescue her, but Stella knew it was no good sitting around and waiting to be rescued. No one ever got anywhere that way.

She took the stairs two at a time, dove into the library, and hastily ran her eye down the spines of the books in the far corner of the room until she found the one she was looking for. She yanked it from the shelf, and to her relief it worked just the same as it had in the dolls' castle—the entire bookcase swung open to reveal a hidden passage behind.

Stella hurried through, drawing the bookshelf door closed after her. Like the rest of the castle had when she first arrived, the secret passageway seemed to come to life in her presence: The sconces on the walls lit themselves, although the passage remained dusty and cobwebby—perhaps because secret passageways were supposed to be dusty and cobwebby.

Stella didn't know where the secret passage led—she just hoped it would get her outside the castle, and she wasn't disappointed. Soon enough she walked up some steps, opened a sliding door, and found herself in a kind of garden shed, filled with skates and sleigh blankets. She opened the door and stepped outside into the cold, frosty air, squinting in the sudden bright sunlight and the twinkling glow of the starflakes. Gazing around, she wondered what had become of their sled and animals. Perhaps there was a stable on the grounds somewhere and everything had been put there?

Stella kept hearing the conversation in the dungeon over and over again in her mind, and it was giving her the most terribly hollow feeling. Even Beanie hadn't tried all that hard to stand up for her, and that stung worst of all.

She told herself to get it together. She couldn't be

thinking about such things right now. She had to find the sled and somehow hide herself on it before it was too late. She had no idea how she was going to do that, given that there wasn't much room to hide on a sled, but she had to at least try to conceal herself under a blanket or something.

But then she saw the sled itself, heading away from the castle with all three explorers on it, the wolves panting and huffing, the unicorn trotting along behind—and her heart sank like a stone into the pit of her stomach.

They had left her. They had really left her at the snow queen's castle.

She was alone.

CHAPTER TWENTY-TWO

FOR A LONG MOMENT, Stella simply stood there, not knowing what to do. Then she became aware of some kind of activity within the castle, and dozens of stone trolls came swarming through the front doors, heading off in all different directions. Stella guessed they were looking for her. They must have discovered the two trolls she'd turned to ice outside her room and raised the alarm.

She turned and stumbled back toward the shed she'd just come from, thankful that her boots didn't leave footprints in the starflakes. Perhaps she could hide in the secret passage for a while, until she figured out what to do. Part of her wondered whether there was even any point. Perhaps she should just turn herself over to the trolls right this moment. After all, she couldn't leave the castle now. Not without a tent or a sled or any supplies at all. Ice princess or not, she'd freeze to death during the first night for sure. But just returning meekly to the castle with the stone trolls would be giving up. There had to be *some* way out of this, something she hadn't thought of. . . .

So Stella ran back into the shed and through the hidden door in the wall. She dragged it closed behind her and then sat down in despair to think on the floor of the secret passageway. And that was where she stayed for the rest of the day. Several times she heard trolls clumping into the shed to search it, but they obviously didn't know about the secret passage, and her hiding place remained undisturbed.

At one point she rummaged in her bag for her little igloo of penguins and felt profoundly sorry for herself when it occurred to her that these were the only friends she had left. The little penguins didn't seem like their usual cheery selves either. In fact, when Stella peeked inside, she saw they were all gathered around a framed photo of a rather grand-looking penguin, shaking their heads and blowing their noses into spotted handkerchiefs. Stella thought that maybe the penguins had a friend who'd deserted them, too.

Finally, once evening arrived, everything seemed to quiet down and Stella risked creeping back out into the shed. The trolls had left the place in a bit of a mess and Stella started sorting through it all—looking for anything that might be helpful. She would just have to start building her exploring supplies up again from scratch. There were blankets in the shed, but Stella would need a lot more than that to survive on her own in the Icelands. She would have to sneak back into the castle to look for the rest of her supplies, but music boxes and jeweled eggs weren't going to help her much, nor were poison apples and spinning wheels. And she'd have to be pretty lucky to find a magic goose or a baby volcano in there.

Stella shouldered her bag and opened the door of the shed, intending to poke around the grounds in search of anything that might be useful. The sparkling starflakes coating the snow and castle turrets continued to give off a soft, silver light, so she could see perfectly well.

And then she saw it. There, over on the other side of the castle, clear as anything in the bright moon and starlight, was the explorers' sled. There were no people in it, but she could see all the wolves, and even Glacier the unicorn stood nearby.

Stella had heard that explorers from the Desert Jackal Explorers' Club sometimes saw mirages—things that weren't really there at all—when they ventured out into the desert, but she'd never heard of this happening to polar explorers before. She didn't waste any more time thinking about it, instead hurrying straight over to the sled.

The cold wood certainly felt real enough beneath her fingers, and so did the warm coats of the wolves, who greeted her happily and tried to lick her hands. As Stella stared at them in wonder, she heard the sounds of a squabble behind her.

She turned back toward the castle, and her eyes widened at the sight of Ethan, Shay, and Beanie, all suspended from a rope they had managed to throw over the turret roof. They appeared to be slowly climbing up toward the nursery window by bracing their boots against the wall and using the rope to haul themselves up. Ethan had reached the window and was staring through it.

"But she must be in there," Shay was saying. "The trolls said she was being held prisoner in the nursery."

"I am not blind," Ethan said coldly. "I tell you, she's not there."

"Tap on the window," Beanie suggested. "Maybe she's hiding under the bed."

Ethan snorted. "That doesn't sound like Stella."

"What are you doing?" Stella said from the ground.

The other three all jerked—and Ethan almost let go of the windowsill. They stared down at her with shocked faces.

"We're . . . we're rescuing you," Ethan said at last.

Before, that would have given Stella a nice warm glow, but it didn't have quite the same effect when she knew they'd gone off and left her earlier in the day.

"Oh, so you changed your minds and thought you'd better come back for me after all, then?" she said.

"What are you talking about?" Shay said.

"I heard what you said in the dungeon," Stella said, crossing her arms. "And I saw you drive off in the sled."

"You idiot!" Ethan hissed. "That was just for show! We planned the whole thing so they'd let us out. It's pretty hard to rescue someone when you're locked up in a dungeon!"

"Personally, I thought you overacted it a bit," Shay said. "All that snarling and slamming people up against walls. It was a bit much, Ethan."

"Beanie didn't mind," Ethan said dismissively. "And anyway, someone had to sell it."

"But why were you arguing about it if it was your plan all along?" Stella asked.

"We thought it would look a bit suspicious if we agreed to leave too easily," Shay replied.

"How could you hear us in the dungeon anyway?" Ethan said. "What were you doing down there?"

"I was coming to rescue you," Stella said.

"Couldn't you have waited until night?" Ethan replied. "Everyone knows the best rescue plans take place at night."

"The best rescue plans *do* all take place at night," Beanie said. "But we're here now, so it doesn't matter."

"He's right," Stella said. "Get down from there and let's go."

"Just because you're a princess doesn't give you the right to be bossy," Ethan grumbled.

"Surely being a princess gives me *every* right to be bossy," Stella shot back.

"Well, I'm not calling you Your Highness," said Ethan. "I'm not bowing, either—magicians don't bow."

The boys hurriedly climbed back down the rope and then Beanie rushed straight over to Stella, took the pom-pom hat from his head, and put it onto hers, which Stella knew meant he was very pleased to see her.

"I can't believe you actually thought we would leave you here!" he said. "There's no way we were ever going to do that." He glanced back at the other two and said, "Was there?"

"Not a chance," Shay replied, walking over to them.

"Absolutely not," Ethan agreed. He gave Stella a sudden smile—the first time she had ever seen him do so—and said, "After all, we're the first joint expedition in history. We can't have one of our members getting locked up in a tower by trolls, even if she is a princess. That would be difficult to explain back at the Ocean Squid Explorers' Club. They frown on that sort of thing."

Stella grinned back at them. She didn't think she'd ever been happier to see anyone, and the fact that they'd never really meant to leave her behind made her feel even more happy.

"It's a shame Ethan's first plan didn't work," Beanie said as they walked back to the sled. "He magicked up some polar beans to see if they could pick the lock on the cell door but they just got stuck in there and waved their arms and legs around, yelling."

"Let's not talk about that," Ethan said hurriedly.

They were almost safely back at the sled—when one of the castle doors burst open and a stone troll came stomping out, shining silver in the moonlight. "There she is!" it shouted. "I told you I heard something!"

The next thing they knew, trolls were running out of every door and jumping out of every window—an entire army of trolls charging straight toward them.

"Run!" Shay yelled.

The four of them ran the last few steps. Ethan vaulted up onto the unicorn and Shay leapt onto the back of the sled, leaving Stella and Beanie to tumble into it in a tangle of limbs. Unfortunately, Beanie landed on Dora, who honked indignantly—but the next moment the wolves were racing off along the snow and starflakes, Ethan and the unicorn galloping along beside them, and the angry yells and shouts of the trolls became nothing more than faint echoes in the distance.

CHAPTER TWENTY-THREE

T HE DELAY AT THE castle meant that there was
no time to lose in getting back to the meeting
point. It had been a fine expedition, but no one
wanted to miss the *Bold Adventurer* and get left behind in
the Icelands. So Stella set the compass for Home and they
raced across the snow, pausing only to eat and sleep. The
compass led them back a different route than the way they
had come, and it was very frustrating to everyone that they
didn't have any time left to explore their surroundings,
especially when they passed by—in quick succession—an
enormous snow shark skeleton, a cottage in the shape of
a mushroom, and finally, an entire colony of polar beans
industriously building an ark.

"Do they know something we don't?" Shay asked as
they sped by.

"Who cares?" Ethan replied. "I've had enough polar

beans to last me a lifetime. I'd never magicked them up before Dad said we were going on a polar expedition."

"What did you produce when you got your spells wrong at sea, then?" Stella asked.

"I didn't get anything wrong at sea!" Ethan replied. But when it became clear that the others didn't believe him, he sighed and said, "It was sea hedgehogs."

"Well, at least you can do magic without running the risk of turning yourself into an evil snow queen," Stella said. "The only thing worse than having no powers at all is having powers that you can't actually use."

They had had to lock the tiara away in the top hat box with the cabbage in the end; otherwise it kept appearing on Stella's head. On one occasion it even materialized there during the night, and when Beanie woke her up the next morning she accidentally froze him solid. They put him in the sled and he thawed out after a couple of hours and was perfectly nice about it, but it was pretty embarrassing just the same, and—worst of all—for the first few moments after she did it, Stella hadn't been sorry, and she hadn't cared whether Beanie was hurt or not. It was his own fault for waking her up. But then Shay snatched the tiara from her head and that cold feeling melted away, and suddenly she was full of guilt and concern and remorse. She had no doubt at all that what the mirror had told her was true—if she used the tiara too much, it would freeze her heart and she'd become cold and unfeeling, like her real parents had been. And Stella absolutely, definitely did not want that.

They made good time, and soon enough they were back at the ice mountain. By Stella's calculations, the *Bold Adventurer* should have arrived the day before, but if the captain still meant to wait one more night and day, as he had promised, then they should just about be in time to catch the ship—so long as they could find some other way to get across the woolly mammoth ravine now that the bridge was gone.

However, they didn't have time to look for another way across, because the moment they emerged from the mountain, they heard a great and terrible thundering behind them. The four explorers turned around and stared in horror at the yeti racing down the mountain. Just like the one she'd glimpsed from the ship, this was a gigantic monster, at least sixty feet tall, with feet the size of sleds, and claws as long as a man. Shards of ice glinted in its shaggy white coat, and its blue eyes were almost lost among all that hair. But it had definitely seen them, and it was coming straight toward them, shaking the ground with every step, its huge hand stretched out greedily.

At the sight of the yeti the unicorn reared up in fright, and Ethan lost his balance and fell off, landing in the snow with a thump. Shay grabbed his cloak and dragged him onto the back of the sled just seconds before the wolves set off running in a blind panic, the unicorn close behind.

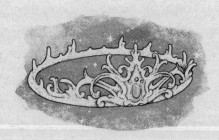

Just like before, they were heading right for the edge of the cliff—only this time there was no bridge, and nothing to stop them from plunging straight to the bottom. The sled would be smashed to pieces and they would all die for sure.

"The top hat box!" Stella yelled at Beanie. "Pass me the top hat box!"

He shoved it over to her and Stella threw open the lid and narrowly missed the jaws of the cabbage as she grabbed hold of her tiara. In another moment it was on her head, and she felt a cold tingling in her fingertips as she stood up and threw out her hands, just as they reached the very edge of the cliff.

Instead of thin air, the wolves' paws landed on solid ice, and the space around Stella fizzed with blue sparks as she concentrated on creating the ice bridge as fast as the wolves could run. The magic didn't just give her a chill this time—it felt like her entire body had been plunged beneath the surface of a frozen lake. From head to toe she was so cold that it was almost impossible to breathe. But if she lost her focus on the bridge for even a moment, then the wolves would tumble into nothing and that would be that. They couldn't die. Not when they were all this close to the finish.

Finally the bridge joined with the other side of the ravine, but the sled slid as it landed, going so fast that it turned over, spilling the four explorers—and Dora—out onto the snow. Stella landed on her front, right at the edge of the cliff, with Ethan close beside her.

Dora was the unluckiest one. The goose was hurled the furthest, and seeing that she was about to fall off the edge, and remembering what the frosties had said about these geese being unable to fly, Ethan lunged after her. But what had looked like solid land was in fact just a clump of snow that fell away beneath his feet the moment he snatched up the goose, and the magician would have plunged straight to the ravine floor below if Stella hadn't grabbed his arm just in time.

On the other side of the drop, the yeti gingerly placed one of its gigantic feet on the ice bridge, but it wasn't strong enough to support the creature's monstrous size and a great slab broke off, shattering the bridge into pieces. The yeti gave a loud, angry cry that echoed all around them, and pummeled its fists against the mountain in frustration.

"That was a close one," Shay said.

Stella looked around and saw that he and Beanie were both getting to their feet and dusting themselves off.

"A little help?" Ethan said below her. "Your goose is pecking my head."

Stella looked down to where the magician was clinging onto her arm with one hand, his boots scrabbling against the cliff edge. He had Dora clamped in his other arm, and the goose was indeed doing her best to peck him.

Stella found it hard to care. Her shoulder felt as if it were about to pop right out of its socket. When he'd flown past her she had grabbed him instinctively, but now she found herself wondering why she had bothered. She looked down at the magician and suddenly remembered every annoying thing he had ever said to her. A strong feeling of dislike surged through her and she said in a cold voice, "You threatened to turn me into a blind mole rat once."

Ethan looked up at her, startled. "That . . . yes, I did say that, but—"

Stella loosened her grip slightly and the magician slipped, his boots knocking big clumps of snow from the side of the cliff as he tried to find a foothold.

"Stella!" he gasped. "Please—"

"You're hurting my arm," she said. "Let go."

"That's the ice magic talking, Sparky," Shay said behind her. "It's not you."

Stella turned her head to glare at him and Beanie. Who did he think he was to speak to her like that? Didn't he realize she was a princess? Didn't he know she was royalty?

"Don't come another step closer or I swear I'll drop him!" she said.

Shay held up both hands and Beanie did the same.

"Just . . . remember who you are, Stella," Beanie said.

But Stella *did* remember now—that was the point. She was an ice princess, and her place was in her castle, with her trolls and her magic mirrors and her dungeons and her iron slippers. Why had she ever let these people talk her into leaving?

She stared down at Ethan—who was still struggling to keep hold of Dora in spite of her continuous attempts to peck him—and she didn't know how she could ever have felt anything like friendship toward him. She hated him. She hated all of them. . . .

Ethan saw something in Stella's eyes then that made him feel truly afraid. He knew that she was going to let him go. He was going to fall to his death, all because he'd tried to save a goose that didn't even like him. First Julian was killed by a squid, and now Ethan was about to be polished off by an ice princess and her deranged goose.

"Tell my father—" he began.

But before he could continue, Beanie said, "What will Felix say?"

Stella froze at the sound of that name. "Felix?" she repeated.

Then she heard Felix's voice inside her head—the words

he had spoken to her back at the Polar Bear Explorers' Club: *Promise me something. . . .*

"What will he say when he finds out that you let another explorer die when you could have saved him?" Beanie went on.

Stella felt something twist in the pit of her stomach. When she thought of Felix—and his laugh, and his smile, and the way he looked at her when he was pleased with her—she suddenly felt warm instead of cold.

"He's responsible for your actions on the expedition, isn't he?" Beanie said. "He'll be disgraced. Thrown out of the Polar Bear Explorers' Club."

I don't want that, Stella thought. *I don't want any of this. This isn't me!*

With her spare hand she reached up for the tiara, pulled it from her head, and flung it into the snow. Shay and Beanie rushed forward to help, and the three of them hauled Ethan up over the side, along with the goose, who instantly flapped off, honking loudly and irritably, obviously quite cross about the whole affair.

"Ethan, I am so sorry," Stella said.

"It's fine," Ethan said, holding up his hand. "It's fine. I like dangling off the edge of a cliff while a goose pecks at my face. Really."

Wordlessly, Beanie handed him another penguin bandage, and Ethan stuck it over the new cut on his cheek.

"I'll find some way to make it up to you," Stella said, feeling awful.

"I've only myself to blame," Ethan replied. "I should never have threatened to turn you into a blind mole rat. That was terribly rude of me."

He gave her another one of his rare smiles and Stella couldn't help hugging him, despite his complaints.

"Thank you for saving Dora," she said. "I'm sorry she pecked you."

Stella felt she never wanted to see the tiara again, and was all for burying it in the snow and forgetting about it, but the others persuaded her to take it home. At the very least, an ice princess's magic tiara would make a fine addition to the collection of curiosities on display at the Polar Bear Explorers' Club. So the tiara was put back in the top hat box with the cabbage, and then they all piled into the sled and continued on to the ship.

To their enormous relief, the *Bold Adventurer* was still there, bobbing gently in the icy sea. A few sailors were loading the last of the supplies on board when they approached, so they left the sled and instructed the men not to open the top hat box unless they wanted a very nasty surprise, said good-bye for now to the animals, and then hurried on board. There were lots of explorers from both the Ocean Squid and the Polar Bear expeditions milling around on deck, who immediately rushed over to greet the junior explorers when they appeared. They were the last to arrive, and everyone was pleased and relieved to see them all in one piece.

"Captain!" Stella called, spotting Captain Fitzroy on the other side of the deck.

He turned at the sound of her voice and gave Stella a low bow as the junior explorers made their way over. "Miss Pearl," he said. "I am delighted to see you. And the rest of you too, of course. We were starting to fear the worst."

"Do you know where my dad is?" Shay asked.

"Captain Kipling is in the luggage room, and so is your uncle, I believe," Captain Fitzroy said, looking at Beanie.

The two boys hurried off in the direction of the luggage room.

"What about Felix?" Stella asked. It seemed strange that he wasn't there, watching out for her, and she was suddenly afraid that he might have been hurt—or worse, lost—during the expedition.

"Mister Pearl is currently involved in an altercation with some other explorers," Captain Fitzroy replied, tilting his head. "It sounds like a most energetic argument. But then, explorers do specialize in those, I understand."

Stella could clearly hear the sounds of an argument somewhere close by.

"It sounds like it's coming from the wolf pen," Ethan said.

The two of them quickly made their way over to the other side of the bridge. Stella could hear Felix's voice, and he definitely sounded very angry, which wasn't like him at all. Stella wondered what on earth they could be arguing about. Ethan pulled back the canvas flap and the two of them peered inside, to see a dozen or so explorers crowded into the wolf pen.

"You can't take the wolves," one of them was saying. "They're the property of the Polar Bear Explorers' Club."

"And they will be returned to the club in due course," Felix replied impatiently. Stella saw him then, right at the back of the pen. There was stubble on his jaw, and he looked rather more disheveled than usual, but other than that, he was the same as ever. "I will pay for the use of the wolves when I return to the club."

"But you *won't* return to the club, you madman!" the explorer replied. "You'll be a skeleton in an igloo!"

"If I am to be a skeleton in an igloo," Felix replied, "then that's surely no one's affair but my own. I cannot prevent this ship from leaving, but I can take these wolves to go and search for Stella and the others by myself."

"You won't be by yourself," another explorer said. It was Ethan's father, Zachary Vincent Rook. He stepped forward to stand beside Felix. "This man may talk a lot of silly nonsense about fairy rights and so forth, but he is quite right about this matter—we cannot leave our children behind in this forsaken frozen wasteland. They will certainly perish. And I will not abandon my son. We must remain behind to search for them. These wolves are coming with us, and anyone who attempts to prevent us from leaving will be turned into a singing cucumber without any further warning."

Stella heard Ethan gasp beside her. He raised his voice and said, "That won't be necessary, Father," but his words were drowned out beneath a chorus of furious responses from the other explorers.

"No one threatens to turn me into a cucumber!" one of them cried. "No one!"

"It's an outrage!"

"An affront to the clubs!"

"You shall both be reported."

"I say that allowances ought to be made for Rook," a large explorer with a red mustache said. "After all, he's recently lost one son, and who can blame him for not wanting to lose the other?" He pointed at Felix. "But your behavior, sir, is inexcusable. Inexcusable! Why, that strange, white girl isn't even your real daughter! In fact, many of us feel you should never have brought her back from the Icelands at all."

"You would prefer that I leave an infant to freeze to death alone in the snow?" Felix inquired, his face turning an interesting shade of pink. "Surely no human being with a shred of decency would contemplate such a thing for even a moment? Stella is the most precious person in the world to me; I would give my life for hers a hundred times over."

"Who knows where she came from or what she is?" the red-mustache man insisted. Then he shuddered and said, "That girl gives me the creeps with her white hair and those icy-blue eyes. They stare right through you, like there's no soul in there at all. If you ask me, she ought to be—"

He didn't get any further, however, because Felix hit him, with a clean, straight punch directly to the chin. Not expecting it, the explorer toppled over onto the floor with a heavy thud.

Stella clapped both hands over her mouth in shock. She remembered how Felix had occasionally mentioned being a boxing champion back in his youth, but she had always thought he was joking.

"Stella has ten times the soul you have, you ignorant, bigoted fool!" Felix ran a hand through his disheveled hair, took a deep breath, and said, "I have never once hit another man outside of the boxing ring in my whole life, but if you speak about my daughter like that in front of me again, I—"

"Felix!" Stella cried, and this time everyone heard her, and the explorers all turned to stare as one.

"Good heavens! Stella!" Felix exclaimed, staring at her.

Taking advantage of the momentary distraction, the explorer on the floor scrambled to his feet and lunged toward Felix. Before he could reach him, however, Zachary

Vincent Rook threw up his hand and the explorer instantly turned into a singing cucumber, rolling along the wooden boards before coming to a stop beside Felix's boot.

"Bad form attacking a man when his back is turned," the magician said, shaking his head in disapproval. "Extremely bad form."

Felix nodded his thanks to Zachary before carefully stepping over the cucumber—which was singing a sea shanty with great gusto—and running toward Stella as she hurried toward him. They met in the middle of the wolf pen, where Felix caught Stella up and lifted her so high that her feet came right off the floor. Stella buried her face in the curve of his neck, breathing in his familiar scent of soap and peppermint.

"My dearest girl," he said, finally setting her down. "Believe me when I say that I have never been more pleased to see you in my whole entire life."

CHAPTER TWENTY-FOUR

Two weeks later

A WARM WELCOME AWAITED THEM back at the Polar Bear Explorers' Club, and a feast was held in honor of the returning explorers. After the collapse of the first ice bridge, the adult explorers had been unable to reach the coldest part of the Icelands, but they had still managed to make a number of interesting discoveries during their expedition—including a yeti pool, a fairy polar bear habitat, and a boisterous dancing penguin colony. They'd even brought one of the dancing penguins back with them—his name was Monty, and he delighted the diners all evening with his enthusiastic show of jigs, slip jigs, barn dances, and cancans.

It was the junior explorers who were enjoying the limelight, though. The president of the Polar Bear Explorers' Club was thrilled to have another first for the club—even if it was a joint first with the Ocean Squid explorers. They had made it to the coldest part of the Icelands and that was something worth celebrating. Both clubs would take turns displaying the expedition's discoveries, starting with the Polar Bear Explorers' Club—which lost no time putting the carnivorous cabbage, starflakes, and ice princess tiara on display.

The president even asked whether they might consider handing Dora over to be stuffed and placed in the front lobby along with the other captured beasts from the Icelands. Stella turned this request down flat and Felix backed her up, as she'd known he would. This line of inquiry clearly made him nervous about Monty the dancing penguin's safety, however, for Stella noticed Felix sneaking him into his bag when he thought no one was looking. Pinching a penguin—and a magic one at that—was a clear breach of club rules, but Stella knew that Felix turned a blind eye to the rule book on occasion.

The discovery that the president of the Polar Bear Explorers' Club was the most pleased with, however, was not the tiara, the cabbage, the starflakes, or the magic goose— but the mustache spoon Stella had stolen from the frosties. The president proclaimed it the most ingenious invention ever created and it seemed likely that Stella would even get some kind of special reward for bringing it back with her.

The feast was in full swing, and for once there was an almost pleasant atmosphere between the Polar Bear explorers and those from Ocean Squid. Everyone seemed happy with the way things had turned out, although Zachary Vincent Rook kept saying things like: "Of course, if it hadn't been for my boy, Ethan, they would all have probably been killed by that cabbage."

And Ethan kept saying, "It was a joint effort, Father," and then rolling his eyes at the others apologetically.

Stella didn't really mind who got credit for what. Felix said exploring wasn't about personal credit and that any explorer who only did it because they wanted to be famous was doomed to fail. You had to love exploring for the thrill alone, and Stella definitely did.

The junior explorers stayed at the table through dessert—none of them wanted to miss the miniature igloo ice cream cakes, after all. When Stella cracked into hers she found a family of frosties inside, in honor of their discovery. They consisted of sugared shards of white mint with chocolate claws, and Stella relished the crunch they made as she ground them up with her teeth.

After the dessert had been cleared away, Stella glanced at Ethan on the other side of the table and signaled to him that they were leaving. The magician nodded, and a few moments later the four junior explorers managed to sneak away undetected, and they headed straight to the Hall of Flags to see their expedition flag, which had been given a special spot as the flag from the first joint expedition in history.

Beanie had written their Flag Report during the voyage back to Coldgate, carefully leaving out any mention of the outlaw hideout at the Yak and Yeti, as per Captain Ajax's request. They had even changed the name *Snow Queen* to *Snow Goose*, just in case. They owed Captain Ajax, after all, and none of them wanted to be responsible for forcing him back into the perilous life of returning stolen treasure maps to ungrateful pirates in the Seventeen Seas.

"I thought exploring with all of you would be a total nightmare," Ethan said as they all gazed up at their flag. "But there were parts of it that weren't terrible."

"What was your favorite part?" Stella asked. "Getting bitten by the frosty?"

"Getting proved *right* about the frosties," Ethan corrected her. "I never tire of being proved right about things."

"The president has been in contact with Captain Filibuster," Beanie said. "When the new edition of his *Guide to Expeditions and Exploration* comes out, they're going to include a section about treating frostbite with mustache wax."

"Dad thinks this new knowledge will save a lot of lives," Shay said.

"And fingers and toes," Beanie replied.

"The Icelands were fun. Where would you most like to explore next?" Stella asked.

"Don't you want to just enjoy being home for a little while?" Beanie asked.

"I *have* enjoyed it for a little while," Stella replied. "I enjoyed the hot chocolate when I arrived. I enjoyed the buttered crumpets in my room. I enjoyed having a bath. I suppose I'd like to go home and say hello to Gruff and the dinosaurs and my unicorn. But then I'd like to start planning another expedition. Felix says that the president is so pleased with the mustache spoon that he's bound to grant me permanent membership in the Polar Bear Explorers' Club. So where would you go next if you could choose? Volcano Island? Cactus Valley? The Scorpion Desert?"

"Isn't the Scorpion Desert bandit country?" Beanie asked.

"I've always wanted to see the Floating Island of Diamond Waterfalls," Ethan put in. "I don't think they have bandits there."

"We should plan another expedition together," Stella said tentatively. She suddenly felt shy. What if the others didn't want to go on another expedition with her? They'd been thrown together by force the first time, but organizing it by choice might be a whole other matter. "We do all *want* to go on another expedition together. Don't we?"

"Count me in," Shay said at once.

"Me too," Beanie said.

"Ethan?" Stella prompted. "What about you?"

There was a pause. Then the magician gave a sudden grin. "I wouldn't miss it," he said. "Besides, you all would be completely lost without me. Dead within hours, probably."

"We will need someone who can create polar beans out of thin air, Prawn," Shay agreed.

Ethan snapped his fingers obligingly—only instead of polar beans, a tiny scorpion materialized and scuttled off into the corner of the room, clicking its pincers together in a most threatening manner.

"Don't blame me!" Ethan said, as the four explorers fled from the room. "You shouldn't have mentioned the Scorpion Desert!"

EPILOGUE

FELIX HAD ALWAYS SAID that the first night spent in your own bed after a time away traveling was one of the greatest pleasures life had to offer. When they arrived home after their long journey, Stella found that Felix was indeed quite right about this.

They had hot chocolate and cheesy toast together by the stove in the kitchen, with Gruff snoozing happily in front of the flickering flames. The polar bear had almost flattened Stella in excitement when she walked through the door, and Felix had had to drag her up by the hood of her cloak to set her on her feet again. Stella didn't mind, though. She was absolutely delighted to see her polar bear again too, and to feel his warm tongue on her face—even if he did get slobber all over her explorer's cloak.

"It'll come out in the wash," Felix said breezily. "Most things do."

When Stella went upstairs to bed, Gruff came with her, and Felix agreed that she could take Buster too, as a special treat. She sat down on her bed and took her Polar Pets from her bag, then peered into the igloo to see what the penguins were up to. A pot of hot chocolate warmed on a little stove, while the penguins divided up a bag of blue marshmallows between them, honking happily at one another. The marshmallows were fish-shaped and, in fact, the penguins gobbled most of them down before the hot chocolate was even ready.

Stella placed the igloo on her bedside table, changed into her favorite unicorn pajamas, and fell straight between the sheets, delighting in how comfortable and familiar and warm it all felt, right down to the sparkling mobile revolving slowly above her bed.

Gruff stretched himself out on the rug by the fireplace in her room, snoring happily, Buster nestled into the crook of Stella's arm, his little claws curled tight around her thumb, and Stella soon fell sound asleep, happy to be back home, surrounded by her beloved pets.

And for a little while after that, everything was quiet. Then, all of a sudden, Stella's suitcase started to move by itself. It jerked around several times before falling over on its side, causing the clasps to snap open. Gruff snorted in his sleep, but didn't wake up, and nor did anyone else.

A few seconds later, a little wooden hand poked out of the case, followed by an arm and then a head. Slowly but surely, the puppet witch from the ice castle's nursery climbed out of Stella's luggage, the strings jerking around her as if an invisible puppet master were controlling them.

The witch's burned, blistered feet landed on Stella's snowflake rug. Her gnarled wooden hands brushed at her skirt, knocking away the bits of fluff she'd picked up in the suitcase. She patted her pointed hat, making sure it was still attached to her head. Then she looked up, and gazed slowly around the room, taking in her surroundings before finally settling her painted eyes on Stella, sleeping soundly in her bed—completely oblivious to the fact that a witch puppet had just crawled out of her suitcase.

All by herself.

Acknowledgments

I would like to thank my new agent, Thérèse Coen, who championed *The Polar Bear Explorers' Club* from the very beginning, first at the Madeleine Milburn Literary Agency, and now at Hardman and Swainson. Many thanks to everyone at both agencies.

I would also like to acknowledge Carolyn Whitaker of London Independent Books, who sadly passed away last year. She became my literary agent when I was nineteen and offered a wealth of advice, wisdom, encouragement, and opportunities over the eleven years that followed. She was the first person from the world of publishing who believed in my writing, and I could not have become a published author without her. Given that this is all I have ever wanted to do—I owe her a great deal.

I've got to mention New Orleans as well. This city is full of music, creativity, and magic, and I happened to visit during a low time when my artist's soul was very much in need of nourishing. I had almost made up my mind to put the manuscript for *The Polar Bear Explorers' Club* away in a drawer, but this trip gave me the drive to submit it, come what may. Thank you, NOLA, and *laissez les bons temps rouler* again one day, I hope.

I'm delighted that *The Polar Bear Explorers' Club* found a home with Faber, and would like to thank Leah Thaxton,

Natasha Brown, Hayley Steed, Hannah Love, and everyone else there who has shown such love and affection for the book. You're all amazing.

I'd also like to thank fellow writers Sarwat Chadda, Natasha Ngan, James Noble, Louie Stowell, Jane Hardstaff, and Ali Standish for cocktails, fun, and all the bookish chat in London. Writing is a solitary business and the friendship and support offered by other authors is extremely special. Plus, they all write fantastic books—go and buy 'em!

Finally, much gratitude as always to my family, who put up with all the ups and downs of the writer's life with such good grace. Particular shout-outs for my parents, Shirley and Trevor Bell, for taking me to New Orleans when they did; my boyfriend, Neil Dayus, for keeping me supplied with whisky cocktails during edits; and my dear little Siamese cat, Suki, who is the very best at cuddles. Gold medals for everybody!

Turn the page for a sneak peek at the next adventure:

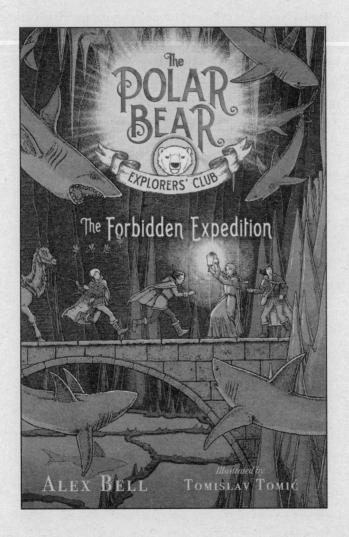

The POLAR BEAR

EXPLORERS' CLUB

The Forbidden Expedition

ALEX BELL

Illustrated by TOMISLAV TOMIĆ

S
TELLA STARFLAKE PEARL SAT down on her favorite ice bench in the backyard and sighed. Her recent expedition with her friends Beanie, Shay, and Ethan had been extensively covered in all the papers and expedition journals—not just because the four junior explorers had been the first to reach the coldest part of the Icelands, and not only because Stella was the first girl to ever be admitted to the Polar Bear Explorers' Club, but also because it turned out that Stella was actually an ice princess.

She looked over at the witch puppet she'd brought back with her from the Icelands. When she'd discovered it was a magical thing that could move around all by itself, she'd been delighted, but her adoptive father, Felix, had insisted on taking the puppet away and shutting it up in the top room of the East Wing.

From her position on the bench, Stella could now just

make out the pointed outline of the witch's hat as the puppet walked up and down the windowsill of the turreted bedroom. Every now and then the witch would stop and rap her wooden knuckles on the glass. The sound carried clearly to Stella through the frozen air, making her shiver.

"She won't be locked up forever," Felix had promised. "But we can't be too careful. This puppet is an exact likeness of Jezzybella. Not only did she kill your parents, but she tried her best to kill you, too. I've heard of witches making images of themselves and then being able to see through their eyes. If that's what this puppet is, then we can't have it anywhere near you."

Stella knew that what Felix said was perfectly sensible, and yet deep in her gut she couldn't help feeling that he was wrong about the puppet. Yes, it was a toy version of the witch who had killed the snow queen and king, but Stella had felt compulsively drawn to it back at the ice castle, and she still did somehow now.

The small, sad sound of the puppet rapping her tiny knuckles against the glass carried through the air once again, and she had to force herself not to run up to the turret to let her out. Felix had sent for a puppet expert from Coldgate, and until he arrived she would leave the witch where she was.

Stella smoothed out the powder-blue skirts of her dress and ran a finger lightly over the sparkly silver crowns stitched into the fabric. Her magical tiara had been put on display with other curiosities at the Polar Bear Explorers' Club, and word of the junior explorers' adventures had traveled fast. In the two weeks since she'd been back, gifts had poured in from people Stella had never even met. There had been dresses, lace gloves, beautiful boxes of pink jellies dusted with powdered sugar, tiny unicorn dolls, and more besides.

At first Stella had been delighted. Everyone likes getting presents, after all, and people send rather nice ones to ice princesses. But they send not-so-nice things too. Letters saying that ice princesses did not belong in civilized society, that they ought to stay out in the wilds of the Icelands, nursing their frozen hearts and casting their evil spells. Felix had taken those letters and tossed them straight onto the fire, telling her to pay them no heed and that everything would die down soon enough, but Stella still felt a cold little stone of worry about it, right in the pit of her stomach.

She was distracted from her concerns when her pet polar bear, Gruff, came lumbering over to her across the snowy lawn. Felix had rescued Gruff from the snow just like he had rescued Stella, and the great white bear had been her best friend for as long as she could remember. Visitors to the house were often startled by his enormous size—especially when he stood up on his back legs, which he did whenever he really wanted to show off and look fantastically handsome. He stood more than ten feet tall, towering over even the tallest man. He'd done this the first time he'd ever met Aunt Agatha—Felix's overbearing, bossy sister—who had let out the most terrible shriek and then fainted dead away in a cloud of petticoats and perfume. Stella had thought the screaming and fainting was terribly rude, especially as Felix had made Gruff look very handsome with a fetching bow tie he'd had specially made for the occasion.

Gruff shoved his black nose into the pockets of Stella's cloak in search of his favorite fish biscuits. She gave him a gentle shove and told him to sit. He flumped down obediently in the snow, and Stella rewarded him by tossing him a treat. The bear crunched it up happily, spraying crumbs everywhere, then licked Stella's cheek before lumbering off toward the lake. Felix had told Stella once that polar bears were very fast runners and could reach top speeds of twenty-five miles an hour, but Stella had never seen Gruff move any faster than a sedate lumber. This may have been because Gruff had been born with a twisted paw, but then again, perhaps he was just a big old lazy bear (which is what Stella really thought).

She stood up from the bench. There was no point moping around worrying. Felix always said that if you were feeling a bit anxious or upset, the best solution was to jump straight into doing something useful and/or fun. Preferably fun, of course, because fun things were much more effective at cheering up a person than a useful thing could ever be.

Stella glanced over to where Felix stood on the terrace, examining the glass fairy globe the fairies had given him the day before. Fairies were terribly fond of Felix, so it made sense that his explorer's specialty should be fairyology. There were several fairies flitting about him now—Stella could see the sparkle of their wings from across the yard.

Felix looked up and gave Stella a wave. She waved back and then settled herself down in the snow to make a snow bear. She would have much preferred to make a snow unicorn, but they were a lot more difficult and she had never managed to get one quite right. She put her gloved hand down, ready to scoop up her first snowball, when a crackle of blue sparks leapt from her fingertips.

She froze. There before her was a perfect, sparkling snow unicorn. It was no more than four inches tall, but Stella could see each individual strand of hair in its flowing mane, the twists in its white horn, and even a collection of fine, feathered eyelashes. The unicorn's beautiful snow eyes gazed directly at Stella, as if it could really see her—as if it was waiting for her to say something.

Stella gazed around in confusion. Had someone else come into the backyard and made the unicorn? But there was nobody around except for Felix, and even he couldn't make snow animals as detailed and perfect as that. And surely it hadn't been there just moments ago. One minute she had wished for a unicorn made of snow, and the next, sparks had shot from her fingers and one had appeared. Almost like magic. But Stella couldn't do ice magic. Not without her tiara. And that was miles away in a cabinet inside the Polar Bear Explorers' Club. . . .

Slowly, she reached out a hand toward the unicorn. As her fingertips got closer, she could have sworn that one of its ears twitched, just slightly—

The sound of breaking glass made her jump, and she snatched back her hand.

"Stella!" Felix shouted, and she was alarmed by the sound of panic in his voice.

She turned to look over her shoulder and saw that he had dropped the glass fairy globe, which lay in sparkling fragments at his feet. Stella clapped both hands to her mouth in dismay. Fairy globes were one in a million, and Felix wasn't likely to come across one ever again. What could possibly have caused him to drop something so precious?

"Stella, above you!" Felix shouted at the exact same moment that a monstrous dark shadow fell over her.

She looked up, and a cry of fear lodged itself in her throat. A gigantic vulture loomed over her like something out of a nightmare, its twenty-foot wingspan flapping out icy ripples of frozen air. It had bedraggled, dirty gray feathers, a long, stringy neck, and a completely bald head. Stella saw the sharp, hooked beak, the curled claws, and the cold gleam in its predator's eyes. If she had had her tiara she could have frozen the vulture, but without it she had no choice but to turn and run, her fur-topped boots kicking up great clumps of snow behind her.

The house seemed so far away. She was never going to make it. Behind her, the vulture let out a terrible squawk, which seemed to pierce the air. The next moment the giant bird swooped in so close that Stella could smell its damp, dirty feathers and the putrid scent of rotting flesh on its breath as it gave that screeching squawk once again, so loud that it seemed to slice right through Stella's eardrums.

She gasped as she felt the vulture's talons clamp down on her shoulders. Her boots were coming up off the ground, and she realized that the bird had caught her and was going to fly away and there was absolutely nothing she could do to stop it—

But then Felix crashed into her, and her cloak ripped free of the vulture's claws as he dragged her to the ground. Stella found herself pressed facedown in the snow, pinned there by Felix's weight as he shielded her from the vulture, which immediately tried to throw him aside. There was the sound of fabric tearing, and Felix's breath caught sharply in his throat.

Stella tried to push him off, because she didn't want his protection if it meant he was going to get hurt instead, but Felix was too strong and kept her tucked firmly underneath him as the vulture screamed into the air. The thought flashed through Stella's mind, clear as crystal, that the vulture was going to kill them both. There was no way they could fight it off, and there was no one around for miles. Even if one of the servants saw the attack from a window, Felix kept no weapons in the house, so there would be absolutely nothing they could do to help.

Suddenly she became aware of the ground trembling beneath her and looked up to see Gruff racing across the snow, faster than she had ever seen him move before, his huge paws kicking up tall fountains of beautiful, glittering ice. The great bear thundered up to them, putting his massive body between the humans and the vulture. His black lips pulled back in a ferocious snarl, and he let out such a deafening bellow of a roar that Stella felt it in the very ground beneath her.

She had never realized quite how many teeth Gruff had, or how cruelly sharp they were, and she had never seen him roaring and snarling in fury in such a terrifying way. The vulture squawked in alarm and drew back a little. Gruff stood up on his hind legs, towering at his full ten-foot height. He swiped at the vulture with his huge paws, landing a solid blow that sent the giant bird reeling farther into the sky.

Felix gripped Stella's arm, and she found herself being dragged to her feet. Then he scooped her up in his arms and sprinted back toward the house. Over his shoulder Stella saw that Gruff had thumped back down to all fours, but he was still roaring over and over again at the vulture, which had flown higher and was circling warily above.

Felix threw open the door to the library with one hand and set Stella down in the doorway. Worried for her polar bear, she tried to see past Felix, but he was already turning back to the door.

"Gruff!" he shouted. "Come on."

The polar bear turned and lolloped across the snow toward them. The vulture had flown so high now that Stella could no longer see it. The moment Gruff padded through the doorway, Felix slammed the door closed and drew across the bolts.

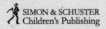

"You're a tracker, Jack Buckles, like your father and his father before him. . . ."

James R. Hannibal takes readers on a thrilling adventure through history—with a touch of English magic.

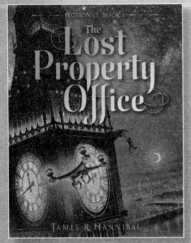

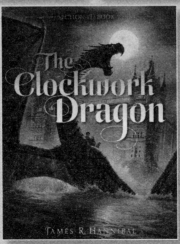

Once invited, you must take care, lest you vanish between the here and there. Welcome to the

Hotel Between.

"Magic and mystery draw you into *The Hotel Between*, and I couldn't leave until I knew all its secrets. Can I make a reservation yet?"

—JAMES RILEY,
New York Times bestselling author of the Story Thieves series

CRACK THE CASE WITH *NEW YORK TIMES* BESTSELLING AUTHOR STUART GIBBS IN THESE WILD MYSTERIES!